Discover the world of
P.I. Jack Hagee . . .

. . . and the acclaimed mystery series by
C. J. Henderson

SOMETHING FOR NOTHING

Hardcase investigator Jack Hagee is hired to
track a wayward husband. But when the curious wife is
murdered, he's after a killer in the streets of New York.
A man they call The Outliner . . .

"A FINE SHARP EDGE . . . NO-NONSENSE
P.I. . . . CLASSIC."
—Gary Lovisi, editor, *Detective Story Magazine*

NO FREE LUNCH

P.I. Jack Hagee thought he'd seen it all. Until he
searches for a small-town girl in the seediest depths of
New York's nightlife—and uncovers the shocking
secrets of her own very private hell. The hottest,
toughest, sexiest thriller of the year!

"RAW VITALITY . . . HENDERSON IS A BORN
STORYTELLER."
—*Armchair Detective*

MORE MYSTERIES FROM THE
BERKLEY PUBLISHING GROUP . . .

INSPECTOR KENWORTHY MYSTERIES: Scotland Yard's consummate master of investigation lets no one get away with murder. "In the best tradition of British detective fiction!" —*Boston Globe*

by John Buxton Hilton

HANGMAN'S TIDE	TWICE DEAD
FATAL CURTAIN	RANSOM GAME
PLAYGROUND OF DEATH	FOCUS ON CRIME
CRADLE OF CRIME	CORRIDORS OF GUILT
HOLIDAY FOR MURDER	DEAD MAN'S PATH
LESSON IN MURDER	DEATH IN MIDWINTER
TARGET OF SUSPICION	

DOG LOVER'S MYSTERIES STARRING JACKIE WALSH: She's starting a new life with her son and an ex-police dog named Jake . . . teaching film classes and solving crimes!

by Melissa Cleary

A TAIL OF TWO MURDERS	HOUNDED TO DEATH
DOG COLLAR CRIME	SKULL AND DOG BONES

GARTH RYLAND MYSTERIES: Newsman Garth Ryland digs up the dirt in a serene small town—that isn't as peaceful as it looks . . . "A writer with real imagination!" —*The New York Times*

by John R. Riggs

HUNTING GROUND	ONE MAN'S POISON
HAUNT OF THE NIGHTINGALE	THE LAST LAUGH
WOLF IN SHEEP'S CLOTHING	DEAD LETTER

PETER BRICHTER MYSTERIES: A midwestern police detective stars in "a highly unusual, exceptionally erudite mystery series!" —*Minneapolis Star Tribune*

by Mary Monica Pulver

KNIGHT FALL	ORIGINAL SIN
THE UNFORGIVING MINUTES	SHOW STOPPER
ASHES TO ASHES	

TEDDY LONDON MYSTERIES: A P.I. solves mysteries with a touch of the supernatural . . .

by Robert Morgan

THE THINGS THAT ARE NOT THERE	THE THING THAT DARKNESS HIDES
SOME THINGS NEVER DIE	

JACK HAGEE, P.I., MYSTERIES: Classic detective fiction with "raw vitality . . . Henderson is a born storyteller." —*Armchair Detective*

by C. J. Henderson

NO FREE LUNCH	SOMETHING FOR NOTHING
	NOTHING LASTS FOREVER

FREDDIE O'NEAL, P.I., MYSTERIES: You can bet that this appealing Reno P.I. will get her man . . . "A winner." —Linda Grant

by Catherine Dain

LAY IT ON THE LINE	SING A SONG OF DEATH

SISTER FREVISSE MYSTERIES: Medieval mystery in the tradition of Ellis Peters . . .

by Margaret Frazer

THE NOVICE'S TALE	THE SERVANT'S TALE

NOTHING LASTS FOREVER

C. J. HENDERSON

BERKLEY PRIME CRIME, NEW YORK

Chapters One through Four appeared under the title "The Things We Do" in somewhat altered form in *P.I. Magazine*, copyright © 1991 by C. J. Henderson.

NOTHING LASTS FOREVER

A Berkley Prime Crime Book / published by arrangement with the author

PRINTING HISTORY
Berkley Prime Crime edition / April 1994

ISBN: 0-425-14209-4

Berkley Prime Crime Books
are published by The Berkley Publishing Group,
200 Madison Avenue, New York, New York 10016.
The name BERKLEY PRIME CRIME and
the BERKLEY PRIME CRIME design
are trademarks belonging to Berkley Publishing Corporation.

PRINTED IN THE UNITED STATES OF AMERICA

10 9 8 7 6 5 4 3 2 1

A book about being one's own man—no matter what the odds—about following one's conscience and doing the right thing, could have been influenced by several people in my life.

However, if that book is to also be about quiet dignity and the sacrifices a person must make to do the right thing without ego, fanfare or gross reward . . . well, that narrows the field considerably.

Thus, I dedicate this book to my uncle,
Gene Henderson.
For the lessons, gently taught,
over the years . . .
Some of which may finally be sinking in.

"No man is so exquisitely honest or upright in living but that ten times in his life he might not lawfully be hanged."

—MONTAIGNE

"You k'n hide de fier, but what you guine do with de smoke?"

—JOEL CHANDLER HARRIS

"It is often easier to fight for principles than to live up to them."

—ADLAI STEVENSON

CHAPTER 1

I WATCHED THE cab pull away through the frost etched across the front bay windows.

"Well . . ." I thought, as it rounded the clean mounds of snow neatly piled along the hedges edging the driveway's end, "that's that."

The house was mine. Mine and the dog's and the kid's. Well, I thought, especially the kid's. After all, she lived there all the time. The dog and I had only been rented for the weekend.

My name's Jack Hagee; I'm a New York City-based private investigator. The dog was Balto. He's mine. Half-husky, half-German shepherd. One hundred and ten hard-muscled pounds of two-year-old playful energy—sometimes a pain in the ass, but pretty much my best friend in the whole world. And, trust me, the statement is not just campaign rhetoric. There've been times when that hundred and ten pounds of lung and life and unquestioning love has made the never-ending nights bearable enough that I could stand to see the dawn.

The kid was Leslie Stadler, the daughter of my client, Ms. Karen Stadler. I was the baby-sitter. Double my daily fee, just to eat and live better than I usually do and make sure nobody bothered the house. Or the kid. Maybe Sally and Hubert were right, I thought. Maybe it *was* time to start living my life as if there were a tomorrow. Truth to tell, I'd found myself doing a lot of thinking on that subject lately. It hadn't taken much to get me started, either.

A week earlier, simply because I'd taken pity on a woman with a bad marriage and the brothers and sisters of my

1

cleaning girl, Elba—a bunch of good kids who deserved a better lot in this life—I'd ended up being hunted by several gangs of drug dealers, the police, and the media. Without even trying, I'd fallen into about as bad a deal as you can find—one that came with a serial killer, crooked cops, corrupt city officials, machine-gunning maniacs, sex clubs, gang wars, and riots in the streets. During the whole thing people tried to kill me with clubs, knives, handguns, and automatic weapons—sometimes by themselves, sometimes in pairs, sometimes in groups. It was a lot of fun.

To keep from having to rehash the whole lonely story, I'll just say that I managed to clear my name and bring the bad guys low. I wasn't able to do much for this lady or her marriage, but at least I made the people hurting her pay—plenty. I know when all is said and done that really isn't very much, but sometimes it's all we have to offer.

As for the kids in need of a better life, I'd managed to swing a deal where they could stay with their aunt instead of getting split up by the city. It meant that instead of just Balto's and my mouths to feed, I suddenly had a few more, but hell, I figured, what's money for, anyway?

And besides, when everything was finally over, I had found myself with my first four-figure bank account in a long time, a positive position in the community thanks to an embarrassed media, and a beautiful lady friend. The two of us hadn't turned into Tracy and Hepburn yet, but it was getting close. I have to admit that it was a hell of a way to get ahead in life. But, I'll also admit that if someone had to do it, all in all I'm glad it was me.

And that was really what had started me thinking. Suddenly, besides the weight of the responsibility for Elba and her siblings, I also had a comfortable position in life and a very attractive, possibly loving, female companion, all with thirty-five still a few years off. The morning I met Ms. Karen Stadler I was firmly convinced that, despite all the debits I'd piled up over the years, I was finally on a winning streak—finally in sight of the big chance. I was also firmly convinced that a man on a winning streak should not goof up the big chance.

Determined to see that firm conviction through wherever it led, I'd walked through the doors of Morrison, Mason, and Merzon, the city's third biggest advertising firm, fifteen minutes before my meeting with Ms. Stadler. Her secretary had made the appointment the day before, his tone promising that promptness was still a virtue that got rewarded in some circles. He met me in reception with a handshake, passing me a menu and taking my hat and overcoat while we walked to the elevator bank, apologizing for the fact that while I might be on time, Ms. Stadler was going to be "Oh, just a *wee* bit late."

Watching my face carefully, looking for a reaction that might betray the fact I'd noticed his boss was not one to practice what she preached, he confided to me,

"She's really stacked up against it today."

"Meaning what exactly?" I asked him, putting the most innocent spin on the words that I could.

"Oh, God—I mean, oh my God," he answered, stopping abruptly in his tracks, spinning around so he could face me. "It just means madness. I mean crazy madness." His tone slipped to a quieter, conspiratorial level as he continued to feed me confidences.

"Forgive me. I mean, you'd *know* if you were in the business. Trust me when I tell you that it is just brutal this time of year. Just brutal. Campaigns for the new fall season—everyone's first, everyone's best, everyone deserves everything—oh, what a headache." His hands flew up in front of him, his elbows tight at his sides, emphasizing how frazzled he was as he sighed dramatically through his chatter,

"Anyway, if you could jest *pleasssseee* forgive us, Ms. Stadler wanted me to tell you she could be delayed up to fifteen minutes. But, she swore it wouldn't be any longer, though, and she told me not to let you get away. So, that simply leaves me to *beggggggg* you to bear with us."

Although the sighing stopped, the chatter continued. It continued into the elevator, while we rode upward, exited, and worked our way back to the boss lady's office. I learned that it was time for lunch at M. M. & M., which explained the menu—thus making our meeting a tax write-off, so I should get whatever I wanted—just *whatever* I wanted. I learned that the firm handled *alllll* the big ones, just *alllllll* the big ones—that the competition would give just *anny*, *annnything* to get their hands on what his boss was doing for the Radiant account so they could use it—that Karen Stadler was one very heightening woman—and that the coffee bar was around the corner, just over there . . . and that it had, well, you know, anything I desired.

Just anything.

I gave the menu a once-over then ordered a pair of medium-to-well-done bacon cheeseburgers with lettuce and creamy mustard, an order of onion rings, and a tall lemonade. He gave me a smile that told me there was fun in my future and asked me to take a seat. I gave him a nod that I'm not sure told him anything and sat down.

I told myself not to scowl, not to let on that I was pissed as hell—that it was indeed annoying to be told to wait after how snidely I'd been instructed to not keep anyone there waiting. I held it in, somehow. I couldn't have five years earlier. Could have done it a year earlier, but wouldn't have bothered. That's the game, though. They know they're raking your ass over the coals. They—all the "theys"—do it on purpose. The deal is to find out if you're a good little monkey, one they can trust to feed their inflated egos.

I've learned a lot of the lessons the hard way. When a man hits thirty, though, he begins to think more seriously—suddenly some of the things that never seemed important before begin to take on new meanings—things like wives and kids and a home in a building to which only he and his family have the keys. I've never come close to any of those things before. Of course, a quick review of my life makes it easy to see why.

My "adult years" were not what most people would call "calm." Living in a world without jobs, I joined the service straight out of high school. Some Military Intelligence jokers came around looking for muscle to protect their geniuses behind the lines. A lot of guys wanted to make the cut—it meant higher rank and more pay. I liked the thought of being an officer. Mostly I liked the thought of the pay increase that came with the rank. To a basically naive guy from, as they used to say, "humble beginnings," it'd seemed like an easy way to step into a more honorable place—one with a higher calling. When the word came down that I'd made the grade I considered myself lucky.

The things I saw and did over the next six years soured that feeling. I left the service fairly disillusioned about honor and higher callings and the such. Despite what I'll label "the tension between us," an officer I had little other use for, Major Rice, pulled a few strings that got me a spot in the Pittsburgh Police Department. I did their street thing for a while until I got myself into the middle of a race riot the brass decided to pin on me for lack of a better scapegoat.

Usually that kind of plan never fails. Luckily for me, however, it backfired in their faces. The people of Pittsburgh—white and black—instead of howling for my blood, howled for a hero. The department was forced to give me a detective's shield instead of the bum's rush they would have preferred. I got married after that to a woman more in love with my headlines than myself. She cut out when no more headlines came along. I cut out a little while after that.

Where she went, I don't know. Don't really care, either. I went to New York and used the last ounces of juice left in me to try just one more time for a life. Getting myself a P.I. license, I opened an office and set out to put my life back together. That had its ups and downs and, in its own way, tried to kill me just as hard as either the military or the police force had. Up until a week ago I'd been getting more and more tired—weary, really—weary from being shot at, from worrying about being shot at, from a life that seemed to consist of not much more than me and the dog and the smell of gun oil. Sure, I had friends and the diversions most people can afford, but there'd been no purpose to my life that I could see, no goal down the field or even a clear direction in which to run.

But, as I sat there in the outer lobby of Morrison, Mason, and Merzon, thumbing through their magazines, I smiled to myself as I rolled over the notion in my head that maybe, finally, that had all changed. Sure, I reminded myself, I'd thought the same thing when I'd left the service, when I'd made the police force, when I'd been married, when my divorce had come through, when I'd moved to New York, and even a couple of times after that.

For a smart guy, you'd think I'd learn.

CHAPTER 2

I GAVE UP on the magazines pretty quickly. The perfume cards were nauseating and the subject matter was mostly snooty or childish, what little politics there was to be found naive to the point of humor. The models used in them didn't do much for me, either. It wasn't their shapes or their hair or their outfits. It was their sneers—the condescension they wore as perfectly as their makeup. I'm not afraid of women, but I'm damn tired of the ones who think I'm supposed to be.

Waiting for lunch, I studied the architecture around me. It was the usual midtown Manhattan throw-together of easily erected and equally easily destroyed corners, arches, and cardboard facades—the kind one finds everywhere nowadays. The walls were strewn with plastic block-protected art—half of it blowups of some of M.M.&M.'s more chic campaigns and half of it fine art prints—none of it telling me anything essential about the corporation, about its character. Then again, I thought, I wasn't being hired by the corporation.

About ten minutes after I tired of trying to entertain myself, Ms. Stadler's flunky took two calls; one told him lunch had arrived—the other told him to get it and deliver it and me to his boss. Seconds later, a small platter of vegetable slices—green pepper, carrot, mushroom, and some things I didn't recognize—a platter of bacon cheese-burgers, and myself were all presented to Ms. Karen Stadler, senior vice president in charge of special network promotion. Handshakes she did not deem necessary. She told Flunky to turn on her fan as he left so it could pull the meat smells out of the office. The look on her face had me wondering if she was referring to me or the burgers.

As we sat on opposite sides of her desk, I tried to drink in everything around me quickly. Ms. Stadler herself was a fairly nondescript woman. Her height and weight were average; her hair a neutral shade of brunette, cut to a functional, easily maintained length, in a functional, easily maintained style. Her eyes were guarded, made up in a minimal fashion, okay enough, but nothing special. She was not an unattractive woman, just one who did absolutely nothing with what she had while projecting an air that said she couldn't understand those who did. Her suit and office decorations fell much into the same range.

"I've got a very tight schedule, Mr. Huggie . . ."

"That's Hay-gie."

"Excuse me . . . ?"

"Hay-gie. Gie—rhymes with lee. Please, don't worry about it," I insisted for the four millionth time in my life, almost sounding as if I meant it. "Everyone gets it wrong. You were saying?"

"Ah, yes." She drew a pepper slice to pop in her mouth, encouraging me to eat. I did. "I'm sure my assistant explained everything to you."

"Yes, ma'am," I assured her. "You're going to Hawaii for the weekend to work on the set of one of the network's new shows. I'm to provide security for your home, grounds, and daughter. A registered nurse will be staying with us to act as chaperon, and obviously as nurse, if necessary. Everyone is their own cook. You have an alarm system, but after the two B&Es in the area last month you don't want to chance your home being hit."

I took a breath, glanced at her eyes just long enough to make sure she was getting the fact that I was jumping every hoop in sight for her, then I leapt for the next set.

"I've already studied what newspaper clippings I could find on the two incidents as well as the diagrams of your property which you had sent to my office. I've already discussed my possible presence with your local police as well.

"Your daughter has last weekend rehearsals for a school play, which is why she has to stay in New York. The nurse is already installed in the house. I have three different numbers for you in Hawaii—hotel, studio set, and the network's mobile remote wagon. I also have the numbers of your father in Westchester, your friends, the Crandells— three doors down to the left—and your doctor's. I have two routes to the school memorized. I will take her to rehearsal by one, wait for her to finish, and then bring her back home by another.

"I also have Xeroxes for you of my insurance, my license, weapon's registration, and my carry permit."

I took another bite while she studied her copies. The burgers were done perfectly, the thin line of soft pink in their centers the only bit of them not bursting with hot, tongue-pleasing juices. The bacon was perfect as well, four long, thick pieces to a burger, all of their folds covered with a thick layer of sweet, bubbling mozzarella. As I was finishing the first of the artery-cloggers, Ms. Stadler said,

"You seem to have everything mapped out, but there is one more thing. No one comes near Leslie." She swallowed another bite and then added, "Especially her father."

"I wasn't told anything about this."

"Don't you dare think you're going to walk out on me at the last minute . . ."

"I didn't say anything—"

"Or run your charges higher . . ."

"Excuse, me, Ms. Stadler," I blurted sharply, loud enough to force a pause, soft enough to not chase away a big-money client as long as I was still entertaining dreams of settling down and maintaining a regular life. Having regained her attention, I continued, saying,

"All I said was, nobody has given me any information about this. I'll need your husband's name . . . a photo . . . some idea of why I should be worried about keeping him from her. Would he harm her? Kidnap her? What are we talking about here? Would he use a weapon? Would he use her as a hostage if he got desperate? Did you break up because of something between the two of you, or between him and Leslie?"

Ms. Stadler held up a finger and then apologized.

"All right. I'm sorry. I jumped the gun and I sprang this on you badly and at the last minute. No. No, none of that—not really. I mean, yes, I have worried that John might try to kidnap Leslie on occasion, I'll admit it—but I don't think he really would. Why don't we finish eating and I'll answer your questions as best I can."

From there on I got the last details I needed to know, including all the facts to the inside story on her ex-marriage to her boring, investor/accountant ex-husband. Those details, uninteresting as they were, still seemed to make me a lot less calm about John than she was. Leslie'd been Daddy's little girl, but because of the nature of the breakup, Daddy, whose name I noted was Fitzgerald and not Stadler, was being denied visitation rights by the courts for the moment. They were scheduled to go back to court for further rounds of fighting over when he would get them—if ever—but that was in the future and something that just couldn't be worried about at the moment.

Of course, I thought, maybe that was because she was just delegating worrying over the situation to her newest employee. But then, why not? After all, it was the kind of thing for which she was paying me, wasn't it?

And finally, after some further business conversation, Ms. Stadler turned over a set of keys to me and that was that for Thursday afternoon. Twenty-six hours later I watched her taxi pull out, and then turned to find out what life with a fourteen-year-old was all about. Pointing at Balto, the smaller mistress of the house asked,

"Does he like cats?"

"He tolerates them. Why? Do you have a cat?"

"Yes. And I'd like it if he wasn't eaten by your wolf-hound."

"I think that can be arranged."

Smiling to myself, I bent over and grabbed Balto around the neck, pulling him to me roughly. Shaking him back and forth, I yelled at him,

"No cats on the diet, you monster. Got that? No cats!"

Balto growled out his playtime roar, letting me know he would eat anything he pleased. I responded by flopping him over on his side. He snapped at me, catching my wrist in his mouth several times, but never breaking the skin. I raised my fist, threateningly.

"No cats, you horselizard. Got it?"

Balto barked his version of "yes, sir" and we straightened ourselves up. Leslie might have been amused, but if she was she did an admirable job of covering it up. So much for my vast understanding of the fourteen-year-old mind. Looking at us as if we were both in clown makeup, she told me,

"You're pretty silly for a detective."

"Yeah," I admitted, "my friend, Ray Trenkel, he likes to say that, too."

"Who's he?"

"He's a police captain." Before she could ask anything else, I pointed at Leslie and commanded, "Balto—take the measure."

Understanding that we had shifted into our business mode, Balto trotted forward, sniffing Leslie front and back, top and bottom. She reacted uncomfortably, asking,

"What's he doing?"

"Recording your scent. We're both here to work. To do his part of the job, he has to record everyone and every place here. Once he knows all the smells in the house, he'll know everything he needs to in case there is any trouble."

"Our house doesn't smell," I was told.

"Everything smells. Some things smell bad and some good, and most have such a slight smell that you and I can't smell them at all—but he can."

She looked at me for a moment, trying to convince me she was filled with doubt, her eyes letting me know she wanted a show. Sitting on top of any little-girl giddiness which might have proved embarrassing to her, she challenged me with her best fourteen-year-old disdain, commanding,

"Prove it."

"Okay. Get me something Balto can carry in his mouth."

The girl thought for a moment, and then ran out of the room, returning seconds later with that week's *TV Guide*. After giving Balto a chance to get its odor, I told her to go and hide it. After she returned, I gave Balto the fetch order. He was back with it in a tenth of the time it had taken her to hide it, looking quite pleased with himself. She was impressed.

Before we knew what had happened, Balto was fetching the *TV Guide* from every corner of the house. Every time he brought it back, Leslie's face lit equally with delight and frustration. After the pair of them had gotten to the point where they could play by themselves, I took my bag to the room where I'd been told to store my things. While I was unpacking, Ms. Stadler's nurse stuck her head in the door.

"Hi—welcome to the staff."

"Thanks," I told her with a sour grin.

"The things we do for money, eh?"

She was an attractive woman, late twenties, black hair, dark eyes, not quite long legs but a nice figure—strong Spanish blood in there somewhere—blood that seemed fairly interested in me. Just my luck. Why is it, I wondered, that good-looking women only wander into your life once you have a steady relationship? The evil part of my mind mentioned to me that Sally and I hadn't had a steady relationship for all that long. I beat my hormones back with a stick handed me by the virtuous part of my mind, the part of me stuck in the middle wondering if this adult relationship stuff was all it was cracked up to be. Outside my head, I bantered back and forth with the nurse while I unpacked, the two of us checking each other out.

I discovered that her name was Tori—that she'd been a nurse for seven years, that she'd stayed with Leslie a number of times in the past, that she wouldn't mind doing the cooking if I'd help with the dishes, and that she had a nice laugh and a coltish manner I was sure came unconsciously which is, of course, what made it so attractive.

She discovered that I'm a sucker for women who call me "blue eyes"—that I'd been M.I. and then with the P.P.D., before finally ending up with my private ticket—that I like

Gilbey's gin if I'm going to drink—that I still smoke cigarettes—that I've never been to the ballet and rarely watch TV—except, of course, for never missing "The Simpsons"—but that I hit the movies roughly once a week, mostly to see comedies. She also made a point of finding out if I was seeing anybody. I told the truth. That got a question.

"Can I ask you why you told me that?"

"What d'ya mean?"

"I mean, here we are, man and woman, locked up for the weekend together, and before you find out whether or not there could be a chance for a little whoopee between us, you just blurt out the truth. I'm curious what makes a man do that. I haven't met many who would."

As we headed back downstairs, I told her,

"Not to try and go pompous on you, but my life's been one long look at what lying does for people. Whether it's country to country or person to person, lies ruin everything they touch. They hurt and they maim and they kill everything in sight. I've watched the Russians use lies, the C.I.A.—everyone's local police and all our political leaders. I make my living unscrambling other people's lies and bringing them down for telling them. I hate lies. I'm sick to death of them."

She smiled at me as we stepped down into the hallway leading to the living room.

"You sure come on strong," she told me.

"I know," I agreed. "Sally, the woman I've been seeing, she says the same thing. It's, well . . . like anybody, I harp the most on the chords I need to hear the most. I . . . I saw some awful dirty games when I was in the service. I don't like to remember them. It's easier to forget lies you've told if you don't tell any new ones."

"Wait a minute." She snapped her fingers. "I know you—oh my gosh—you're the guy they were chasing for murder—the one that politician tried to frame!"

I turned sharply, staring at her. People hadn't taken to chasing me through the streets or asking for my autograph, but the media coverage of everything that had happened just a little over a week previous had made me a target for people's comments. Wondering what hers might be, I admitted,

"Yeah, that's me, all right."

"Oh, I know. I remember it—you and that policeman, what was he . . . a corporal?"

"Captain," I told her. "Captain Ray Trenkel."

"Right, yeah," she said, her excitement level growing. "Him and you—everyone was chasing you two. The TV, they were all saying you were guilty as sin—on the news, in the papers, everywhere. And you called them on it and beat them. The cops and the mayor and all of them. The press, they really got nice to you after, huh? Bastards. They trash your life without a thought and then it's 'Oops, I guess you're a hero.' Did any of them ever apologize or come out and say on the air that they had almost gotten you killed?"

I told her they hadn't. She said that the news was no surprise. Looking at me in a different light, she took my hand to shake it, telling me,

"Hey, anyway. Nice job. Wow. I'm spending the weekend with a hero. My girlfriends and I, we talked about you— you know. We all agreed we wanted to—"

I cut her off before she made it too tough on me.

"Yeah, yeah—please. You'll swell my mushy little head and then my girlfriend will throw me out. And," I added, batting my blue eyes at her for comic effect, "well, gee—you wouldn't want that, would you?"

"I don't know," she teased. "Getting you back out loose on the streets. There're a lot of women who might like to add a night with you to their collection." Then, suddenly, her joking demeanor disappeared, replaced by one more disturbing.

"Don't worry, I wouldn't do that to you. There's few enough men left in this world who would pass by an offer"—she stretched her body provocatively against the door frame of my room—"this good. You *are* passing it by—aren't you?" she asked in a humorously silly voice.

"Yeah." I threw a smile at her. It was a lopsided one that

let her know that she had a tempting offer, just to make her feel better while I teased her back, "Not that you're making it any easier on me."

Smiling to herself, satisfied she was only being passed by because I was a one-woman kind of guy, she dropped her *Penthouse* pose and then added,

"I'm impressed. Our rich lady has really hired herself a hotshot this time, huh?"

My neck grew hot and red. I pursed my lips to one side in a frowning grin. Of course I was flattered and a part of me swelled with the artificial importance that comes from being recognized by a stranger, but part of me was also damned uncomfortable. Although nothing had been said at my meeting, and I was certain Tori was not implying anything, I was fairly sure that the dour Ms. Stadler—like a number of other people who had contacted me during the last week—had done so only because of my current television notoriety.

I'd grabbed all the other contracts, of course, taking a fair cut and then farming the work out to my regular stable of free-lancers. Money is money, after all. But, it was leading to something I had always thought I never wanted—a big agency, one with employees under me, health benefits, an ad box in the yellow pages . . . stability. Somehow, every conversation I was having was leading me back to the same subject—one I was going to have to think about—long and hard. Not wanting to appear too distracted, though, I answered Tori, saying,

"Yeah, that's me. The newest TV hotshot. Move over Magnum—here comes Jack Hagee. I'll admit I've never thought of myself in such flattering terms before, but thanks for the vote of confidence, anyway."

She smiled as if I'd just made her my special confidante. She asked if I was hungry. I told her yes. She agreed that she was as well and headed for the kitchen. As she walked away, I asked her,

"Hey, since I'm a big celebrity, do I still have to help with the dishes?"

"You want to eat," she called out without turning around, "you work."

I headed into the living room, smiling. So much for celebrity.

CHAPTER 3

THE REST OF Friday went smoothly. I took Leslie to her school for evening rehearsal right after dinner, noting how much neater the Westchester snow removal crews were than the ones in New York City. Imagine that, I thought, rich people getting treated better than poor people—what a concept.

A long five hours later we finally left. It hadn't been bad—most of the kids made up with heart what they didn't have in talent. Meredith Willson's had worst done to him in his time. They were doing *The Music Man*—Leslie had snared the part of the mayor's wife. Not a lead, but a good, well-developed character part. She enjoyed playing a strong-willed woman who defied her husband and went after her own dreams the first chance she got. I didn't have to ask where she'd picked up those traits. She also fell naturally into the character's ability to allow herself to be sweet-talked by a flimflammer. I wondered if she'd picked that up from the same drama coach.

I got us back home to stately Stadler Manor as fast as road conditions would allow. We were all back in the homestead, cleaned up, and tucked in—Leslie in her room, Tori in one down the hall, me on the living room couch—long before midnight. The Stadler women did have another guest room—I'd stored my gear in it. I simply chose not to use it. Couches are less comfortable than beds. That makes them better for light sleeping. Also, break-and-enter specialists expect to find people in their beds, not the living room. It's only a small advantage, true, but I've found that most of the time small advantages are all you get.

I'm not sure where Balto slept—I rarely am. Whenever I take him on a security job, he always scouts the area we're watching and then picks his own spot. I think it has something to do with finding the core of a location's sounds, the area from where he can hear the most noises a place has to make. I'm not sure, obviously because he's never told me one way or the other, but it's my best guess. Nothing happened Friday night anyway, though, so it was all academic.

The next morning Leslie found me in the living room cleaning my .38 when she finally got up. The first thing she asked me was where Balto was. I told her I didn't know exactly. She told me,

"He's pretty smart."

"Sure, he's Balto, the wonder dog."

"What're you doing?"

"Cleaning my gun."

"I know that. I mean, what're you doing it for? Why do you have to clean it?"

"Well, in truth," I answered, finishing up, "mostly just because I'm bored. This isn't a full cleaning, anyway. This is just maintenance. I clean it every few days."

"Do you have to?"

"Actually, yeah. You want to keep your guns free of dirt because they'll rust if you don't. Besides—dirt, grease, dust—anything inside the barrel can cause your shot to pull to the left or right. Rust never sleeps." Then, looking at her watch me, I got a thought and said,

"Guess you've probably never seen a real gun before. Would your mother mind if you looked at it?"

"Yeah," said Leslie with a dragging sigh, one I had to admit was probably no different than a fourteen-year-old boy's would have been.

"Probably."

Suddenly feeling like a conspiratorial uncle from an old black-and-white TV show, I held the unloaded revolver out to Leslie with the cylinder open, saying,

"Then, I guess we better not tell her."

Leslie's smile grew wide. She took the gun in her hand,

her eyes popping open in surprise at its weight. The .38 dragged her hand down a foot before she was able to compensate and bring it back up.

"Wow." She whistled. "Just like television."

Then, she flicked her wrist to snap the cylinder into place. I flinched. Reaching out, I took the gun back for a moment, saying,

"Just one of the things TV does wrong. Never close a revolver that way—it jars the mechanism. It's also noisy. Here, let me show you something."

Releasing the cylinder again, I showed her how to lock it back into place correctly by just shoving it in with your other hand, or even against your chest.

"Even a one-handed shooter doesn't have an excuse for treating his gun that way."

"Is everything on television wrong about policemen?"

"Well," I told her, "not everything, but most of it."

"Like what?"

I showed her how to swab the barrel and told her.

"Where to begin? Well, no one gets hit over the head two or three times in one day and then goes off on a date. They die because their gray matter's been denied oxygen."

"Yeahhh?" she asked, fascinated. I weighed going on against possibly upsetting her mother. A lot of people have something against telling their kids the truth. I'm not sure why that is—what they could be so terrified of that they risk lying to their own children to escape it, but whatever it is I've never been that afraid of it. Maybe when I have my own kids I'll find out different. Willing to risk a bit of the truth with someone else's daughter, though, I said,

"Well, maybe they'll be lucky and only end up with some bearable level of brain damage, but 'maybe' don't come along much in real life."

"What else?"

"Well," I said, telling myself *in for a penny* . . . "let me see. Cars can't fly through the air and slam against the street and keep driving. You get a bent axle or a cracked drive shaft—you at least lose your hubcaps. The cops can be the bad guys just as often as they can be the good guys. And not even because they're bad people. Sometimes it's just the law they have to enforce that's bad. Aahhhh, there's so much . . ."

I told her about how boring and truly dangerous police work is. I told her about the long hours and the feeling of futility they induce in those struggling through them. Focusing our physical attention on the gun, I showed her how to hold it, how to aim, and how to support her wrist with her other hand while at the same time I tried to slide everything into place as I told her about different criminals I'd known.

"You have to understand," I said, moving her hand up her arm, tightening her grip on her wrist, "when you come right down to it—nobody in the world thinks they're the bad guy. Everyone has the best reasons for the things they do. What you have to remember is that people who steal, or murder, or rape—do you even know what rape is?"

"Sure, my mom and I had a long talk about it after a TV movie where a guy tried to rape this woman and she caught him and tortured him for it."

"Uh-huh. Okay, well, anyway—the people who do these things, they don't think of themselves as bad people. It's always someone else's fault they did what they did."

"Why is that?"

"Because no one wants to be responsible for their actions anymore. People . . ." Suddenly I stopped. Remembering that what I did with my own children was one thing—what I did with someone else's was another, I asked myself how far I intended on taking my little lecture. I also asked myself if I would even give the same lecture to my own daughter at the same age.

Suddenly I was feeling stupid. Bad enough to risk offending a rich client by teaching her fourteen-year-old about proper weapons ordinance—popping off about the criminal justice system to a grade-schooler was no way to endear myself, either. The whole thing became a grim, weighted reminder of what being a parent is all about. When Leslie asked why I had stopped talking, I got another.

"Oh," I told her honestly, "let's just say I was getting

carried away. Believe me, as any of my friends will tell you, you don't want to hear me go on about the civil irresponsibility of our politicians and legal system and the such."

"Why not?" she asked. "My mother says I should learn about the world any chance I get."

"Maybe so, but I don't think 'The World According to Jack Hagee' is what she had in mind. Besides," I answered, pointing toward the clock over the living room's fireplace mantel, "don't we have a school to get to?"

"Nutzoidal ruination," she shouted, seeing the time. "I'll go get my stuff—I'll meet you in the driveway." She headed upstairs, then stopped to yell back, "Can Balto the wonder dog go with us?"

"To school?"

"Sure, all the kids would love him. He's tiger-ready."

I told her, "Sure, why not?" She ran upstairs. I found my "tiger-ready"—whatever that means—canine, and got us both headed toward the front door. Sticking my head into the kitchen, I told Tori we were off, and then left for the car. Leslie and Balto talked in the backseat. I chauffeured. It gave me another one of those grim reminders.

CHAPTER 4

WE RETURNED IN the wee dark hours. Leslie was exhausted. I was pretty done in myself. Balto bounded out first, showing off his usual endless energy, but was kind enough to wait for us. At least for a moment. As we trudged up over the patches of sludge frozen to the driveway, he raced past us back to the car, then raced back to the house, giving us a playful, "Why, you couldn't be tired, could you?" look. Anyone who has ever owned a dog knows the look I mean.

The play's director, extremely pleased with his cast's progress, had decided to be magnanimous and take everyone out for pizza. I had to go wherever they did, and Balto goes with me. We were both welcomed, teacher and cast all wanting to hear lurid tales of big-city crime. Since there's little that warms my heart like free pizza and a chance to spin a few stories, everyone got what they wanted.

And so, after more pizza, bragging, and stupid pet tricks than are good for anyone, Leslie and I staggered up the driveway, Balto's Speed Racer antics making her laugh through her yawns. I could tell my brain was again testing out the feel of having children around. Deep down I had to admit that I liked the sound of it—the tired laughter, her attempts to keep up with me, my attempts to keep up with her . . . both of us trying to keep up with my half-witted mutt.

"Hey," I told her finally, panting partly for the comic effect, partly because it was the much easier way to breathe considering the way I was feeling. "I'm an old man stuffed to the gills with cheese and pepperoni. Come on, now.

Something's got to give here. I'm usually in bed by now with some hot milk."

"Oh, yeah—right."

I could tell she didn't believe me. Looking as hurt as I could, I asked her,

"How old do you think I am, anyway?"

She stopped in her tracks, turned and stared up at me through the darkness. She scrunched her face up as if she were trying to make a good guess, then said,

"I don't know. What—maybe sixty?"

"What?" I asked her in mild shock. "Sixty? Do I look like a grandfather or something to you? Sixty? Shheee-zit. I'm only thirty-two."

"Sure," she answered, sounding as if she were only taking pity on me. "Whatever you say, Jack."

Then she turned back toward the house, continuing to giggle, making me think she wasn't really convinced. Well, I thought, that's all right. I guess. Then I found myself wondering if she really thought I was the hot milk type. I was beginning to wonder if being around kids was a very good idea for people like me. I'm not used to being that paranoid. Before I could develop a full-blown complex, however, Leslie begged me to let her take Balto to the backyard.

"All right," I told her. Then, looking down at my grinning hound, I told him, "Now listen, horselizard . . . Leslie's in charge. You listen to her, but keep an eye on things—okay?"

Balto barked out his interpretation of "okay." I decided that was good enough for me and headed up the stone stairs to the front door.

I called out for Tori as I went inside, but got no response. Checking my watch, I saw it was even later than I'd thought. It suddenly dawned on me that the pizza celebration had gone on a bit longer than I had realized. But, I figured, what the hell. Ms. Stadler hadn't set any particular bedtime. Looking up at the dark house, I figured Tori must have already sacked out for the night. Fine by me, I thought. All in all, it sounded like a damn sensible idea.

In fact, I found myself smiling. The weekend had turned out to be just the thing I needed. Chauffeuring a kid around, playing with her and the dog, supervising meals and living in the suburbs and all the rest had felt pretty chummy. I'd fit into the patterns of that life a lot easier than I'd ever thought I would—hoped I would, anyway—a discovery that was coming as more of a relief than a surprise.

Dragging myself lazily through the living room, I decided to give Leslie ten more minutes of playtime and then call her and the mutt inside. Never one to be particularly bothered by a cup of bean before bedtime, I went into the kitchen and switched on the percolator. Then, shrugging out of my shoulder holster, I left it on the coffee table near my couch and headed upstairs to the bathroom. As I reached the landing I fumbled for the lights, tired and careless and still not quite adjusted to someone else's living space. That's when he hit me.

The blow came from the side, low and crushing— stinging like hell and just a half inch off from where it would have done a lot more damage. I fell back down the stairs, tumbling and yelling the whole way. I hit the floor—hard—skidding out into the center of the living room. I hadn't had to fall so far, but I was trying to put some distance between myself and whoever it was dealing out the love taps. It didn't work, though. As I tried to get back to my feet I discovered that my attacker had followed me down. Two sharp kicks kept me on the floor—my eyes closed, head spinning. The lights started to flicker out again. From somewhere hidden in the darkness, a voice told me,

"Be smart, big guy. Stay where you are. I don't know who you are. I don't know what you're doing here. And honestly, I don't want to know, either."

My brain started to clear slightly as he talked. I stared at him through the darkness, but couldn't tell anything from what little I could see, especially with the stars still spinning in my head. Blinking caused cracks of pain to shoot across the top of my skull, setting electric flashes off in my eyes. I couldn't tell if my head hurt more with my eyes open or closed so I settled for just not caring. While I tried to bring my hands to my head, my attacker told me,

"To put you at ease, the lady in white is tied up in her bedroom. Cooperate, and that's where you'll go, too. I haven't found what I came for, but something tells me you've got the answers I need."

As my hands finally managed to crawl up the sides of my splitting head, a thought hit me—John Fitzgerald. Somehow he had found out about his wife's weekend absence and had decided it was time to make his move. I didn't want to go hard on him, and yet my job was to keep him from what he wanted to do. Besides, I told myself, it wasn't as if I had a whole lot of choice. The little voice inside was more than happy to point out that he was the one standing with a lead sap in his hand while I was the one rolling on the floor in pain. For a boring investor/accountant, the guy packed a hell of a wallop.

Of course, I told myself, that had just been a lucky blow. The guy would know his own home better than I would. He was probably smart enough to see a man's clothes and know someone else would be coming back. So, when he heard all our idiot noise outside, he just sat and waited and then bushwhacked me.

Okay, I thought, trying to screen out the pain—goody for him. Now it was going to be my turn. All I would need was one good shot at him. After all, lucky shots, hell-of-a-wallops or not, he was still just an accountant. Bouncing guys into next week was more my specialty than it was his.

Figuring I wouldn't hurt him too badly, I dragged myself to my feet, nodding slowly when he motioned me back up toward the bedrooms, acting more hurt than I was. He bought it. As we reached the base of the stairs, I tripped myself—nothing exaggerated, just a short stagger. As I stumbled back past him, I planted my right foot and then sidestepped hard to the left—elbow out—digging. My attacker went down like a fat lady on ice, but . . . so did I.

While I'd made my move, someone else still hidden in the shadows had made theirs, clubbing me from behind. The pain shot over both ears and refilled my eyes with a star

field the size of the Milky Way. I hit on my knees and then
toppled to my side. I was hurt and gasping, holding my
head, forcing back the screams and tears raging at me to
give in to the darkness and forget all about the two
gentlemen with the saps. I couldn't imagine who they were,
or what they wanted. I couldn't imagine anything. The pain
tearing at me made thinking about what was happening too
hard to maintain.

Thoughts sped through my brain, relaying past each other
in a jumble. Whatever was going on, it was not a random
break-in. These two weren't just sneak thieves—this was a
dark blitz team, a well-trained pair, used to working
together—if it was only a pair. Even through the pain, I
knew that whoever they were, neither one of them was John
Fitzgerald. This was something serious, which meant it was
time for me to get serious, but . . . oh God, it hurts—if I
could just . . .

Pain hit again—a kick told me it was the first one, on his
feet again. I'd grown used to his kicks—knew how he
placed them. The little whisper that tries to protect all of us
told me I had to do something, fight back, but I couldn't
react, couldn't focus past the ringing in my ears. Something
finally got my attention, though. The sound of an automatic's hammer sliding into place . . . and the second's voice
saying,

"Kill him."

I tried to react, but it was useless. I was in too much
agony. I could barely open my eyes, let alone start a
wrestling match. If I only had a minute—just sixty seconds
to clear my head and figure out how to get my feet back
under me. Simple things, but impossible ones. As I forced
myself forward blindly, desperately trying for a lucky
connection with one of them, I heard more noise coming
from somewhere. Then gunfire blasted away in the background behind the stabbing agony drumming in my ears.

CHAPTER 5

"NOW, WAIT A minute." Sally stared past the fettuccine on the end of her fork. We'd gone to the Spumoni Gardens, my favorite neighborhood restaurant. We'd already done a great deal of damage to the bread basket, polished off the complimentary order of baked clams they give every couple that orders an entrée, and made decent headway against the platter of fried calamari most places would call a meal for two but which the Gardens merely called an appetizer. Well, I'd done a lot of damage, at least. Eating is one of my favorite ways to celebrate. We were celebrating my still being alive. One of my favorite things to celebrate.

As I stuffed an oversized calamari ring into my mouth, going weak from the taste of its herb-seasoned breading, Sally asked with a little impatience,

"I'm mad enough that you didn't get on the wire and exclusive me with this story. But now you're getting ahead of yourself. Who were those guys?"

I smiled. Never date a reporter if you want to be able to finish telling anything the way you want to.

"Well, dear," I answered, "aside from the fact that I really don't think either of us needs to make this a public romance by tipping people off with me giving you exclusives for no apparent reason, if you *must* ruin the way I'd like to tell this story . . ."

"Oh," she answered, her blue-gray eyes sparkling, "I must. I must."

"Sigh, women." I pouted for a second to make her smile, then finally swallowed my last bite, spread my arms out for emphasis, and told her.

"Well, sweetheart, believe it or not, you almost lost your fabulously talented meal ticket here for the greater glory of the Radiant Lady Cosmetics Company."

Sally looked at me for a second. Her head jolted just a fraction, shaking her black, shoulder-length hair. Then she caught on, waving her fork as she exclaimed,

"Oh, I get it. Corporate spies. They were there trying to steal your Ms. Stadler's notes."

As she slid the last of her forkful into her mouth in triumph, I told her,

"Yes, dear. It seems that they'd already pieced together that she keeps her most important account notes at home, so home is where they came. Not expecting big and powerful yours truly, of course."

"Oh, and a big lot of help you turned out to be." Tapping her fork against her plate, signaling that I'd stalled her long enough, she demanded,

"And speaking of which, you've strung me along with this tale of yours past the point of no return. Spill it—how'd you get out of that mess in one piece, anyway?"

"Well—back before I was so rudely interrupted—that noise I mentioned . . . that was Balto taking down one of the guys. The gunshots, that was Leslie."

Sally looked up from her fettuccine. Her mouth had stopped chewing. I was fairly sure that she had forgotten she had a fork in her mouth. Hoping to nip the jokes I could sense were coming, I said,

"Yeah, when she and Balto came in, she found my .38 on the coffee table. She, uh, knew I needed help so she . . . she picked it up and started blasting."

Sally smiled, the backs of her eyes lighting with mischief. Knowing she couldn't hold in whatever comment she'd come up with, I told her,

"Go on, get it over with."

"Honestly, Jack," she said sweetly, finally chewing again, "I don't know what you mean."

The ever-growing smile she couldn't hide let me know that she would figure out what I meant sometime before the evening was over. I frowned back at her, hiding my mortification behind another mouthful of calamari. For some reason it didn't seem to taste as good as the one before it.

"So, did she kill anybody?"

"No, no. She hit one guy—a nick, really. Balto was the hero of the day. He downed the one with the gun while the other whined about the hit he took from Leslie. I did manage to get the whiner's legs and bring him down. Blind or not, once I was on top of him he was easy enough to take care of."

"Ohhhh," Sally answered breathlessly, "now I'm just all breathless." As she batted her eyelashes at me, reminding me of my clowning around with Tori, making me feel guilty without even knowing it, I made a motion indicating I'd like to bounce her head off the back wall. She took it as a compliment to her comedic skills and laughed me off. Knowing I stood no chance I changed the subject.

"Ms. Stadler didn't like the results much, lot of blood on the living room carpet—to say the least—but she agreed the consequences would have been worse."

"What do you mean?"

"My playmate wasn't lying when he said the nurse was in the bedroom. He did lie about her condition, though. Tori'd been roughed up pretty bad. She'd also overheard talk that has her absolutely convinced they were going to kill her once they had what they wanted. Since I know they were going to kill me, nobody seems to have much doubt that they wouldn't have had any compunction about killing Leslie, too." I forked up another jumbo ring and then added,

"The police were glad to get their hands on the pair, too. They think they can tie them in with some other nasty jobs with the same M.O. Official thinking is that they keep anyone they come across alive until they're finished just in case they get caught. A pretty sick pair to be operating in the business espionage field, but there are stranger things in this world. Anyway, Leslie and Tori are both okay." I concluded as I swallowed,

"And that's pretty much that."

"I think I'm disappointed."

Knowing I was being teased again, but no more immune to the effects of it than the next guy, I asked,

"Okay, I'll bite. What's so disappointing?"

"Well, heavens, what kind of hard-boiled detective are you turning into? I mean, you take a rich client you can hardly stand, you pass up a chance to sleep with a sexy woman, you don't even raid the liquor cabinet . . . then, you let two hoods beat you up, a puppy and a little girl have to save you . . . I don't know, I don't know. What happened to all the beating and shooting you're so famous for? This doesn't sound like the tough guy that swept me off my feet."

"Wha—haven't you heard, all that tough guy stuff is *tres passé* these days. Why, I don't think I could ever do the wild kinds of things you're suggesting anymore. Oh no." I suddenly switched my voice to my best "Masterpiece Theatre" imitation of an upper crust British accent,

"No . . . I've grown far too refined in your company to even contemplate such things ever again."

It was her turn to smile. She stared at me a moment, eyeing up her prey, then leaned forward.

"Oh, yeah?"

"Really," I told her, keeping up the accent. "I've seen the error of my ways, dearest Sally. From here on I'm looking forward to a far more genteel and contemplative life."

" 'Contemplative,' is it?"

"Oh, yes. Quite right."

"No more fun or excitement now, eh?"

"Well," I said, the accent breaking as I suddenly grew a lot more serious than I'd thought I was going to. "Maybe, Sal . . . I was thinking of trying a, I don't know, *different* kind of fun and excitement."

"Why," she answered, "now you've got me curious. What did you have in mind?"

I looked at her as if I were doing it for the first time—not that I wanted to be that enamored again, that much in awe, but I couldn't help myself. Putting down my fork, I knotted my hands in front of me, not knowing what else to do with them. Moving my head from side to side, sometimes looking at Sally, sometimes not, I dropped the accent completely and told her,

"I don't know, exactly. I've just been thinking a lot. Ever since I sorta became responsible for Elba and her brothers and sisters and all, I've been thinking about a lot of stuff. You and Hubert have been harping at me to expand my agency, capitalize on my notoriety and all, and . . . well, I've been thinking that you're both right."

Sally looked a little stunned, the way most people do when you agree with them and tell them that you think they're right when they tell you how you should run your life.

"You do?"

"Yeah. When I took the Stadler job I farmed out a lot of other cases that came in. I've done it in the past. Pete Wei and Vinnie and Grampy—they're always looking to pick up some loose change—Hu and Maurice are always willing to skim a percent to dig up someone for me. The thing is . . . well," I said with a stall in my voice, needing time to hear the words, convincing myself as well as Sally.

"I've been thinking that maybe it wouldn't be so awful to be the boss. I might like that. Set my own hours . . . get to take a vacation once in a while. Not always be the guy who gets shot at—that'd be nice. I mean, the P.I. business is not supposed to be so dangerous. It's actually *supposed* to be kind of boring—you know? It's *supposed* to be just a lot of research and digging up facts and records for lawyers and, well, a lot of other dull stuff. But me—I mean . . . it seems like every time I turn around somebody's trying to do me in."

I searched her eyes, looking for the cue that would tell me she understood and that I was on the right track. Not seeing it, but assuming it was just around the corner, I fed her a little more bait, saying,

"I'm tired of all these little boy's games, Sal. I never asked to be anybody's hero. I want a life—a real one—just like everyone else. And I want all of it—do you know what I mean? The whole bit—the home of my own, grass to mow, regular dental checkups, something in the refrigerator besides restaurant leftovers in tin pans . . . kids. And a wife . . . to go with them . . . that would be nice."

Still looking in her eyes, I saw her reaction to my bait. It wasn't quite the reaction I'd been looking for.

"What are you saying, Jack?"

"Don't worry. I'm not proposing," I told her honestly. "I'm just talking. Talking about where I want to go and, sorta hinting about who I'd like to go there with. Some of it I want to do now, some of it I just want to start working toward. I thought, was hoping, anyway, that you might be thinking something along the same lines. Guess not."

"Jack." I heard what was coming in her voice and it froze my spine. Sap, I told myself. Fucking sap. Spend a weekend in the suburbs—a weekend that almost gets your brain rearranged—and suddenly you're thinking about being fucking Ward Cleaver. I hadn't expected her to jump up and down and squeal with delight, clapping her hands like some second grader who'd just finished counting her valentines in the back of homeroom and found out she'd gotten more than any of the other girls, but I thought I'd been on at least something like the same wavelength with her. It wasn't the first time I'd thought wrong about such things in my life, though. Ask my ex-wife. Hell, ask anybody.

"I, I," she stuttered, "I just wanted us to . . . get to know each other. I mean, maybe . . ."

"Don't say anything else, Sal."

"Maybe later if, I mean when . . ."

"Drop it. Let's just eat. Forget about it."

"I mean we haven't known each other that long and I never thought that you would be . . . that you could be . . . I mean, this is so fast and . . ."

"Sally," I said her name harder than I meant to, throwing it at her like a lit match. "Drop it. I was wrong. You've been good enough to let me know that."

"Jack, I don't . . ."

"You want to keep talking," I spat, not talking even out of pain, but from hurt and anger. A nasty, growling defensive voice rose up from within me, steering me toward the driver's seat, ready to make sure that if I was going to feel bad, everyone around me was going to feel worse. "Fine. I'll give you a topic. What the hell have you been going out with me for anyway then? Laughs? Sex? I'm good enough that you can bear to waste my time and money—but to think about something permanent—to think about the future with a guy like me, that'd be out of the question—right? Fuckin' right?!"

"Jack, don't . . ."

"Don't what? Don't start in on the truth? Don't cut off your string of bullshit clichés about wanting to just date and not get serious like we were in high school or something?"

"You're a real bastard."

"Don't start us on name-calling. I used to be a tough guy—remember? I'm pretty good at that one."

"Stop it, Jack."

"Or maybe we should—nice screaming match—maybe it would give us that elusive something in common you must think we have missing from our 'relationship.'"

The little voice inside did its best to let me know that perhaps I was making a horse's ass out of myself, but like most horse's asses, I didn't care. Going all cold inside, my voice got quiet as I said,

"You want to start us out, or should I?"

Sally sat staring at me, her eyes sad and hurting. Then, suddenly they boiled up, her brows folding down, making her face as cold and harsh as mine must have been. Quietly, her hands both clenched into fists, she looked at me and said,

"And I thought I hated you before."

"Yeah," I told her, my brain telling me to shut up before it was too late, "I remember that night, too. Another guy doesn't fuck you the way you like it, and so you take it out on the first guy who does. There's some typical female logic."

She stood up then, grabbing her coat from the chair next to her. If there was anything in her eyes asking me to stop her, I couldn't see it. Maybe there wasn't enough of me that wanted to see it. Maybe it just wasn't there.

"Good night, Mr. Hagee," she said coldly. "Enjoy your meal."

I turned from her, pulling my cigarettes from my jacket pocket. Bending my head down to the glass candle bowl in the center of the table, I lit up easily from its flame. Bringing my head back up, I exhaled deeply, letting go a big cloud. By the time I did, she was gone.

Knowing I was in the nonsmoking section, realizing I'd only lit up to annoy her, I crushed the cigarette out in the center of the calamari. I didn't feel much like smoking anymore. Obviously I didn't feel much like eating anymore, either. I looked at the last thread of smoke leaking out of the crushed cigarette in the middle of my meal. Anger tore at my insides. I wanted to smash the butt, knock the plates from the table, hurl food and glass and china in every direction. My fingers tried to curl into fists. My anger pounded in my head—screaming at me—blind, red lines of hate crisscrossing over my eyes, pushing me toward violence.

I controlled myself, though—somehow—feeling stupid enough for one evening. One idiotic performance per night, I told myself, forcing the blood pounding in my head to calm down or, at least, figuring out how to ignore it. Signaling the waiter, I apologized for disturbing anyone we might have disturbed. Then, I paid for our meals and tipped him some ridiculously high amount and headed out for the parking lot.

Part of my mind wondered where Sally had gone. Did she know the neighborhood well enough to know where the nearest car service was? Did she have someone take her to one? She wouldn't have taken the subway . . . would she? Would she have taken a ride from some stranger who'd only come there to pick up a pint of spumoni? Could she have possibly . . .

As I unlocked my car door, listening to the frost eat into the mechanism as I turned it, to the door's hinges as I swung it open, the voice in my head that always has the stupidest things to say told me,

What do you care? What's the difference where she went? Fuck her. Let's just get out of here.

I threw myself into my car, slamming the door behind me. Having gotten out of the restaurant without causing a scene, my brain congratulated me by giving me another chance to be an idiot. Gunning the motor, I fanned my cooling anger with any stupidity I could think of in the hopes I could keep it going long enough to get home. There I knew I had an almost full bottle of Gilbey's. At that moment, an almost full bottle of liquor looks good to a lot of people. Especially those that have been hurt but haven't lived enough to realize that the only pains that don't go away are the ones we inflict on ourselves.

CHAPTER 6

"GET AWAY," I snarled—dried phlegm crusting my throat, strangling me. I coughed—hard and tearing—spitting bits of something or other across my desk. I didn't know who could possibly be knocking on my door, and it was certain that at that particular moment, I didn't much care, either. My head was throbbing—my brain banging with rapid spasms of pain that were fast turning the insides of my eyes red and curling the fingers of my fists in a crippling agony. When the knocking started again, I grabbed one of the empty bottles from my desk and then hurled it through the doorway connecting my inner and outer offices, screaming,

"I said *get away!*"

The bottle hit the wall, cracking against the outer door, but going wide of the wired glass inset in its center by a good half foot. Disgusted with missing—hating the sight of the reversed black block letters spelling out my name and all they stood for, I yelled again,

"Get out of here!"

I tried to stand from behind my desk, using black hate to push me up in place of strength. I made it halfway, then tottered and stumbled, falling back toward my chair. I hit it badly, my hip catching one of its arms, knocking it over. I tumbled over with it, cracking myself against one of its wheeled legs. My body screamed in red fury. Drunk as I was I knew I hadn't broken anything, but I also knew I'd bruised myself a good one. As I lay on my back, panting—dragging in the cold air running along the floor, one agonizing lungful at a time—I heard Peter Wei's voice coming through the locked door.

"Jack," he called from the hallway, his voice filled with both concern and confusion. "Come on, man, open the door. What's going on? I talked to Elba. She told me what she thinks happened. Bummer, man—but, you know, you can't sit around feeling sorry for yourself. Remember John Donne . . . 'But I do nothing upon myself, and yet I am mine own Executioner.' Despair's not the way, man. Open up."

Shit, I thought, cursing Peter, my stupidity, and everything else around me in general—he was right. I had to do it—I had to open the door. I had to make it up off the floor. I had to untangle myself from my chair and somehow stand, get across two rooms, and then unlock both the locks on my door. Wondering what it was that made me let some of the things happen to myself that I do, I got myself up onto one elbow, the pounding in my temples doubling from the effort.

"Yeah, yeah," I managed to croak out in a half-sober voice, gasping past the pain. "Okay—wait up. I'm comin'."

I pushed myself upward again, almost shrieking at the level of pain running through my side. My fingers went stiff and straight from the feel of it, trying to balance me. I froze at the first touch of the raging agony, desperate to find a way of moving that wouldn't aggravate it any further.

Gritting my teeth, I listened to the bubbles of spit hissing through them as I tried to both stand and ignore the drumming battle raging in my head. Part of my brain was growling at Peter, hating him for showing up on time, hating him for showing at all. It screamed at me to open the door and clobber him, to beat in his head for catching me at my worst.

Another part was growling at me for getting myself into the mess I was now in. It wanted to know how I could have let things get into the state into which they had fallen—again. How could I have let Sally walk out of the restaurant? it asked—screaming at me. How could I have not called her? Not done anything at all except drive home and drink everything in my apartment, then blubber like a fool to the fourteen-year-old girl who cleans it? Then drive into Manhattan and drink everything in my office?

How—it screamed at me—*you fucking moron*—vibrating my skull, demanding answers at a crippling volume level which bowed my head and hurt my eyes.

How?!

Ignoring both the voices as best I could, I staggered to the doorway between my inner and outer offices. Holding onto the doorjamb for balance, I began to move forward when suddenly I wondered if I was wearing my pants. I didn't want to look down—it felt stupid to not know if I had clothes on. But, I was forced to admit, between the pain in my head and that in my side, I simply could not feel if there was anything against my legs or not. Finally, I looked down and saw that there was. I was missing both shoes and one sock, but at least I had my pants on. And even a shirt which still had a few buttons.

Oh, good, the sarcastic voice told me, for a minute it looked like you were going to make a horse's ass out of yourself. Glad to see we avoided that.

"Jack? What's going on?"

Suddenly unable to control my temper, part of me still wanting to attack the innocent man in the hall whom I was sure was actually honestly concerned about me, I screamed out—angry and embarrassed,

"I'm staggering across the office to unlock the fucking door! Does that answer your fucking question?"

Peter didn't say anything else. Weaving only slightly, I finally made my way the entire twenty-five steps to the door. Slipping the first dead bolt, I had to stop and lean against the wall to catch my breath, the effort of twisting my fingers sapping all my strength. Sucking in a deep breath, cursing again the stupidity I should have dropped when I was a teenager, I flipped the second dead bolt and then fell away from the door onto my waiting room couch, gasping for air. Peter turned the knob at the sound of the lock being released and then pushed the door open. Peeking inside, he asked,

"Should I bother to come in, or are you just going to keep on screaming?"

"Fuck you and John Donne both. Come in and shut up and just make some fucking coffee, will you?"

"Sure," he answered, scratching his head at the same time—annoyed but willing to put up with things for the moment.

"Anything for my sturdy Caucasian pal."

I pulled my legs up onto the couch. Curling into a sloppy ball, I told him,

"Good. Wake me when it's ready."

Closing my eyes, I gave into the fatigue clawing at me and set to work at passing out again. It was an easy job. The last thing I saw was the look on Peter's face. One of definite confusion, trying not to turn into one of disgust. I could accept that. Why not? I thought. After all, it was pretty much the way I was feeling about myself at the moment. Why shouldn't everybody else?

"Okay," I heard Peter's voice later, cutting through the blackness. "Up and at 'em. Java time."

I opened one eye, wishing I didn't have to expend so much energy. A fumbling look at my watch showed me that it was already after twelve. Peter had let me get a little over two hours more sleep. It had been a wise decision. I felt better than I had before. I still wasn't much in the way of fit company, but at least I wasn't homicidal anymore. Peter was willing to settle for it.

"Come on, Jack—up and at 'em. We have exactly one hour before company arrives. We should at least *try* to look like we know what we're doing."

My brain went blank for a moment . . . then I remembered—the good folks from the Chinese Consolidated Benevolent Association were coming to pay Peter and me a visit. They wanted to talk to me about something "highly sensitive" as they had put it. Being Chinese, they didn't give me anything over the phone they weren't prepared to, telling me all would be explained when we met. Considering that working for the C.C.B.A. always meant checks made out for the right amount that both came on time and didn't bounce, I was willing to wait and see what was what until we met.

What little they had told me, however, let me know that it was going to definitely be more than a one-man operation. I'd called Peter figuring that if I had to hire a freelance operative on for a Chinese case, then they might as well be a Chinese operative. Peter is also one of the best in the business, which didn't hurt the decision-making process, either. I've thrown him a lot of work during my time in New York. He's even managed to return the favor once in a while.

Of course, that was all some twenty-four hours in the past, back in a time when I still gave a damn about at least a few things. Now, I didn't care what they wanted. Not about checks coming in on time or how high they bounced. All I wanted was to go back to sleep and rest up enough so I could go out and buy a few more bottles and get back to doing something I enjoyed. Who knew—maybe I could let my fingers do the walking and find a liquor store that delivered.

Forcing my head upward, I took in the figure of Peter Wei standing over me. He was tall for a Chinese, hitting six one, which put him just an inch under me. His body was taut and well-tapered, topped with knobby, solidly muscled shoulders. His dark eyes were intelligent and gentle. He had a high forehead crowned with a lot of hair, which he wore neatly trimmed in a bristle cut that stood straight up like a well-manicured lawn. It was a look that would have been awful silly on most guys, but it somehow worked on him. What didn't work were the circular-lensed glasses he wore. They gave him a college student look which usually doesn't do much for the image of a field investigator. It hadn't hampered him too much so far, though, so it seemed there was no talking him out of them.

Trying to talk him out of pushing me into our meeting instead, I told him,

"Look, you've taken a lot of business off my hands

before. Consider this a Christmas present. You take the case. You can use the money and I can use the rest."

"No deal," he told me, handing me my razor. "The C.C.B.A. wants the hero who proved Chinatown wasn't flooding the city with Black Dreamer. You gave the Chinese community back their pride. Even if you tell them to use me . . ."

He swallowed, letting me see him choke down his own pride just so he could guilt me into moving,

"You've worked Chinatown long enough to know what will happen. They'll just nod politely and thank you very much and go away. Those old men—they're shopkeepers. They like to think everything's just like in the movies. They feel big because they took on the Communists. Yeah, sure, you and I know they took them on by running away but, in their minds, they came here and made big successes out of themselves. They're not peasants anymore. Peasants hire guys like me. Them—they want Big Jack, the man who took on City Hall."

Noticing that his voice level had been going steadily upward, Peter stopped shouting at that point, giving my throbbing head its first rest since he woke me up again. Not finished torturing me, though, he added in a gentler tone,

"And you are right, I do want their money. So get out in the hall and wash yourself and get shaved. *You* can't be bothered to earn some money—suits me. Just prop yourself up long enough to get them to fork over the advance. I'll do the work and you can go back to drowning yourself in gin."

I pulled my head up to the point where I could look at Peter, fighting the agony in my neck as I did so. My mouth tasted like ash-stuffed cotton. My eyes were half-glued shut by sleep crusts and just plain gravity. Turning my head from side to side—gasping involuntarily at the burning pain the maneuver produced—I continued trying to wrench some of the tension out of my neck and shoulders while I took the razor out of Peter's hand with a leadened grip. Muttering at Peter, I told him,

"Pretty harsh stuff you're slinging around, kid."

"Guess I've been hanging around with you too long."

"Not what I meant," I said. Pulling myself up off the couch, feeling the effort in every limb—my body wondering what in the hell I had done to it this time—I told him,

"No, I was thinking more about the two of us sitting down in Number 11 Mott Street one night, me watching you knock back triples one after another."

Peter's face froze, a bad taste springing into his mouth. Imitating his voice as best I could in my weekend condition, I gave him another mouthful,

"Oh, Si Wan, ohhhhh, Si Wan."

"Very funny, round eyes."

"How can I live without her, Jack?" I said, meanly giving him another bit of memory to chew on. "She means everything to me. Oh, boo hoo hoo."

"Yeah, oh yeah. I can see it's going to be real fun working for you."

"Think so?" I asked facetiously. Putting on the happiest face I could manage, I told him, "That's great. Everyone else thinks I'm a bastard."

"And they say the common man is stupid."

I let him have the last line. He deserved it. I was letting myself fall apart over what was essentially nothing, and he was trying to make sure I didn't blow my future again. It didn't matter that he stood to get just as much out of what was coming as I did. He was still right and I was still wrong. So, with a meek "Thank you, Mother," I pulled myself out into the hallway and got to work.

Ducking into the janitor's service room, I stripped to the waist and then scrubbed myself down with a floor brush and sink cleanser—rough going, but the best of what was available. There's nothing like grinding Bon Ami into your armpits and then having nothing but ice-cold water to splash it off with to wake you up. I put the brush aside when it came time to do my face, just rubbing the gritty cleanser in with my hands. I put a lump of it in my mouth with a handful of water and rinsed away the foul tastes as best I could, hoping the scent of sink polish would smell better than ten layers of booze.

Hell, it should work, I thought grimly, spitting it out. It tastes better.

After that, I finally felt awake enough to put a razor to my throat. Using the magnetic mirror with the nude picture of Madonna etched into its glass that the janitor keeps hidden behind his garbage bags, I managed to both de-bristle and get my hair into something that looked reasonably like a style instead of a mop. Then, I looked into my eyes, searching for an answer as to what had gone wrong the night before.

What was it? I asked myself. What was the answer? After all, I reminded the pious voice in the back of my head, the one playing Peter's game of trying to guilt me into admitting that everything was my fault, let's look at the facts. It might have been mean of me to say it, but the first time I'd met Sally, it had been her idea for us to sleep together. Then, she'd gotten all upset about it, just because I had smiled the same way afterwards that some bastard in her past had. I'd also been the one that bent over backwards to get us back together and now I was the one that was supposed to bend over backwards again.

"Fuck that," I growled, scraping cleanser off my body.

All I'd wanted to know was whether or not there was a future for Sally and me as a couple. That was all I'd wanted.

Well, the little voice inside told me, I guess you got your answer, didn't you?

Staring back into my own eyes, wishing for just once I knew how to lie to myself, I pulled the janitor's mirror down from the pipe I'd stuck it on and slid it back behind the garbage bags. Putting my hand on the utility room's doorknob, I told myself that maybe we'd be lucky. With my shirt in my other hand and my upper body still dripping water and wet Bon Ami in the February cold, I thought, maybe the C.C.B.A. might want me to go to some faraway deserted island where I wouldn't have to worry about dealing with women for a while.

Opening the door, I stepped out into the freezing hallway, letting the stupidity of how I'd been running my life sink in. At thirty-two I had a few dollars, an office in a run-down shithole of a building, no girlfriend, and no life. The only creatures that loved me for what I am were a dog and the girl who cleaned my apartment. True, it was better than some guys had, but—like most people—I wouldn't have minded having a little more.

I reminded myself that maybe I'd been poised on the brink of success a few too many times to be able to throw this chance away as well. I'd made the press big-time twice in two weeks—four times since I'd come to New York—more than most people see in a lifetime.

"Now, fuckhead," I told myself out loud, "now is the time to hit while the iron is hot. You are going to go back into your office, get dressed, meet these people, find out what they want, do it for them, take their money, and then move on to the next bunch. And then the next and then the next and then the next. You are going to open a real agency, get a real office, a real girlfriend, a real bank account, and a real life."

Then, finally closing the utility room door behind me, I added one last line to my pep talk, finally getting everything down to the heart of the matter.

"I'll show her."

Then, after that, I shoved the throbbing in my head off to the side, telling it I had better things to do. Crossing the hall, I went into my office, shut the door behind me and, much to Peter's relief, started in on my big plan.

Yeah, I thought to myself again, I'll show her all right. It would have been good if I had remembered the last time I'd said something like that. It had been back when my first wife had left me and I'd gone out and got drunk and then pulled my life back together by showing her how easily I could wind up in the hospital by getting shot.

CHAPTER 7

"BIG HAGEE," SAID Smiler, his eyes bright enough to make mine hurt. "We meet again."

I stared across my desk at a Chinese man ten years my junior—one tall and thin and very well dressed. His name was Jackson In, and he was the man who had saved my ass from the slab two weeks earlier. Two or three times, actually. I'd done him some equally big favors at the same time, though, so we had gotten past the point of worrying about who owed who what. I could see that his presence was throwing Peter, however. It was understandable. Beside being a C.C.B.A. executive board member and a pillar of society, Smiler is also the head of Mother's Blood Flowing, a ruthlessly successful tong which makes him one of the most powerful gangsters in Chinatown.

Considering he had saved my life and all, I had left him with the thought that he and I could be friends as long as he never asked me to do anything that crossed any of my personal lines. Considering my mood at that moment, however, I wasn't sure how much there was that he wouldn't be able to talk me into. Of course, since he'd come under the auspice of his title as C.C.B.A. board member, I wasn't expecting whatever he wanted to be very illegal.

"Jackson In," I said just to show Peter we were all friends, straining for a smile against the dull ache still running through me, "it's good to have you here in my office."

Peter had brought me a suit from home as well as my razor. I was forced to keep myself behind my desk because, just as he hadn't grabbed my toothbrush or comb, he hadn't brought me a pair of shoes, either. I was still wearing the slip-ons I'd worn to the restaurant. I'm surprised that when Elba let him in she hadn't thought of that. A guy in his twenties not thinking of toothbrushes or matching shoes I can believe, but a fourteen-year-old girl? Maybe she was just tired.

I shook Jackson's hand, and then those of the three men and the one woman who had come with him.

"You know Gerald Chang, of course . . ."

"Certainly. How've you been, Jerry?"

Chang laughed. I was the only person who ever called him Jerry and for some reason he always got a charge out of it. We shook hands as he said,

"Very good. Very good. Saw you on TV. I knew you didn't kill that woman. Good you show the city what kind of politicians we really have."

"Well," I told him, "I did have help. If it wasn't for Jackson here, you'd probably be gathered at my funeral service today instead of my office."

"No way." Chang laughed. "No way. You number one best detective in America. You always get to truth. No one ever going to stop you."

"Well, thanks for the vote of confidence, Jerr," I told him, motioning my hand to point him to a seat.

Turning to the others, all people I did not know, I found them to be Ton Chin, Christopher Lun, and Sharon Chee. They were all agreeable enough people. Like Jackson and Jerry, Lun and Chee both dressed in a modern, western style. Lun was the only one among the five C.C.B.A. representatives to have settled into a more traditional Chinese style of dress. Of course, he could have been dressed like a Vegas chorus girl and it wouldn't have mattered to me. I'd forced down a handful of ibuprofens with coffee before everyone had arrived. At that point, all I was concerned with was trying to stay in one piece through the whole meeting.

Shaking hands with the entire crew, I introduced Peter to them as my partner and then got us all into seats. He handled the intro without batting an eye. I figured we could straighten out what exactly the word "partner" meant later. At that moment, it was time to get started.

One of the things you learn fast handling cases out of Chinatown is that the Chinese are never bothered by cutting through the bullshit as quickly as possible and getting right down to business. Considering how many meetings I've held with people in a hung over state, it's easy to see how I came to prefer Chinatown as a home turf in the beginning.

Peter had set the place up remarkably well in the short amount of time he'd had. The office looked a lot cleaner than usual. He'd brewed some awfully good coffee as well as setting up a small bar area off to the side with tea and soft drinks to the ready. He took orders and started filling them without an unnecessary word. Doing my part, I fed our future clients a little banana oil of my own, saying,

"Well, this is indeed an honor to have the ruling heads of the C.C.B.A. here. I would have been more than willing, of course, to come to your offices."

"Big Hagee here," said Smiler with a grin I could see had been designed to embarrass the others with him, "is fishing for the real reason a bunch of hotshot Chinese millionaires have dragged themselves out of their nice, warm offices today . . . out into the freezing cold through the miserable traffic of this falling-apart dump we call a city when they could have easily gotten him to come to them."

Smiler turned, flashing me a look which asked if he was wrong. Sending him one back that said he wasn't, along with an eyebrow raise suggesting that he might have been more tactful, I watched as he just laughed, making a hand gesture which surrendered the floor to Lun. The older man made a small sound with his lips and then said,

"Mr. In is most correct. At any other time in which we required your services, we would have had you come to us . . . as a matter of propriety. But I must admit on a personal level, it is somewhat exciting to be here in your office. You are a most famous figure throughout Chinatown. Stories were told of you long before your deeds during the New Year. It is not a great loss to sacrifice a bit of formality and comfort to be able to see you here in your

own . . . environment. It is, how can I say it . . . worth
the price of admission."

I gave Lun a most humble smile of thanks. He was a
player from the old school, and a master of the art of
negotiation. Okay, there was some reason they had come to
my office instead of having me come to them. Rather than
humble himself, though, Lun had turned it around, making
their coming to see me more on the order of a field trip, a
visit to a TV set. And yeah, sure, I could have embarrassed
him more than he already was by calling him on it—by
rubbing his face in whatever his real problem was—but that
wasn't smart business. A wisecrack at a rich man's expense
made one a big shot at the bar with the boys, but it didn't put
any money in your pocket to buy the next round.

Lun noted my humility, giving me a flash of the eyes that
he was impressed with a man as young as me who could
keep his mouth shut. It was clear he would expect it of a
Chinese but not an Occidental. Flashing him a look back
that let him know I understood and agreed with him in all
things brought a tiny exhalation from him. If he was
relieved to that degree just to know I knew how to play the
protocol game, then he and his fellow board members were
really in something serious. Suddenly, my headache quieted
to the point where I almost couldn't feel it anymore.

"But," Lun started again, "that admitted, perhaps we
should come to the point of our visit."

"If you feel comfortable . . ."

"We have not been a comfortable group for some time
now, Mr. Hagee. Do you know the name, Kon Li Lu?"

"That rings a bell," I answered honestly, not letting on
how tiny a bell it had rung. Throwing the ball to the only
teammate I had, I asked,

"Did you get the information on Li Lu put together yet,
Peter?"

"Ah, sure," he answered, surprised, fumbling a little but
covering with a look that said to the audience that he hadn't
expected to be called on while pouring tea. He handed Chee
her cup, while saying,

"Kon Li Lu was one of the organizers of the Tian'anmen

Square uprising back in '89—one of the focal people the students rallied around. He was the only one with real power to escape the Communist sweep for the movement's leaders."

I looked back to old Mr. Lun who supplied a bit more information.

"Yes. He beat the murderous warlords. And he did it by hiding in their own buildings . . . the Workers Gymnasium, the Zhonglou Bell Tower, even in one of their own Friendship Stores and in their five-star tourist hotel. He is a legend. He is the craftiest man to defy the emperor since Whut Yuen."

I knew that reference. Yuen was a poet who spoke out against the Chinese emperor some five hundred years ago. The emperor's Army chased him across the country, but they couldn't catch him. There are a lot of stories about him and his exodus, but they all end up the same way. The Army cornered Whut Yuen against the ocean. Rather than apologize to the emperor, though, he threw himself into the water and escaped punishment through suicide. In many ways, a very Chinese story.

Interrupting the flow of the conversation, Ton Chin leaned forward, suddenly adding,

"Much like Yuen, Kon Li Lu escaped the government by throwing himself into the water. The government tried very hard to capture him. Very large rewards were offered. None would help the Communists. Kon Lu was hidden in any basement available, by any who found him. Soldiers hid him—Red Army soldiers, enlisted *and* officers—they hid him. He is a hero."

Leaning forward, not having to feign interest, I listened while Lun took over again.

"Kon Lu made it to Hong Kong. He spit in the government's face. His angry words covered their thieves' hands with blood. He screamed the truth and then went underground, before their agents could find him. And they have tried. On two different occasions, they have managed to infiltrate meetings of people who gathered to hear Lu speak. Twice now, he has been fired upon in public. And there are rumors of more attacks. Kon Lu has had to make his every move in secrecy."

"How tight is Red Chinese control of Hong Kong now?" I asked, certain I was not as up on the subject as my guests. Lun answered,

"It is very bad. Officially they pretend that they have no influence, but it is more obvious with every visit I make that they plan to take over in '97 as ruthlessly as they can."

While everyone assembled nodded their heads in unconscious agreement, suddenly Sharon Chee spoke up, saying,

"You must understand, Mr. Hagee, Hong Kong is everything the controlling dogs of the Chinese government need and yet fear at the same time. They need Hong Kong's wealth—they need its open access to the free markets of the world. And yet, it frightens them for it is far too democratic for them. They fear its influence, the 'baggage' that comes with it—private property, open markets, wealth in the hands of peasants, free enterprise. This is not the Communist way.

"And please," she said bitterly, the venom added in case I might be one of those people who thinks socialism is a good idea, "let us make no mistakes about the noble goals of Communism. The masters in Beijing are in no way friends of the people. As we saw in Tian'anmen, they are not above using the People's Army—which it had always been vowed would never be used against the people—to gun the people down in the streets like dogs. Do not believe their lies of hundreds only wounded. Thousands died during the student rebellion. *Thousands.* And thousands more were imprisoned. But since China has no oil, President Bush sent only congratulations to his old friends, the murderers who bleed our country."

"What a lot of the American press missed, while they were still allowed inside the country," said Lun, as impressed with Chee's fire as I had been, "was that the students were not even trying to call for an end to Communism."

Taking a long breath, Lun's face fell abruptly into sadness

for a second, then quickly hardened over. Sitting tall in his chair, his voice grew louder as he shouted,

"They were not asking for freedoms—they were not screaming about toppling the government. All they were asking for was that their rulers be good Communists. That they stop sending their children abroad for educations normal Chinese are forbidden. That they stop giving their children and friends all the best jobs, despite their inability to do them . . . that they stop bleeding China. All they were asking the foul little pigs who gathered in the reins of Mao's horses was to keep them running on the same path—to not try and replace the old emperors with themselves."

"I think," said Smiler, after a long moment of silence, "that our good Mr. Lun is trying to impress upon you how strongly we all feel about the Communists. I know it's a popular myth to say of gangsters . . ." Several of the other C.C.B.A. members reacted noticeably at the mention of the true nature of In's business. He waved his hand in the air, dismissing their embarrassment with the gesture, adding,

"Please, we are here to lay all our pieces face up on the table and to beg for help. Leave your manners in Chinatown." Then, turning back to me, Smiler said,

"As I was saying—a lot of left-wing people in this country like to believe that gangsters say they hate Communism only so they can align themselves with the right wing for protection. But, we don't hate it out of convenience. We're against fascism and communism, and even socialism for the same reasons as everyone else. Free enterprise is for us. We supply people with what they want—with things governments don't want them to have. Anyway, Big Hagee, Tian'anmen gave a lot of us hope that the government would have to open up—that the people would finally rise up and kick them in the ass."

Smiler stopped talking. For a second it seemed that he was about to blow up and make a speech of his own, but he pulled back, saying quietly,

"Anyway, all I wanted to say was that there are a lot of Chinese people in the world who want the Communists out of China. When Kon Lu escaped the mainland, made it to Canada, made it to the States, we were all happy. It was like a holiday. We had our living hero to celebrate with, to give thanks to, to, to . . . to dream with."

I started to think I had an idea where our conversation was going. Knowing me pretty well from the dozen-odd times he'd hired me in the past, Chang could see it in my face. Shaking his head slightly to let me know I was correct, we both sat back and let Smiler tell the story.

"Lu started raising money everywhere he went, funneling it into secret accounts. He was filled with passion. Let me tell you, Big Hagee, it was something else to sit in a room and listen to him talk—to see the people's faces light up when he spoke of funding rebellion on the mainland, of freeing the people. We both know that no one ever believed the old-liners from Taiwan would do it, but Lu . . . Lu they believed."

"And so," said Peter, drawing all eyes to himself, "they opened their wallets and their purses and their bank accounts and they gave him a lot of money to make that belief come real—didn't they?" As everyone's silence attested to the correctness of Peter's observation, he said in a quiet but hard tone,

"And now, after he's gotten every dollar he could from every Chinese enclave in the world, he's suddenly disappeared with everyone's money. Correct?"

The silence deafened all in the room once more. Breaking it as delicately as I could, I asked,

"Jerry . . . how much did the C.C.B.A. donate to the cause?"

He took a moment to get down enough air so his voice wouldn't choke up on him when he spoke. Spreading his arms to include himself and all the other board members, he said,

"Between us we gave Kon Li Lu roughly fifteen million dollars."

And suddenly, it was no longer a mystery as to why the board had decided this was one meeting best held away from their headquarters.

CHAPTER 8

"THAT'S A LOT of money," I finally managed to say. No one seemed inclined to disagree with me. In fact, now that they had gotten what they had to say off their chests, no one seemed inclined to say much of anything. I took a long sip of the tea Peter had poured for me earlier, hoping someone else would fill the silence. Everyone else seemed content to wait. As Peter played "Mother," refilling my cup, I tried to coax something else out of any one of them, saying,

"Didn't you think that was a lot of money?" As the quiet continued, I prodded them along a little bit further, asking them in turn,

"Any of you? Jerry? Mr. Chin, Ms. Chee? Mr. Lun?" I purposely didn't bother to ask Smiler. I knew he'd give me his opinion when he'd let the others stew long enough first. True to form, obviously feeling that that moment had come, he said,

"Yeah, Jack, fifteen million dollars—fifteen . . . million dollars . . . aauugh—the moon's sweet tears—it makes me cringe every time I think of it." The king of Mother's Blood Flowing took a moment to catch hold of himself, then added,

"*Yes!* Oh, yes! It is one fucking hell of a lot of money. Yeah, sure—I know it looks like I'm laughing at my fellow board members here, but try to remember that quite a big chunk of that fifteen was mine." In's face went tight, his smile growing awfully strained.

"So, I'm laughing at *all* the noble C.C.B.A. members at the same time."

"Don't you dare," snapped Ms. Chee, showing more fire

than I would have given her credit for. Chinese women are like that. They cloak themselves in a veil of quiet respectability, but it's just a prop—one they can drop instantly if they need to. Ms. Chee had just felt the need. Pointing at Smiler, she spat,

"The store owners, the merchants and their workers and their suppliers, all of them—they gave to the cause because we had checked everything out for them. *We* gave the approval. *We* gave the big donations that started the ball rolling. Don't you dare laugh at them. All you can laugh at is our stupidity—their only crime was in believing us."

"That's enough of a crime to convict in my book," answered Smiler, pulling a cigarette. I slid my ashtray, a ball-and-cone affair shaped like the symbol of the '39 World's Fair, toward him as he answered her,

"And who are we?" he asked bitterly. "Just more gullible fools."

"We don't know that!"

I was as surprised as anyone else in the room when Ton Chin finally broke his silence. We encouraged him to continue with our stares. He obliged us, saying,

"We have no proof Kon Li Lu is a criminal. None! Maybe it will be that he is. Maybe it will be he is not. But we do not know yet. And that is why we are here."

Once again, everyone stayed quiet. Feeling it was my duty to cover this silence, I said,

"It sounds to me as if we're finally getting down to the gist of what it is you folks wanted to meet with me about. Why don't I do a little talking for a while and see how much of this I've got right?"

Everyone involved seemed to think that was a good idea. Just as I started to talk, however, the phone rang on my desk. Peter grabbed the entire unit and moved it quietly toward himself as far as the cord would reach. Then he stretched the receiver to its end and answered the call discreetly in the background as if we'd been doing our act together for years. More and more he was making all my partnership talk look like a good idea.

A shake of his head let me know it was nothing important.

Taking his word on it, I turned back to the others, picking up where I had left off.

"Okay, Kon Li Lu makes a name for himself in the world of democracy. He helps plan the student protest in Tian'an-men Square, helps bring the whole thing off, and manages to get out and make the Commies look like fools doing it. He resurfaces in Hong Kong and starts telling the world that he wants to lead a revolution that will topple the old men with their foot on China's neck once and for all. People believe him. He makes a few passionate speeches, and more people believe him. He starts traveling the world to raise funds and ends up ducking an assassination team or two. He lives through them, however, and ends up raising a lot of money everywhere he goes."

Taking another sip of my tea—needing the caffeine—hoping it wouldn't start my head to pounding, I gave the room a chance to jump in. No one did. Figuring it was still my show, I set my cup down again, and then continued, saying,

"Finally, he brings his act to New York. He does his song and dance and scores big again. Now, my guess is, he and all the funds have disappeared, and from what Mr. Chin says, people don't know if he made off with the bundle, or if the Commies did him in and just want it to look that way."

"Now you see?" demanded Chin, upset and relieved at the same time. "Now, you see?! Even this man, an outsider to our community, can recognize the possibility without having it suggested to him." Light filled the old man's eyes as he added in a fervent whisper,

"It *is* possible."

Chin sat back in his chair then—once again silent—his point made. Smiler added,

"Ton, nobody ever said you were wrong." Cracking a wide smile, the youngest head man in the history of the Chinatown gangs lit a fresh Winston, taking a deep drag as he said,

"Personally, I think there are enough crooks around already. I'd certainly like to believe that that pack of dogs from Beijing did him in and not that Kon Lu was no better than the rest of the world. But," he turned away from the others to focus on me at that point, "this is why we need you, Big Hagee. We want you to find out what happened to Kon Li Lu. Did he run away to the Rivera with all our dough, or did some death squad out of the Forbidden City bring him down and take all our green back to China?" Spreading his hands wide, Smiler added,

"Hey, I know it's a big question. That's why we came to the big guy."

"Well," I started, stifling a smile, searching for a humble balancing point to stand on so I didn't get knocked off the negotiating floor now that the time had come to talk money, "I'll admit that it certainly is a big question . . ."

"No time for false modesty, Jack. The board here knows who you are. They know your M.I. work bounced you all over the South China Sea. They know you've got a lot of the language down—that you're not some rummy white-shirt left-handed fork-eater who's just going to walk the streets asking a lot of stupid white-boy questions. They know you've got the score." The gangster pointed to his chest, waving his Winston, saying,

"*I* know. I watched you take apart the Time Lords myself. First, two giants, down—boom. Then, two knifers and two clubbers, down—boom. In the streets, on the ice, with just your fists. We know that if anyone has the will to see this thing through to the end, it's you."

Smiler took another drag on his cigarette, then exhaled. The break gave him a chance to lower his voice a bit for dramatic effect. Talking through the smoke, he reminded us,

"We know, man—we all know—that there is nobody better for this job. You've got deep connections in the government . . . and outside the government, too. Big pluses. Also, you know your white devil's path, but you can also walk ours. You can get visas to go wherever you might need to and you can take care of yourself when you get there." Taking another drag, Smiler dropped his voice again as he added,

"This is a dangerous thing we're asking of you. Nobody is giving anything away for free here. No matter what the truth is, whether or not Lu has taken the money, or if he is dead somewhere and others have taken it from him—somewhere out there is a lot of money that people have already been killed over . . . a lot of money that many people want back. I am sure other parties are hiring their own people to look into this thing as well as us."

Taking one last pull, Smiler crushed out his Winston and then blew the lungful of smoke away, saying,

"To show you we are most serious, we have even come prepared to put aside our normal love of haggling. We are ready to offer you your usual rate, plus fifty percent, for as long as you are willing to stay on the job. We will cover all expenses and open as many doors as possible for you. All we want from you is the answer—did Kon Lu steal the money or didn't he?"

Smiler paused, on the surface just to light another cigarette. His pause was too calculated, though. He followed through casually enough, however, almost making it sound like an actual afterthought.

"Although," he started, taking a series of short, starter puffs, "if you should happen to be so fortunate to recover the missing cash, we are also willing to give you the standard fifteen percent recovery fee that such jobs usually get."

I looked at Smiler, suddenly knowing that everyone in the room was as serious as I thought they were—that if I accepted the case, it was probably going to be one of the most dangerous things I had ever done in my life. From what they had said, there was no doubt in my mind that there would be other teams searching for the missing cash. Lots of them. Some of them sophisticated enough to play by some rules. A lot of them not so sophisticated. Whoever had the money, they would be real dangerous, and probably not very inclined to give it up. Why would they be? I wouldn't be. Neither would anyone else.

My mind weighed everything I had heard once more, totaling the effect on both sides of the scale as quick as it could while I smiled politely on the outside—sipping my tea. Part of my brain tried to remind me of what I'd been thinking about the past few weeks—security, settling down, not getting shot at anymore. Another part, however, reminded me who all those notions had been centered around. The two pretty much canceled each other out, leaving me to wonder if I could even make an intelligent decision in my current state.

I wasted a few seconds making eye contact with Peter, pretending that the opinion of a guy in his mid-twenties that I threw some work to once in a while could influence me when thinking about putting myself within the gunsights of one of the most dangerous powers in the world. Again. His opinion, flashed back in his more openly honest face, was that he was ready to move on a moment's notice.

I sighed to myself on the inside, thinking that kids never do get any smarter. Stretching to give myself another minute to think before even beginning to show what I thought of the job, I said,

"Well, Jackson, I have to admit that fifteen percent of fifteen million dollars is a pretty easy figure to come up with, even for a guy with my meager math skills, but . . ."

And then, Smiler laughed, smoke flying wildly from his mouth. He had been caught so off guard by whatever funny thing I'd said that he couldn't help himself. Jerry found it funny, too. The others just showed another side to their embarrassment. When he finally caught his breath, Smiler told me, laughing as he talked,

"Oh, Big Hagee, that's why I love you. You're such a straight guy. Fifteen million? Fifteen million is just what this group of fools before you here in this room gave up. We talked the rest of the C.C.B.A. into raising well over *twice* that for Lu. And, and . . ." Smiler bubbled with his own humor again, barely capable of adding,

"You're forgetting everywhere else he went. Oh, Big Hagee, the last word we had, his revolution bank accounts had almost three billion dollars in them."

CHAPTER 9

PETER AND I sat in silence for a long time after the C.C.B.A. board of directors left my office. How long, I'm not really sure. The sun didn't set and rise again or anything quite so dramatic, but it took the two of us one long moment to be sure. Peter, being the healthier of us at the time, was the one who finally found his voice first. Being a direct kind of guy he used it to take us to the heart of the matter.

"Do you know what fifteen percent of three billion dollars is, Jack?"

"Not off the top of my head, no."

"It's four hundred and fifty million dollars." He was winded when he finished his sentence. He had a right to be. In awe of the figure, he said it again.

"Four hundred and fifty million dollars." And then, suddenly there was no stopping him. Getting up from his chair, he began pacing in front of my desk, telling me,

"Four hundred. Four hundred and fifty. Four hundred and fifty . . . *million* . . . United States of American green dollar bills, Jack. Four hundred and fifty mill—"

"Okay, okay," I growled. "I get the idea. I understand, all right? Yeah, yeah, four hundred and fifty million dollars. Yeah. All right. That's *if* we can find it. If we can find *all* of it. If it's even still out there to find, and if we can get anywhere near it even if we do find it."

I sucked down a deep breath, held it in for a moment and then let it out slowly—calming myself, trying to keep my migraine from staging a coup. Staring levelly at Peter, I told him in a quieter voice, "Try and remember, they still haven't been able to get the Philippines' money back from the

Marcos clan, and they even know where that's stashed. And that's two countries trying to do the retrieve. We're just two guys."

No longer pacing, Peter crossed his arms over his chest, drumming his fingers restlessly on his biceps. Suddenly he wasn't sure what I was telling him and so didn't know how to attack next. Finally trying to establish just what was going to happen next, he asked me,

"You did tell Chang and the others that we were going to take the case, right?"

"Yes," I admitted, nodding my still aching head wearily. "I told them we'd sniff around and see if we could find any kind of a trail. Although after seeing Jackson's package . . . who knows how much of a pot there'll even be at the end of that trail?"

Peter nodded, acknowledging the nine by twelve envelope on my desk. As the group had been leaving, Smiler had held back for a moment, telling the others to go on and that he would be right with them. Then he had given us the package on my desk, one containing fifteen photos of Kon Li Lu. Several were early shots of the man, just there for the purpose of being able to recognize him. The others were something more, however.

The remaining twelve were all shots of Lu spending money wildly—gambling at the tables of the Riviera, in Macau, at racetracks, in card games, et cetera. Some were blowups—copies from Polaroids, others were grainy cutouts from other people's photos. But one, one was a clear picture of him enjoying himself in the company of some unnamed, unAsian woman of stunning beauty, one that made it seem fairly obvious that all the money he had collected might not be earmarked for overthrowing the People's Republic of China. Smiler's only comment had been,

"I have not shown these to anyone else. People like my companions . . ." he shrugged his shoulders, showing a compassion I would not have expected from him, "they need their beliefs. Me, maybe I've been in the 'trade' too long. Me? I guess I'm not so surprised. Anyway, Big Hagee, try and get our money back. This could be good for all of us—eh?"

And then he had slapped me on the back and hustled out the door of my outer office to catch up with the other C.C.B.A. board members. I had stared at the photos for a long time, feeling a bit of the sucker myself for having let Chin and the other's rhetoric pull me in. Peter, on the other hand, didn't seem to be suffering nearly as much over Lu's apparent fall from grace as I was.

"Hey," he answered me, "I'm willing to go on the assumption that even a Chinese gambler couldn't blow three billion dollars that fast. So, if we are going to look for him and his loot, what's the difference if we think a little about what we could get out of it if we find them?"

"Because," I told him, feeling the space behind my eyes begin to tighten, "doing that is what gets guys like you and me killed."

I wanted to keep talking but suddenly found that I had to break off. The effort of playing "clean and sober" for the C.C.B.A. board members had finally caught up to me. Try as I might to stay calm, the pain started shooting through my head again, twice as bad as it was earlier, shutting my eyes and making me wince from the effort . . . hoping to make up for lost time, I supposed.

Understanding the look on my face, Peter got me the ibuprofen bottle and a fresh cup of tea. I fumbled the lid off as best I could in my blind state and popped three of them into my mouth, washing them down as fast as I could. The pain forced me to keep my head bowed, unable to look up, unable to talk above a whisper, unable to understand how I could have done such damage to myself—over a woman—*again*.

My first marriage had never been anything to write home about, to say the least. After all—at the first complaint everyone would have been saying "I told you so." All the parents involved had been against it, and most every friend in sight—my friends, her friends, our parents'—all of them. I'd known best, of course—known everything was going to be fine—known that after what I'd already been through in my life that God or karma or *something*, anyway, owed me, and that my marriage lasting forever was how I was going to collect. Sometimes Hubert jokes that I take some of the shit that happens to me so well because nobody's topped the trashing my ex-wife gave me. Sometimes Huberts' jokes aren't all that funny.

But that wasn't the problem here—Sally was my problem this time. Yeah, I told myself, I'd done it again—handled things the wrong way and then reacted badly when I didn't get what I wanted. Life never changes. Trying not to think about it anymore, though, I turned my thoughts away from the woman I wanted in my life and how I'd chased her out of it. There would be a time for thoughts like that later, I told myself, but not then.

I worked at getting a handle on both the pain in my head and my heart as best I could and then tried to explain my other concerns to Peter.

"All right," I said. "Follow me here, will you? Think for a second. Just think. Do you honestly believe that In and his pals are the only people looking for their lost money? Do you think we're the only guys who are going to be out there? Do you think we're going to be the toughest guys out there?"

I downed another sip of the rich but bitter tea Peter had served, feeling the pain behind my temples retreat a little bit further. Blinking, I found I could finally crack my eyes open a slit without screaming. Taking another sip of tea before I replaced my cup on its saucer, I said,

"Try and get a little perspective here—okay? Every intelligence network on the planet must know about this thing by now. Every rouge player in the entire world . . . do you understand me? In . . . the . . . entire . . . world. All of them are looking for that money right now. How many C.I.A. agents do you think wouldn't push their grandmothers down the cellar stairs for four hundred and fifty million dollars? How many K.G.B. men? Or MI5 players? By now every player on the board, from Scotland Yardbirds to the worst street punks, they're all going to be tearing up the countryside looking for that dough—and call me a cynic, but I figure they're all perfectly willing to gun down anyone who gets in their way."

Stretching my arms upward, rolling my head around on my shoulders, I felt parts of my headache break loose and dissolve, others intensify. Cramps in my shoulders and neck broke apart, driving a wedge of pain through me so harsh I squawked in surprise. Peter made a crack about not being sure about working with an old man. I made one back at him.

"Old men have brains, junior. I was only telling you what some people in this world would do for four hundred and fifty million because that was the figure you fell in love with. What my tired old bones are reminding me of is the fact that it's three billion that's missing."

Dragging myself around in my chair, I fumbled through my top desk drawer, sure I had an old pack of Camel extra-wides in it somewhere. Finding them, I shook one free and dug my lighter out of my pocket while I said,

"Three billion makes a man a player. I don't care if he was lying in the gutter yesterday. I don't care if he's got the skeleton of a dead rat in his pocket and pus-filled sores on his face—people will overlook anything for money. There are women who'll crawl up on top of him and lick that face clean. He could drag his pocketful of rat bones over their bodies and they'd moan as if they'd had Jesus Christ inside them—and they'd mean it, too. Every groan and tear and "Oh, daddy, you're the best," every step down he made them take would just excite them all the more because in their minds they're trading their self-respect for some kind of access to that money."

Getting my cigarette lit, pulling in that sweet blast of double strength smoke, I blew out the first heavenly drag, blessing the R. J. Reynolds Company in the back of my head as I took another and told Peter,

"And let's not forget how many men would lie on their backs and let our newfound multibillionaire piss in their faces for that same chance."

"You're getting to be kind of a bummer here, Jack."

"Oh, well, excuse me, but that was my goal. It's not that I want to take all the fun of having money away from you—it's just that I don't want you spending money you don't have. We've got to approach this like any other job." Catching Peter's eye, I held it with mine, telling him,

"We're looking for Kon Li Lu. And that's it. Period. Accept it up front—we will look for the money only to the extent that it will help us discover what happened to our target. And I mean it. Getting caught up in a search for wealth is a one-way ticket to the trash heap. God knows," I said, the image of what I'd looked like a few hours earlier—what I looked like then—flashing through my head, "I'm pretty good at trashing myself. I don't need any help. Not from a bunch of greedy fucks who wouldn't think twice about knifing their mothers and not from a partner who thinks he's part of a TV script instead of real life."

"Okay, okay," answered Peter, a bit miffed at my going on at length as I had but enough of an adult to be willing to admit that I'd been right, "I think I get the idea. So now that we've established who's boss, what do we do next?"

"Next, we're going to head out for my apartment. I'm in no shape for moving around, but well, hell—now that I've got you, I can get drunk all I want. You'll do the driving. Before we take off, get Hubert on the phone. Tell him to bring Maurice if he can and say that I want them both to be at my place at eight for dinner."

"What should I tell them we're having?" asked Peter.

"Tell him we'll be having whatever he wants," I said. "Then tell him he's bringing it."

CHAPTER 10

BY SEVEN O'CLOCK I was finally feeling something like a human being again. Not completely, but something like one, anyway. After Peter had gotten in touch with Hubert, we'd rung up a few more people and then called it a day, heading for Brooklyn. I had napped both in the car and once more when I got home, done some stretching exercises, showered, walked Balto, and then just a little of this and that to get myself back to somewhere near the normal feel of things.

Peter went with me while I walked Balto. He said he wanted the air. I needed it. Balto needed what all dogs need when they get outside. The two of us talked out a lot of things while Balto indulged himself, including an agreement that I wouldn't mention the fool he'd made out of himself over his Si Wan if he would do the same for Sally and myself. We also came fairly easily to an agreement on just what this "partner" stuff we had been throwing around all day was really about.

I leveled with him. Since I'd set up in New York I'd collected myself a small but strong clientele, a group of faithful repeat customers with whom I had solid relationships. The media had gone out of its way to build me up to the public once. After I let it all slip away, they tried to crucify me, but I beat the devil and left them with no choice but to build me up again. This time I was in the position where there was some real money to be made and I was going to capitalize on it.

"So," I told him, "I've spent the past few years getting my head kicked in to get where I am right now. I'm tired of it. Someone else gets their head kicked in from now on."

"I'd like to think that there might be more to get out of saying yes than a weekly head-kicking."

"We'll work out the money end later. I'll be square with you, Pete—you're young and I'm feeling old. You've got a knack for the computer stuff—those bail skippers I told you about are coming due and I'm still trying to get that genealogy program to run. You're also a good man on a corporate case—I've watched you tear through the civil docket and the federal tax lien records, and I've seen you call a trend just by reading through a few TRW profiles. You've got a lot to offer. So, you want to get worked like a dog to get a piece of what I've built up, you got it."

Looking down at Balto, watching the silvery breath steam out of him as he trotted alongside us, Peter answered,

"You don't treat your dogs all that bad."

"Well, not the ones I like, anyway."

Peter laughed sourly and I smiled, the action of it making me feel twice as good than all the painkillers I'd gobbled throughout the day. We headed back for my apartment after that, dropping Balto off at Elba's on the way up. She and her brothers and sisters love to play with him and he loves them which is fine by me. He would have just been underfoot when everyone started to arrive, and that was going to be trouble enough. I thanked Elba for the dog-sitting assist and then Peter and I headed upstairs to my place, getting there only ten minutes before the first of our guests. Hubert rang the buzzer with his customary craziness. When he got upstairs, I asked him what he had been trying to do. He told me,

"I was p-playin' 'Solitary Confinement' by Bim Skala Bim. Didn't you recognize it?"

The hard thing about dealing with Hubert is making up your mind over what he's kidding about and what he isn't. Five foot six, straight whitish-blond hair, round, animated face and only slightly insane eyes, he had walked through the door in a 1920's "Oh You Kid" raccoon fur coat under which he had hidden a dark purple suit. He had chosen to wear that with a gold shirt and tie with matching pocket hankie and boots. When I asked him how he had managed to match his hankie to his boots, he told me,

"Hell, I don't do any clothes shopping. Maurice does all the stuff like that for me."

I turned to the small, willowy Jamaican, Hubert's right-hand man, and gave him a look that asked just what he was thinking dressing Hu in such a getup. Then, I took a good look at the brightly colored, beaded and spangled vest he was wearing over his hairless black chest, and decided purple and gold suits were as conservative as Maurice got. Taking the twenty-five pounds of fur and leather he called "his wrap," I threw it on the bed along with Hubert's rug and then went back into the living room to get the show on the road. The first thing I did was ask,

"So, what's for dinner?"

"Knowing that we were dealing with the lowest of the underclasses, we stopped at the" —I knew it killed Maurice to say it— "at the 'Colonel's' for the night's providential blessing."

"Ahhh, dry up. Don't pay any attention to him," added Hu. "I've seen this guy go through six p-pieces of extra-extra crispy without battin' an eye—and that's not even m-mentionin' watchin' him then tear up a family portion of mashed potatoes and gravy all by himself."

"A man must eat," answered Maurice simply.

Before anyone could add anything else, though, the buzzer sounded again. It was a combination of shorts and longs that let me know it could only be Grampy. When he came in, Maurice gave Grampy his customary stare of disapproval. Grampy hits the scales at 260, is balding with a shaggy beard, and shops at the Goodwill. Grampy also lives in the streets. Whether he had to do that out of necessity or not was academic. Ever since he'd mustered out of the service before me with a shrapnel wound, he hasn't liked having an address that made him easy to find. To say that he and Maurice come from different worlds is putting it mildly.

Before either of them could start in on the other, however,

I grabbed up the bags Hubert had left by the door and brought them over to the table, announcing,

"Hey, hey—let's eat."

I hadn't actually been able to contact Grampy, of course. Instead I had called Carmine Cecolini, a tall man whose specialty is long jobs. I'd wanted him there at the meeting anyway and I knew he'd track Grampy down if I asked him. I said my hellos to both of them but then, before I could throw the bags on the table, the buzzer rang again, meaning that Francis had arrived. Dumping the chicken quick, I then crossed back to buzz in the new arrival while Peter headed for the plates and glasses. Grampy and Carmine threw their coats in the bedroom. While Grampy went straight for the john after that, Carmine brought a bag he had had in his coat pocket out to the kitchen. Unwrapping it, he asked,

"Where's Balto, Jack? Me and the old lady and the kids had steak last night."

"I took him down to Elba's to keep him out of the way. Throw the bones in the fridge. I'll make sure he gets them."

Carmine stretched out his beefy frame, then stashed the bag on one shelf while he grabbed a beer from another. Cracking it open with one hand, he knocked back a good blast, then said,

"I don't know. I wouldn't want you scorin' points with my little Rosa's favorite dog. She left half the meat on hers just for him. My wife almost had a fit."

"Jeezit," I said with mock anger. "You'd think I didn't feed the mutt or something."

Carmine laughed, taking another healthy slug. Then, getting down to business, he asked, "So, what's up, Jack? What's the big mystery?"

"Grab some chicken and start stuffing your face and think about whether or not you'd like to work for me."

Carmine, always one to follow orders, dug his hand into the bucket of honey barbecue roast and pulled out a thigh. Pulling half its meat away with one bite, he answered while he chewed.

"Sure, why not? I mean, I always like whenever I'm workin' for you good enough."

"I'm talking full-time," I told him.

"Well, well, well," crowed Hubert. "So, big Dick Tracy finally grows a b-brain inside his inch-thick skull."

"Eat some chicken," I told him. "Bones and all. I hear they're good for you."

Maurice looked up from the wing he was eating to ask, "And so is that why we are all here, big brutal white person, to get fitted for our chains? Shall I sing a spiritual for you, old Massa Jack? Would you be liking that?"

"Yeah," I told him, in no more of a mood for taking his shit than I ever was. "How about 'The Camptown Races'?"

That got a laugh. Unperturbed, Maurice answered,

"You know the arrangement—you polish my stem until I smile like the sun and I will sing 'The Camptown Races.'" Maurice let a beat go by, then turned innocently to the rest of the crowd, saying,

"He loves my voice, you know."

Grampy, still in the toilet, was the first to laugh. I don't know who was the second. I'd asked for it, though, so I took it. True, he had started the wisecracking, but anyone who tries to trade insults with Maurice is asking for it. I was tempted to tell him to shut up and eat his chicken, but I knew he would've just bounced back with some line about me licking his fingers for him, so I let well enough alone and just went back to answer the door. As I had thought, I found Francis Whiting on the other side.

"Food," he said, sniffing the air and licking his chops in an exaggerated manner while rubbing his still-gloved hands together. "Yes—that's definitely food. How thoughtful. You must have known a law student was coming."

"Yeah, come on in." I stepped out of his way, telling him earnestly, "You'd better grab something quick if there's even still anything left."

He peeled his heavy gloves and scarf and coat in seconds, throwing them to me or just throwing them away, I wasn't really sure from his aim. I caught them and took them to the bedroom, though, figuring I could barely begrudge the kid a crack at the buckets before Grampy got out of the john.

Once the two of them were squared off at the same table it would be every man for himself.

The next half hour went smoothly enough. I spent at least half of it on my feet, mixing drinks and stuffing extra beers in the freezer, microwaving portions of potatoes and gravy, getting the mayo for Grampy, the mustard for Hubert, salt and ketchup and extra bread and then butter for the bread and then cheese for the bread and opening bags of chips and flash-fried cheese curls and slicing down a stick of pepperoni and every other task my collection of dinner guests could think up.

Peter stepped into his role of partner again, slicing plates of oranges, making both the tea and coffee, clearing the garbage as it grew, as well as any other chore he could take over without looking like the hired help. By the time the assembly had gone through everything Hubert had brought as well as half the stores I had on hand, they were all in better moods, even Maurice. While Peter tied up the tops of the three shopping bags of trash we had created, I called our meeting to order.

"Okay, okay, let me get to the point here. I'll make it short and simple. I'm going to expand my agency. I'm extending invitations to all of you to join me. Obviously each of you is being asked for different reasons. Some people I'd want in the office every day, some people I'd want to work out other arrangements with. But, I want all of you on my team, in some capacity or another. What's everyone say?"

"That's fuckin' short and simple all right," answered Grampy. "You talkin' benefits and paychecks and drug tests and the whole nine yards?"

"Well, outside of the drug tests, maybe." Everyone laughed. I continued, though, telling them, "But, yeah. I'm serious. I'm talking a real business, nine to five or whatever. We work like a team and we take cases and we solve them. We track down information and we provide security units and we do background checks and we trace skip jumpers and we throw ourselves an office Christmas party at the end of the year and all the other happy horseshit you can think of."

"You sound p-pretty serious there, Dick Tracy."

"I am serious, Hu. And I'm not expecting everyone to come running to the head of the line to sign up . . . even though it is a recession," I added dryly, rolling my eyes upward as I finished, "and, Congress being what it is, there isn't a man in the room who couldn't use a few more dollars these days."

"Speak for yourself." Maurice smiled. "I am quite comfortably situated these days, thank you."

"I did say 'man.'"

The cheap laughs started again. Maurice glared at me, caught off guard for once with no rejoinder. I was so happy to see him that way I smiled my first smile of the day that didn't hurt. Not wanting things to get out of hand, though, I cut the comedy short, saying,

"Okay, cheap shot. I admit it. But look, let me get rid of the garbage here. You bozos drink up some more of my beers and whatever else isn't nailed down and I'll be right back so we can work out some details."

Then I grabbed up two of the trash sacks, letting Peter get the third. I didn't really need the help, but it gave us both an excuse to leave the apartment, which gave everyone else a chance to say whatever they might want to without either of us hearing. I walked slowly to the garbage chute halfway down the hall, giving the boys as much time as I could. Peter asked,

"Think they'll go for it?"

"I don't know. Hope so. I'd like Carmine in the office every day . . . Grampy, too, if he's up to the routine. I know we could never nail Hu and Maurice down, but I'd sure like to get an exclusive out of them. Francis . . . he's a hell of a research man. He'll dig through City Hall records all day long without a lunch break if someone's paying him. And, he usually finds what I want without too much trouble, too."

Stuffing the first two bags down the chute, I took the last from Peter's hands and slid it in after the others as I told him, "I've got some other people in mind—second-string replacements for anyone who doesn't want to join up. We can worry about that kind of stuff later, though."

Letting the door to the garbage room close behind me, I turned to start back for my apartment when Peter asked,

"So, who did you have in mind to replace me if I told you 'no'?"

Just as I started to answer the floor jumped beneath our feet, knocking both of us violently to the floor. A monstrous explosion pounded our ears as splinters of glass and brick and wood bounced off of us—dug into us. The hall lights were smashed at the same instance, leaving us blinded by the darkness and deafened by the noise.

CHAPTER 11

I SAT IN the emergency room of Coney Island Hospital, feeling alone and cold and very, very near the edge. Peter had taken on the responsibility of handling the police. With all the other bodies around, no one seemed to think there was anything suspicious about me being quiet along with the rest of the corpses. The day had been too much for me. First destroying myself over Sally, and then the C.C.B.A. and their bombshell—then someone else and theirs. I'd overloaded from the pressure, withdrawing into my brain, trying to put it all together when I wasn't busy blaming the one on the other. It was a vicious circle—one from which I couldn't seem to find any way out.

If I hadn't been angry over Sally—started the defensive voice in my head—if I hadn't been looking for some way to punish her, I wouldn't have taken the kind of job that attracted guided missiles. Of course, I reminded myself, if she hadn't left me cold, I wouldn't have been angry. Then again, it said, if I hadn't pushed her she wouldn't have been angry herself, and I wouldn't be angry and on and on and on.

I could still see it all perfectly clear inside my head, the cold part of my mind replaying the events of the previous three hours over and over, looking for clues. I saw my apartment door rip off the hinges, blowing out into the hall. It slammed off the opposite wall, shattered by the contact—propelled by force and flames and a stream of burning debris that used to be most everything I owned in the world. Before all its pieces could settle to the floor I was running

73

back the scant few yards that had separated Peter and myself from the blast.

Climbing into my apartment, I burned my hands on the door frame, filling them with splinters and gashes as I threw aside the wreckage. I called out names but got no answers. Everything inside was smoke and shadows—all of the lights were blown—the only illumination coming from the fires burning in various corners. The first body I found was Carmine's. Most of it was sizzling, flesh burning along with the melting plastic threads of my couch cover which had fused themselves to his skin. Half his head had been sheared away, his mouth hanging open, teeth falling out of it like rotted plaster from an ancient wall.

I saw his wife in my mind's eye and suddenly, my eyes filled with tears. I saw his three kids, saw his house on the auction block, his wife and boys begging for coins in the street. I turned from the charred and broken corpse, breathing smoke, choking as I bellowed everyone else's names. Peter caught up to me then, trying to get me to leave.

"Jack, we don't know what exploded. We've got to get out of here."

"Not without knowing!"

"Knowing what?" he shouted back.

"Knowing who's alive and who isn't!"

"Jack, come on, we've got—"

I knocked his arm away from mine, spinning around, grabbing his shirtfront. His hands grabbed mine. As we started jerking each other around, I screamed,

"Listen up, boy—you want to go . . . then, all right—go! But I called these men here. This is my fault. I can't leave them here to die."

A look filled Peter's eyes, one meant to remind me that he'd made some of those phone calls as well. Both of us understanding what the other was saying, we let go of each other and then started looking for the rest of our friends. I waved Peter over to the stove area, telling him where he would find my fire extinguisher and emergency flashlights. As he moved through the darkness a voice called to us from the outer hall.

"Mr. Hagee. Mr. Hagee. What happened? What happened? Mr. Hagee. Are you in there?"

"Yes, Mrs. Buddenhagen," I called, trying to keep the old woman from entering the apartment. Thinking of a way that worked to my advantage, I shouted to her in slow sentences, repeating myself often. "Don't come in, Mrs. Buddenhagen. Don't come in. I need you to call 911. Tell them there's been a very bad explosion. A very . . . bad . . . explosion. Tell them to send police and ambulances right away. Police and ambulances—right away. Okay, Mrs. Buddenhagen?"

"Police and ambulances. Police and ambulances. I'll call them, Mr. Hagee. I'll call."

I heard other neighbors moving in the hallway, coming closer. Taking a flashlight from Peter, I sent him toward the doorway to keep them back. I found Francis as Peter moved away. He had become such a part of the wreckage I hadn't even noticed him at first. Pulling in on my emotions, I scoped the apartment with my inner eye, trying to determine what had happened. Pushing my hysterical side down made everything a lot easier.

Some sort of projectile explosive had struck the outside wall, pushing it inward. Francis the student, still at the table, still eating, had taken the brunt of the flying bricks and glass and steel. It had smashed him backwards across the room, driving his body into the refrigerator—the force so brutal it had shredded him and the frig, mixing flesh and metal and plastic like freshly shuffled cards. Ignoring my emotions, fighting down my grief like they'd taught me in M.I., I headed back toward the bedroom, looking for the others.

I found Grampy unconscious in the bathroom. His constant need to flush his system had saved his life, only leaving him with a cracked skull and some possible broken bones. Hubert and Maurice I found in the bedroom, both half on the floor, half on the bed, both semiconscious. What had made them move back there I didn't know and I didn't care. They were alive and looking unharmed and that was all I cared about at that moment. Hu looked up at me, wiping at his face, his hands and arms moving as if guided by strings and not human muscles. Choking on the smoke now beginning to curl its way into the bedroom, he asked me,

"Jack—Jack, wh-what, what . . . ?"

"Got no idea, Hu. First we've got to get out of here. Are you all right? Can you stand?"

After he found he could make it up and stay there without too much trouble, I helped him get Maurice going as well. Once we made it as far as the bathroom door, the three of us managed to pull Grampy to his feet, shaking him from his stupor. He was stunned but not out as I had originally thought. He did have some kind of problems, though.

"What hurts, Grampy?"

"Fuckin' ribs are screamin'. Owww—fuckin' shoulder, too, looks like." Pushing his own way up off the floor with his one good arm, trying to pull his pants up at the same time, he glared at me, grumbling,

"Great fuckin' parties you throw, man."

"Just shut up and keep moving," I told him, too hot under the collar to allow myself to give in to cheap releases. Playing my light in the hall, I showed the way for Hubert and Maurice. As Hu helped his assistant out, I held back, knowing Grampy needed someone to lean on, but also knowing it would kill him to show that kind of weakness in front of Maurice. Homosexuals were just one of the types Grampy had had trouble dealing with since he'd gotten out of the service.

As we moved through the remains of the living room, I noted that the frigid winter air had begun flooding in from the outside now that I no longer had a living room wall to keep it in check. Still in my survey mode, I also noted that Peter had contained the fires and taken up a position at the doorway, keeping all of the curious out in the hall. He started to speak, but before he could, suddenly Balto bolted out of the stairwell, racing for the apartment. He sniffed at each of us as we came out, then crowded inside past us. I knew why.

Carmine had always been his favorite out of all my friends. The two of them had hit it off on some level the first time they'd met and that had been that. In some ways the two had grown so close that, if such things were possible, I could have almost been jealous. I'd been sure earlier that the bone with all the meat on it had been his and not little Rosa's. Now, the bone was gone, and so was the man who had brought it.

Crowding back inside through the legs of the wounded, Balto went straight for the couch, straight for Carmine's body. He sniffed it up and down a few times, then suddenly he howled long and loud. It was an earsplitting mourn, a horrible wail that no one present had either wanted to hear, or would ever forget. I didn't blame him. I wanted to do the same thing.

After that, things had moved in a haze. More neighbors had arrived. Elba came as well, telling me how Balto had gone insane when they had all heard the explosion, howling and barking and clawing the door. They had let him out and followed him up. As had practically everyone in the building. Eventually, though, the cold and the soon on-the-spot police and emergency medical teams drove most everyone back to their homes.

Only Elba and the super stayed after that. Balto took up residence in the hallway to the bedroom, refusing to budge. With his breeding—half-husky, half-German shepherd—he was a winter dog. I knew he could guard whatever I had left in one piece until I got back, unfazed by the cold. The super said he would get some plywood and cover the door, a temporary measure to keep the cold from freezing the rest of the building, as soon as he made sure the gas line to the stove wasn't ruptured and that there were no live wires exposed anywhere. After that, the police and the medical teams moved those of us still living downstairs to the waiting ambulances and off to Coney Island Hospital. And, once they'd put me in a chair in the emergency room waiting area, there I had sat, lost within my own head until a familiar voice decided to intrude on my thoughts.

"Oh, isn't this a pleasant sight? Big, bad private dickhead Jack Hagee all upset and lost and alone in the world. What'sa matter, Jack, life getting too rough for you all of a sudden?"

The voice was that of Edward Raymond Fisher, captain of the precinct that stood guard over my neighborhood. To say that we were not friends was to put the case mildly. I'd turned up some dirty shenanigans early in my career, involving diamonds and drugs and payoffs and Brooklyn cops—Fisher's cops. It had never been proved or even very strongly suggested that he might have had any knowledge that anything was going on, but for whatever reasons he had, he'd been a thorn in my side ever since. Not having time for his nonsense at the moment, though, I told him as calmly and evenly as I could,

"Fisher, two of my friends died tonight and I'm in no mood for any of your regular shit. You want to act like a cop, fine. I'll do anything you want to help you find out who did this. You came here to use this as just another chance to get back at me, I'll put your eyes out."

I hadn't put my head up, hadn't made eye contact with him yet, but I could tell from the change in the air around us that I'd rattled him. Good, I thought.

Normally I'll go to the lengths that most people will to not antagonize the police needlessly, but the times weren't normal then and I'd kept myself under control as long as I could. I was reaching the end of my string and didn't have the strength left to withstand any of Fisher's nonsense. Feeling him getting ready to make some kind of noise in my direction anyway, though, I looked up, letting him see who he was getting ready to tangle with.

The look in my eyes shook him, made him take a small backward step. Raymond Fisher was not a small man—not a weak one or one easily intimidated. He was also not a stupid man. He was a cop with a lot of years, one who could tell when a man was near the breaking point. After all the times I towed the mark when he'd cracked the whip since our personal troubles had first begun, he knew I was in no mood for our normal Mutt & Jeff routine. Not giving an inch, though, he told me,

"Okay, you're all busted up inside for your pals. Good. Maybe it'll give you some idea how I felt when you trashed twelve good men's careers. I won't debate what they were

doing or why with you, I'll just remind you that there are
better ways to handle every situation—just like now. So
keep playing it cool and so will I—this time—as long as
you start singing. What the hell are you mixed up in now,
dickhead?"

All the voices in my head screamed at the same time. The
beast within me wanted my hands to just reach out and start
plastering Fisher across the scenery. The more rational ones
debated the merits of telling him everything, telling him
nothing, telling him choice bits, et cetera. I had no idea if
anyone had talked to Peter yet, or what he might have told
them if they had. Hoping to jar loose a clue as to what the
captain had already found out, I said,

"I was in the hall getting rid of the trash when my place
blew up. There, now you know as much as I do."

"The chink gave out with that version, too, and I'm not
buying it from you any more than I did from him. Now get
real, scum wad. What were you all doing at your place?"

Choking down my anger, trying to keep my feelings for
Fisher from interfering with either him doing his job or me
doing mine, I told him truthfully,

"I'm getting ready to expand my organization. Everyone
was at my place tonight to hear what I had to offer and then
decide whether or not they wanted to sign up."

"And that's why someone blew the shit out of your
place—because they didn't want the mighty Jack Hagee
Agency to be formed?" I glared, trying to force myself to
blink as the captain paced back and forth in front of me.
"What? You think you're Doc Ass-licking Savage? You
think you're that fucking important or something?"

"I don't think anything, Fisher," I growled, trying to keep
myself in my seat. "I don't know why my apartment was
bombed. I don't know why my friends are dead. But I plan
to find out. Maybe if you were really a cop you'd want to
find out, too, instead of strutting around here in front of me
with a tin whistle shoved up your ass."

Without thinking, the captain launched a slap at my face.
Just as quickly and with as little thought, I blocked his arm
with one hand, my other shooting out, catching his shirt-

front. Before I could stop myself, I jerked him downward, slamming his knees against the hospital floor. Fisher howled in blind pain. Three of the other cops there in the E.R. moved forward, hands fumbling for their guns. That was all I needed.

I pushed myself upright, reaching behind myself as I stood. Bringing my chair around, I drew back, ready to hurl it at the first cop who drew his gun. In the same split second, nurses and patients screamed, some of them scrambling to get out of harm's way, some of them trying to help others to escape. Two of the cops had their flaps unclipped, guns almost drawn. I was finished with my windup and ready for the release. Just before I could, however, a voice cracked through the room, freezing everyone in their tracks.

"*Stop right now!*" the voice barked from the sidelines, demanding everyone's attention, draining the situation of its tension. As my chair went back to the floor and those guns in the air went back in their holsters, the voice stroked us sarcastically with mock praise.

"Why, now, that's much better. What intelligent types they have fighting the good fight in this city."

The speaker walked forward toward us. He was a tall man, roughly sixty, maybe more, maybe less. Closely cut salt-and-pepper hair, hard jaw, bristly clipped moustache, strong shoulders, no gut, cold eyes somehow staring down everyone in the room at the same time. His heavy, ankle-length trench coat was dripping, which meant the wet sleet rains had started again. Despite the drizzling cold from which he had just come in, though, his cheeks were clear, unflushed.

Walking past Fisher, who had just started to make his way up off the floor, he ignored the police captain as if he did not exist, speaking to me instead.

"Long time, soldier."

"Long time, Major."

CHAPTER 12

MAJOR RICE, PETER, and I sat in a booth in the Del Rio Diner, the closest all-night place to the hospital worth going to. Their specialty is their burger platters, big tasty ones surrounded by more fries and onion rings than most people can choke down. Their double bacon cheeseburger platter is my favorite. Knowing my tastes, when I gave him my opinion of the menu, the major shut his and placed it facedown on the table, ordering without looking it over any further. Still fairly full from earlier, Peter let his sweet tooth guide him, ordering a monstrous slab of chocolate cake, one decked with strawberries and some sort of hard white frosting which ran in swirls down its side—just one of the desserts from hell in the Del Rio's glass-walled revolving "treats" display case. I ordered a cup of coffee.

I couldn't eat. I had no trouble sitting with Rice and Peter as they did, but try as I might I couldn't entertain the notion of food. I kept seeing Francis and Carmine in my mind's eye, kept remembering how hard it had been to keep Balto back when the ambulance workers had begun their work, trying to separate Carmine from the couch. I couldn't eat then. Hell, I couldn't even touch the coffee.

"Good food," said Rice, hoisting one of the Del Rio's gigantic, hand-cut french fries. "Not quite the old service standard rations, is it, Jack?"

"No, sir," I said automatically, wincing that I had given Rice even that token of respect. Catching the gesture, he said,

"Oh, come now. Those days were a long time back. You've come a long way and done all right by yourself.

Most of the lads whose careers I've decided to follow over the years haven't made it quite so easy for me as you have. Stopping dread assassins, foiling corrupt politicians, saving fair young millionairesses. One would think you could spare an unbegrudged salute for your poor old major."

"I take it you two were in the service together," said Peter, barely looking up from his dessert thing.

"Ouuuu, sharp lad, sharrrp," replied Rice as he downed the fry in his hand. "No wonder you're making him your partner. Someone to handle the brain work."

"Fuck you, Major, *sir*," I snarled back. "I will be glad to flip you your unbegrudged salute and a case of chili peppers if you want, if your help in getting me untangled from Fisher was just the generous gesture of an old commanding officer for one of his spuds. But somehow, knowing you and the Red Dog Team, I don't think it stops there. So, why don't you stop pretending to give a rat's ass about me and get to the fucking point."

"Why," Rice drawled innocently, almost meekly, his eyes laughing at me, "whatever could you mean?"

"Don't play innocent with me."

"I'll play any game I like, soldier. I'm dealer here, because all the cards are in my hand. So why don't you tell me what you think you know and I'll tell you whether or not you're any brighter than Number One Son over here."

Peter looked at the major through cold eyes drawn into slits. A large, false smile on his face, he said in his best pidgin Chinese accent,

"Oh, miss-ta soldier, sir. Oh, you make velly funny joke on Peter thele, sir. Ha ha, yes—velly funny."

Turning his body to face my partner, Rice reached down into the gravel in his throat and said in a cold whisper,

"Now you listen to me, boy. I'm here on business. Jack knows it, and if you had any brains you'd know it, too. If a joke that harmless is going to set you on boil, in all honesty, friend, you'd better find another line of work."

"I'm just sitting here eating my dessert, old man," answered Peter. Calmly forking up another mouthful, he said, "I will tell you two things, though. One—you're not the only one here on business. And two—and you'll have to trust me on this one—if you think I can be pushed to boil with that kind of crap, then you're the one who can't take a joke."

Rice took a big bite of his second bacon cheeseburger, answering as he swallowed,

"All right, let's call a clean slate, shall we? I don't have time for these games and neither do you. We've got a lot to talk about, and the quicker we get started the quicker we can be done with each other."

I picked up my coffee to take a long sip. I made my movements slow, dragging out the action to give myself time to think. The physical layout was easy to sum up. After not having seen Rice for over seven years he suddenly shows up in my life on a night when I needed the type of intervention his kind of clout could provide. Because of some special deal he hadn't seen fit to explain yet, he had the power to swat Fisher and sent him packing. Official business—all of a sudden my government had need of me.

There was no doubt in my mind that Rice wanted to steer me in one direction or another concerning Kon Li Lu. It was the only thing that made sense. It would be no surprise to me that Rice could know about an assignment I had only picked up that day. No surprise either, if that was the case, that he was already in New York ready to manipulate me into doing his bidding.

One truism everyone had agreed to in the old days . . . Rice had pull. When I'd been with Military Intelligence, a part of his code-named Red Dog Team, unofficially known as the Suiciders, he'd never had any trouble getting whatever he wanted when he wanted it . . . *exactly* when he wanted it.

My problem at that moment was whether or not to play along with him. No matter how much I hated Rice for reasons of my own, I had to admit that he had always played me fair. I had to remind myself that although he might represent the government, he himself had never lied to me. Truth to tell, I'd never heard of him lying to anyone.

I also knew that if I didn't agree to whatever he had in

mind he'd throw me back to Fisher in a New York minute. Figuring that there was no sense in asking for trouble, I put my cup back down and told the major what I knew. I gave him everything I had—Smiler, the C.C.B.A.'s troubles, the money, the assassination attempts, all of it. Then, I asked him,

"Now, you tell me why all of this is so interesting to you."

"First off, I'll confirm everything you just told me. Our intelligence has come up with all the same stuff over the past few years." When I gave him the old M.I. "draw them out" stare, he chuckled and told me,

"Yes, of course. Did you think we wouldn't be watching someone like Lu? Charismatic, intelligent, raising billions of dollars around the world so he could lead a bloody revolution in the last major Communist stronghold? Yes, everything your clients told you is true. And it is almost all we know about the situation as well. We have some other tidbits which I'll feed to you later. At the moment, however, let us move on to more important matters." Pulling out the duffle he had stashed under the table earlier, Rice slid a large, drab olive-green fiberglass tube from inside it, asking me,

"This was found in your neighborhood. Still recognize one of these?"

"M-47 Dragon mini-rocket. You telling me this is what took out my apartment?" The major's head went up and down, the nod sufficing for an answer as he took another hefty bite of his last bacon cheeseburger. I said,

"Dragon's got a seventy-five yard minimum range. It won't even go off if it's triggered from closer than that. Where the hell they launch from?"

"Straight line, sixty-two degree angle from a building fronting on Bay Parkway. Would explain how they missed you. They can see your apartment from that vantage, but they were cut off from full view. Didn't know when you'd ducked out with the trash."

"How long has the Dragon existed?" asked Peter.

"Thought about that. Good question but bad answer.

Unfortunately there's nothing new about these beauties. The Dragon's been in production since the '70's. Anyone could have their hands on one by now."

"So you have no better idea who took out my place than I do—right?"

"Hardly," Rice answered sharply. Taking another, smaller bite of his burger, he finished it off quickly, then said, "We know who the major players on this board are. You're the one who hasn't the foggiest. What is puzzling to me about that is, A, who could have known you had moved onto the board . . . B, what made them think you could know anything more than the scores of players already involved . . . and C, why would they try to eliminate you in such a sloppy, open manner?"

Peter started to protest Rice's last point, but I cut him off. The major was right. In fact, he was seeing things a lot clearer than me. Who outside of someone watching the C.C.B.A. could have known about me being brought in? Why would anyone be watching the C.C.B.A.? And, even if they—whoever "they" were—knew about me being brought in . . . so what? What was the big deal? What could there possibly be that made me so dangerous to anybody's plans? Especially—what made me so immediately dangerous that they would risk pulling a stunt like setting a Dragon off in public without even guaranteeing that it would get me?

Without looking up from his plate, Rice showered another generous portion of both salt and pepper onto his fries as he said,

"So, curious now, are we, Jackie boy?"

"Yeah," I admitted. "I'm curious. So what?"

"So, I'm here to help you, lad."

"Help." The new voice was Peter's. "And what in your eyes constitutes 'help'?"

"I've already got a report on the M-47. I can tell you where it came from, and where it probably was last. I can also get you to that place—clear of this charming city of yours and its equally charming Captain Fisher."

"And what do you want for all that?" I asked, knowing

the major wouldn't be sitting across the booth from me if he didn't want something. Angry at the thought of working for Rice again in any capacity, I asked,

"And what's the list—what's my fucking patriotic duty this time?"

"Jack," answered Rice, "you never were much of a team player, but this isn't one you can lay at our feet. You've gotten yourself into this scrape. I'm here offering to bail you out. In return for a favor I figure I'm owed one. If I get your word on it, you get your lead and clear passage for two."

"Make that p-passage for f-four."

I turned away from Rice, looking over at the sight Hubert and Maurice presented standing next to the Del Rio's dessert display case. The trays of cakes and pies and puddings revolved next to them, red and white lights glaring against them as they walked up to us. Their spotlight effect brought out the white of Maurice's bandages against his dark skin, heightened the smears of blood soaking through Hu's.

"And why would I do that, little man?"

"'Cause, you prick-nosed motherfucker, some cock-sucker bit off more than he could c-chew tonight." Hu thought for one long second over whether or not he should blow his stack. He is not one for hostile confrontations on a personal level. Not unless there's no way around one. A second was all it took for Hu to tell. Blowing air out through his nostrils, his hand shaking in the major's face, he growled,

"I came c-close to buyin' it when your fuckin' hardware blew a hole in the wall and two of my pals. I don't like almost buyin' it. It upsets the hell out of me. It's the kind of thing that makes me nasty."

The major picked up another fry, eating it in calm, measured bites as he said to me,

"Your monkey has me terrified here, lad. Whatever will I do?"

"Fuck you and your mother's fat ass, MacArthur."

Turning to me, Hu shifted his eyes back and forth, sending his rage at Rice in aside looks while he told me,

"I'll tell you the major's big secret. The rocket that trashed us came from a shipment of crap they were movin' out of one of the bases the government shut down in the Philippines. There was a big strike. Thirteen G.I. Joes were wasted. Whoever made the hit knew their shit. They got it all, ten trucks of weapons—World War II vintage up to some fairly new crap."

Hubert suddenly made a grinding noise with his teeth, clutching his side, his body bending inward at that point. Hissing his words out painfully, he accused,

"You want that mess sorted out—don't you—you want the weapons found and covered up. You don't want word of this to get out, do you?"

"Yes," the major answered sharply, growing irritated. "Is it so much to ask?" Rice turned back to me and said,

"All I was going to do was point you in the right direction and ask that if by chance you located any information on the weapons to pass it on to us. Your government knows what you did for it, son. It doesn't mind helping you when your interests coincide with its." The major took another bite of cheeseburger, then added,

"And, if that doesn't sound like gratitude to you, I suggest you try and get a grip on the big picture. Men died when those weapons were grabbed—more than anyone realizes. There are plenty of people up to their eyeballs in this one, lad. Plenty of others we could go to—several we already have. I like to take care of mine own, though. If I can help both of us, then what's the horror?"

"None," I admitted. As much as I disliked Rice for my own reasons, I couldn't argue with him. He wasn't lying—it wasn't his style. And, knowing that even if Hu did know everything that was going on, there wasn't much he could do about Fisher, I asked,

"Give me the outline, Major. What do you want?"

"We'd just like to keep those weapons out of the wrong hands and, if we can't, to at least be able to minimize the bad press that will result."

Hubert buckled suddenly, pain in his side forcing him to allow Maurice to help lean him back onto one of the stools

at the counter. As he held what I figured had to be busted
ribs, my mind raced. I wondered how Rice had gotten a
handle on what had happened so fast—how his people had
located the M-47 launcher, how he had known it was my
apartment that had been hit, that I was at the hospital . . .
everything. I also wondered how Hubert had come up with
what he had, trumping the major at his own game. Hu had a
way with digging information out of the woodwork, but this
had been fast even for him. Knowing I had to make a decision,
however, I told the major,

"All right. You've got it. But, I want everything you have
on this situation—both on Kon Lu and your missiles. I want
a list of all the players and I want their CSs and CRs."

I watched Rice's face for a reaction. I knew there was no
way I would catch him off guard, but I did know some of
how he thought. Whatever expression he put on to answer
me with would at least give me some clue as to how he
really felt. With clear eyes and an open face, he said,

"Done. I'll have passports for both you and your partner
in the morning."

"Passports?" I asked. "Why? Where're we going?"

"To visit with the last known owners of your
g-government's property," answered Hu. "That's yer pal's
other big b-bit of news . . . where the weapons ended up.
He figures that's your best bet." Hu grabbed at his side
again, pushing in against new pains, sputtering weakly,

"He's figuring that if you can f-follow the weapons you
can find out who used one on us and that that's yer best
chance at findin' Lu."

"Your chimp does good work," said Rice. Ignoring him
and cutting Hu off before he could answer the major back,
I asked,

"And so let's flip to the back of the book. Where are we
going?"

"The Royal Crown Colony at Hong Kong," answered
Rice.

Hong Kong, I thought, not saying anything at first.
Finally, after a moment, I got over my shock at the fact that
the past catches up to everyone, wondering just how long a
jet trip to the other side of the world took these days.

CHAPTER 13

HUBERT HAD TURNED out to be more banged up than he'd thought. While Rice headed back to whatever sanction house he was working out of during his stay in the city to get his end of our deal rolling, Maurice and Peter took Hu back to Coney Island Hospital to get his ribs taped. At the same time, I went back to my place to see just what that might constitute anymore. In some ways I turned out to be luckier than I had thought.

Balto was waiting for me inside the door. How he can tell the difference between me coming up in the elevator and anyone else I'll never know. I went in, ducking under the yellow police barrier tape stretching from one side to the other, shutting the make-do door that the super put up while I was gone, not wanting to freeze out my neighbors. Keeping my coat on, I watched my breath turn silver as I went inside, stepping over the debris in the foyer. I looked the place over, wondering again why anyone would bother to try and take me out of the game. The Dragon had impacted against the outer wall, throwing it inward. I took a quick inventory, cutting the darkness with one of my flashlights to see if anything had survived. It hadn't.

My living room/kitchen was gone. Food, dishes, television, stereo and VCR—destroyed. Couch and table and chairs—twisted, ruined, gone. All of my books, wiped out. I pulled a large handful of scrap loose from what was left on my bookshelf. It turned out to be Colin Wilson's *A Criminal History of Mankind*. I had only been halfway through it. Now the massive volume was just a wrecked jumble of shredded pages. Dropping it to the floor I turned to head for the bedroom.

The smell of smoke was practically gone. Peter had put out the fires the rocket had started quickly—the February cold and winds had done the rest. Crossing through the short hall, I found that outside of drop damage, everything in the bedroom seemed fairly intact. In fact, the room was even slightly warmer than the rest of the apartment. It hadn't dawned on me the radiators in that room might still be working. Shutting the door to try and conserve some of the heat, I stuffed two towels along its base and then returned to taking inventory.

My mirror was shattered, everything that had been atop my dresser was scattered, but not much had actually been broken. I stretched out on my bed, coat and shoes still on, trying to clear my mind. Balto curled up next to me. It wasn't something he did normally, but then it wasn't a normal situation. There was a hole the size of a refrigerator in my wall. It was freezing cold and to tell the truth, it seemed so right I didn't even question it as he pressed his back up against mine. I had other things to think about.

Why? I wondered again. Why? I just couldn't see an angle that made sense. Closing my eyes, I pulled a quilt over myself, throwing a corner of it over Balto. Then I lay back and tried to see some line I could follow in what had happened.

I break up with Sally and that makes me stupid enough to accept an impossible case from the C.C.B.A. I knew when I did it that I would be in over my head, but I didn't care. I wanted to either punish Sally for breaking up with me or myself for breaking up with her. Looking at things without anger or a hangover, I had to admit that I still wasn't exactly sure who had ended things.

Great, I thought, just great. Some terrific detective you've turned out to be. You get two of your friends killed because you want to prove a point to your girlfriend and you can't even remember what the point was. Jerk, I told myself. Loser. Things don't change for you, do they? You thought the military was going to be your big chance. When that turned out to be a bust you took M.I.'s offer to step up and be an officer—except all they wanted was a grunthead with a knack for killing the enemy to protect their brain boys and girls.

I lay in the bed reliving the nightmare that had been my time with the Suiciders. Rice sent us anywhere in the world there was something dirty to do. It went on for four years—four years during which I watched everyone around me die or get maimed. Swell fucking life.

But I remember vowing, *I'll change all that. I'll quit and make it up to the world.* And so came the Pittsburgh Police Department—a job arranged for me by Rice, no less—a job like the others that had looked like a way out from under, but in the end, had only been a ticket to more riots and more killing and more friends dying. At the very end, when it trashed my marriage, driving me to the bottle and the drugs, it left me confused and alone. When finally I couldn't stand the body count there I left for New York.

"What a laugh," I said out loud. "What a stinking, stupid laugh. What a fucking idiot you are." Adopting a standard television announcer voice, I continued, telling myself,

"Hey, pal, tired of pain and misery? Looking for a way out where you can start over and live free as the birdies? Then, hey—*you* should come to *New . . . York . . . City!* Yes, New York City, home of the most carefree victims in the world. Yeesssss—I said, New York City, with the best of everything—the highest crime rates, the highest taxes, the highest prices. Yes, New York City, where the beggars are the dirtiest, most obnoxious beggars in the world. Where the roads are the worst roads, the subways the worst subways, where the service of any kind couldn't be more awful and . . . where we have the most corrupt politicians—and *more* of them—than any other city in the world."

Then, suddenly, the whole bit just wasn't funny anymore. I dropped the voice, as well as the thought that I could blame New York, bad as it was, for Carmine's and Francis's deaths. That was my fault, my responsibility, and I didn't have the slightest idea in the world as to why. What possible motivation could anyone have had for trying to blow me to kingdom come? Try as I might, I couldn't come up with any ideas.

Before I could waste the whole night thinking about it, though, my phone rang. I couldn't believe it. My electricity and gas were out, but the phone on my hallway wall still worked. Adding "lack of privacy" to the list of things New York has more of than anywhere else in the world, I threw myself out of bed and headed for the hall. My caller turned out to be Maurice.

He told me that the hospital was going to hold Hubert for at least a day. When I asked what Maurice's plans were, he said,

"My employer has instructed me to be on call for you while you are in Hong Kong. I will be preparing for you a list of our contacts in the soon-to-be-abandoned Royal Crown Colony. And then, after that, I shall be returning to our offices and beginning the search for the mad bomber who tried to destroy us all."

"Where do you plan on looking?" I asked, curious to see what he and Hu thought the answer might be as to the identity of our attacker. He told me,

"I have no ideas—yet. But they will come. Somewhere out there is an answer as to who this person is. And I shall find them."

"Be careful," I told him. "I don't see where I have to remind you as to how rough these guys play."

"Be careful yourself," he said in his normal, joking tone. "Big, lumbering, dumb white men make even better targets than perfectly proportioned specimens such as myself." Then, suddenly, his voice went cold as he added,

"Do not worry about me, sweet Hagee. I know about pain—both how to take it and how to dispense it. I am Maurice de Valmoire. I am the last of a long line, one which has never accepted a slight in the past and is not about to start now. No one shoots missiles at me . . . not twice, anyway. We will find these killers, and they will be destroyed. Your two friends, one was ugly and stupid, the other a lawyer. On top of that they were both white. None of these are characteristics I admire greatly. But, they were on our side, and they will be avenged."

Then, before I could add anything, Maurice made an abrupt "good night" and hung up. I started back to the bedroom, but before I could make it, a knock sounded on the super's makeshift door. It sounded familiar enough to trust, but I couldn't be a hundred percent sure.

When I opened the door, though, Balto right behind me, I found that I'd been right—it was a familiar knock. It was just that . . . thinking I was never going to see the knocker again, I'd just assumed it had to be someone else. Reminding myself about assumptions, I said, tensely—guardedly—not meaning to sound that way, but not able to help myself,

"Hi. What brings you here?"

"You just stay a bastard to the end, don't you?"

"Great to see you, too."

I looked into Sally's sharp blue-gray eyes, surprised at how angry and yet scared they looked. She stared up at me, unblinking, waiting for me to say something else. I was afraid to invite her in, afraid to send her away. Part of me was working itself into a panic—not wanting her to see the wreckage, not wanting her to worry. Of course, another part of my brain told me, did I think she was so stupid that she didn't notice the plywood door—or that she was there for any reason other than that she had already heard about the attack? Finally, after letting the silence go on for a long moment, I said,

"I take it you heard about . . . ."

She cut me off, pushing me inside with force as she said,

"Yes, I heard. The whole city's heard. The story hit about a half hour ago. The report said there were two dead and a number of wounded."

"Yeah," I confirmed. "Carmine and Francis. Francis Whiting. I don't think you ever met him."

"I'm . . . I'm sorry. I know you liked Carmine a lot. I . . . I didn't know who had been hurt, or how bad. The report didn't have any of that. Most people are waiting for the follow-up. I wanted . . . I couldn't wait so I came right over. You're going to be up to your ears in reporters anytime now."

"Oh," I said humorlessly, maintaining my hard-guy pose. "So you thought you'd get here first and scoop everybody."

"You bastard!" she screamed, hitting me with both fists, bringing them down as hard as she could on my chest. "You miserable, shit-heel bastard!"

I didn't bother to stop her. She hit me again and again, continuing to scream as loud as she could until finally she collapsed against me. I pulled her close, folding my arms around her. I didn't say anything, not wanting to upset her any more.

"Why?" she asked me. "Why did you do it?"

"Do what?" I asked her softly.

"Why did you take the C.C.B.A.'s case?" I looked at her with a bit of surprise, wondering how the media could have learned so much so fast. Not responding to me or my looks, she continued.

"That's what did this. That's what got your place shot up—almost got you killed. You were lucky this time, but how many times will that keep up? How many near misses do you think there are going to be?"

Sliding my arms up to her shoulders, I moved her back from me only far enough so that I could see her face. Then, somehow pushing aside my bitterness, getting past worrying about whose fault things were, I told her,

"I don't know, sweetheart."

"You don't know what?" she asked quietly, her eyes meeting mine. "How far you can push your luck or why you took such a crazy case?"

"Either one, I guess."

"Oh, don't lie about it." She buried her face in my chest again, saying, "Please, don't lie."

"What do you want me to say, Sally? I could tell you a lot of things, but the plain and simple truth is I got drunk and gave myself a king-daddy hangover and before I knew it I was on the C.C.B.A.'s case."

"And you didn't do it to punish me? To show me how bad I'd feel after you were dead?"

I hesitated, looking for some way to not admit the truth, but it was no good. I'm not much of a liar—I've never had any use for people who lie and can't do it very well myself. If Sally knew anything about me, she knew that. Before I could even try to cover, she said,

"I knew it. Oh God, you big, stupid . . . couldn't you just wait a day . . ." her voice filled with misery as she asked, "just one day?"

I pulled her in close again, telling her,

"I'm sorry, sweetheart. I thought you were gone—that I'd chased you away for good. The first time we split, that first night, that was bad enough. This time, I don't know . . . I just, I mean, without you . . . what was the point?"

And then suddenly, she pushed away from me, breaking my hold. Staring at me through the darkness, her eyes blazing, catching every little glint of light, she said in a louder, questioning tone,

"I mean that much to you? You think I'm gone out of your life forever and so you volunteer for a suicide mission as soon as you're sober? What? I'm supposed to believe I'm that important to you?"

"First off," I told her, "I didn't volunteer for a suicide mission. I got offered a lot of money to do the kind of job I do all the time. True, it held the possibility of being a little rougher than most jobs, but only if I let it get out of hand—or so I thought, anyway. But nothing from what I knew led me to believe anyone would do anything like this." I swept my hand across the gaping hole in the wall, turning to look at it as I said,

"This . . . this doesn't even make any sense."

Then, I turned back to Sally, telling her,

"And second, yeah. You are supposed to believe that you're that important to me."

"Oh, Jack . . ."

She managed to get out the two words, and then suddenly we were tangled in each other again. Our arms intertwined, we held on to each other with desperation. I kissed her, tasting her silent tears. She kissed me back, the force of her telling me she wanted me to drop the case. She pressed into me, the need within her flooding out through her coat, through mine, through the cold filling the room. The silver left our breath as we kissed, the heat of our emotions raising our temperature to the point where we were growing too hot. I told her,

"It's warmer in the bedroom. There's furniture left in there. We could sit down—talk about all this."

She started us walking toward the hallway, saying,

"You're not going to drop the case, are you?"

"I wish you wouldn't . . ."

Before I could say anything further, Sally put several fingers across my lips, telling me,

"You don't have to say anything. I know. They killed your friends. They meant to kill you, but they missed. Now—now you don't even care about the money . . . do you? It's become personal for you—hasn't it? You just want whoever blew up your apartment—whoever killed Carmine."

My mouth drawn in a straight line, I nodded slowly. There was nothing I could do but tell the truth. Like Maurice, I didn't appreciate people shooting missiles at me, trying to kill me, killing my friends. I started to explain, but again she silenced me, saying,

"I know. I knew when I came out. That's why I had to come—I had to see if you were hurt. All the way here, I was hoping you were—hurt, I mean. I thought if only you'd been hurt, maybe you wouldn't be able to follow this one up."

"I'm sorry," I told her.

"Don't be," she whispered. "I knew you wouldn't be able to let this go. I knew. Just tell me, do you have to go now?"

"No, not now. Peter and I will be leaving for Hong Kong in the morning."

"Then," she said softly, starting us back through the hallway, "let's go where it's warm. It's my fault you did this. I knew you were going to push our relationship forward. I wanted you to. But then, when you did, I panicked. I had what I wanted and I pushed it away. I knew you weren't the

·type to play games and yet I tried to get you to play one anyway. It didn't work."

She pushed my bedroom door open and then held out her hand to indicate that I should go inside. Balto followed us as far as the door, but curled up in the middle of the hall, not even trying to go any further. As I went into the bedroom, Sally followed me through, shutting the door against the cold. As I kicked the towels back in place along the baseline, she said,

"So you got drunk and I broke all my plates." I looked at her sideways, surprised. She looked back, grinning, telling me,

"What the hell . . . I eat out all the time, anyway."

As she shrugged out of her coat, I told her,

"I'm sorry about all this, Sally. I really am. All I wanted to do was . . . I don't know. Make us both happy, I guess. Now, now I have to do this. I *have* to."

"I know," she told me, folding her coat over the back of my desk chair. Turning back to me, she took my hand, leading me over to the bed. Sitting on its edge, she whispered,

"Now I have to make sure you come back to me when you're finished."

I went down on one knee in front of her, whispering,

"I'll be back."

And then, we kissed each other again, one long kiss that lasted throughout the darkness until the morning sun flooded the windows.

CHAPTER 14

PETER AND I just made our twelve-thirty out of JFK for the Royal Crown Colony of Hong Kong. Somehow, in just the few hours he'd had, Rice had managed to get both of us valid passports and visas, as well as tickets for a commercial flight to HK, one with only one layover—three hours in San Francisco. And people say the government can't provide for its citizens anymore.

The major met us at the airport, as pressed and cool as ever. He had two expand-files with him, one for each of us. Mine was notably larger. I knew why. Peter's had only his travel papers. The one Rice had for me had all the information his people had on Kon Li Lu and the current situation around him. Or, at least, as much of the information the major's people had gathered that they were willing to release to a civilian. Of course, on top of that, I'd told Rice that I wanted the CS on every player in the game as well as their CRs.

He'd brought them all—every major and minor scrap his organization had, everything his information net felt might be important. All 3,513 pages worth. I looked at the medium-sized bag filled with files and printouts and said, "Thanks."

He told me I was welcome. Only one of us was smiling.

A person's CS is their "Current Status" report—something like what everyone tried to make you believe your permanent record would be. Even back when I was still with M.I. they were tied in to almost all the government's computer networks. I was sure they were into all of them by now. In the old days, if you needed to know where someone was at that moment, how many outstanding warrants they had, how much working capital was at their disposal, who they were dealing with, their addresses back to birth, bank accounts of parents and friends, childhood pets, favorite color—any fact about their lives that had ever been known—it was in their CS. When you wanted to know about things that weren't facts, you called for their CR.

CRs are a person's "Crap Register." The CS lists everything known about a person. Their CR lists everything ever *suspected*. It's a shadow report, filled with suppositions, accusations, petty jealousies, gut feelings, and the personal musings of every official person—F.B.I. agent, cop, teacher, drill sergeant, bank teller, whathaveyou—a person has ever encountered. The report tries to draw as many lines as it can from one entry to another. In a way, a person's CR *is* their permanent record—the one that really does exist.

In my time I had found them to be equally helpful and misleading. The only way I ever found a CR to be truly helpful was to read them with the thought of not taking any of their information as gospel. If in the course of an investigation I found a puzzle piece that fit in someone's CR, then I would use it. I know that would seem to be only logical, but you'd be surprised how many people can look at the most outrageous lie and accept it without a moment's hesitation. Then again, if you've ever attended a corporate board meeting, a high school, or a church social, maybe you wouldn't.

Once we had our seats, I explained what my new case full of paper was all about. Holding up a large handful of CSs for my new partner to see, I told him,

"Have fun."

"Have fun doing what?"

"Memorizing."

He looked at me for a long minute, wondering if I might be kidding. I assured him I wasn't. It was going to take us over eighteen hours to get to Hong Kong. To some people that might seem like a long time to be stuck on a plane. To tell the truth, it seems that way to me, too—usually. Of course, our flight that day was not one of those times most people call "usual." Plastering on my "it's time to get serious" look, I told Peter,

"It's simply in our best interest to try and get through as much of this stuff as we can. I'll be going through their fact sheets, who was where when . . . all that." Passing the files in my hand off to my new partner, I said,

"Start with these. I think this bunch in particular might warrant close study. Rice bundled them in a red rubber band. Red was always his code color. Probably means he was under pressure from above to leave us directionless. He wouldn't have risked giving us a direct communication, but it could be his way of giving us a hint."

"Yeah," agreed Peter. "Then again, it could just be a red rubber band and that you're getting awfully paranoid in your old age."

I looked at my junior partner, knowing there was nothing I could say in response. There was every possibility he was right. One of the worst things about getting mixed up in the dirty games that go on in this world is that after a while, you never know quite what is part of the game and what isn't. Is your cabdriver a man come to kill you? Did that woman peek at me from behind her menu? Is the room bugged? Am I sitting in front of a window? Is my back to the wall? Does this place have a rear exit? Is it safe to close my eyes? Can I sleep tonight?

Before long the game becomes all-consuming. It takes you through the worst the world has to offer, showing you every aspect of greed . . . towns and fields and forests burned, bombed, people murdered—all ages, in all manners—skulls stacked in piles—women, children, raped, tortured—flesh sliced, burned, knotted, shocked, broken—blood spilled and dollars collected. It wearies everyone it touches, filling them with the knowledge that their life has no more value than any of the hundreds they've seen taken—some for revenge, some for wealth, some just as an amusement.

And soon the time comes when every shadow seems to conceal something—every bush holds an assassin, every person you meet is hiding an angle. Your nerves begin to scream from the pressure of trying to keep you alive. Before long you find yourself scarred and growing hard— incapable of trust, or love, or even friendship. You go into the game with a handful of people you know—after a while either you're dead or they are and new people are brought in . . . new people you and the rest of the survivors don't know—and don't trust.

I did manage to resign my commission before the paranoia consumed me, but that was only because I had had my own reasons. If I hadn't, my nerves would have gotten me soon enough. Just thinking about what I was getting myself into had me looking over my shoulder already. Not wanting to pull Peter into my despair, I told him,

"Hey, old age is the best time of all to get paranoid." Then, as he started to flip through the files, I said,

"I'm serious, though. Take a close look at this bunch— get into their heads—figure out who they are. The one thing we have going for us is that we're the loose cannons. Most of them don't know we're coming. And those that do, don't know why. Oh, they might think they have a good idea— some will think it's just the fee, some will think we're trying for the whole ball of wax. Some will think we just want vengeance. Doesn't matter, though."

"Why not?"

"Because their confusion over what we're up to is our ace in the hole. They're not going to try and kill us until they find out if we know whatever they want to know."

"Not most of them, maybe," said Peter, his voice thick with apprehension. I couldn't blame him. The hole in my living room wall proved that he had a point.

"Yeah, well," I answered slowly, "what that clown's story is we'll find out when we catch up to him. But for real players, trying to kill people before you know what they know is just a waste of time."

"But, Jack, we don't know anything."

"That's my point. I've been wondering if whoever shot at us is even connected to this. It seems like they should be, but it just doesn't make any sense. Right now, I don't care. The rocket they shot at us came from a shipment stolen from the government. Rice says the only lead they have is that the weapons were supposedly stolen for Kon Lu's big revolution, and that they were shipped off to Hong Kong. So, if the weapons are in Hong Kong, that's where we go. We look for them, and if they lead us to Lu, so much the better. If we find Lu and that leads us to the weapons, that's good, too. I don't care. I just want the son-of-a-bitch that killed my pal."

Peter let my little speech roll around for a minute. Then, indicating the folders in his hand, he asked,

"So what do all these people think we might know? Besides where the money is?"

"There's that," I admitted. "Some people are sure to only want the money. But there are going to be some who only want Lu. Some, of course, are going to want both. Then there are going to be those who only want to stir things up to embarrass people, or just cause trouble, who don't care about the money or Lu."

"Sounds like a lot of fun."

"Yeah," I answered, settling into my seat, flipping open a folder, "loads of it."

Over the next eighteen hours we had all the fun we could bear. Since neither of us was up for any of the three movies they showed, we got a lot of reading done. I didn't think the food was bad, but anyone who's been in the military really isn't much of a judge of such things. They fed us a lot—two hot meals, two cold ones, and lots of snacks in between. But it only took up so much time, and besides we're both the kind of guys who can read and eat at the same time. Peter actually managed to cop a nap—an ability I envy immensely.

Like most ex-soldiers, I can catch a quick forty anywhere. I've slept in trees, ditches, the backseats of cars, the rider cabs of eighteen wheelers, on boats in more than one storm, in boxcars, on subways, once in a sewer and once on a mountain ledge two feet wide and half a mile straight down. Heights don't bother me, not as long as I'm attached to the ground. But planes . . . I don't know what it is—I'm not afraid of flying, which is good, since I can pilot a few small aircraft, but sleep in a plane . . . I can't do it. I've tried—I even tried again on the way to Hong Kong, but after a while I just gave up and went back to reading. It wasn't like I didn't have interesting material.

Of all the stuff the two of us plowed through, I could see that any real trouble would be coming from only five potential sources. The first was Bill Slaner—C.I.A. He'd only first been introduced onto the scene at about the same time I'd left the Far East, but I'd heard plenty about him. Dedicated, totally committed to the Agency and the country, and pretty much in that order. He was younger than me, tough and intelligent—a real dangerous combination. One I never went out of my way to confront.

The next was Sil Hung, a Chinese Communist operative known in the trade as Sil Hung Yee—"Yee" being the Chinese expression for "auntie." She was thin and good-looking and a lot older than she looked. Like Slaner, I'd never met her, but the word was that Auntie Sil was good, and that she'd brought down a lot of people everyone had at one time thought were a lot better at the game than she was . . . "at one time thought" being the phrase to pay the strictest attention to in that sentence.

Two of the players on the top five list I'd met before— Louis Perreau and Saul Cronberg. Perreau was French. Cronberg was Israeli. Cronberg was okay. He had a good sense of humor and even something of a sense of honor— not a trait highly prized in the Mossad, but tolerated in an agent as sharp as Cronberg. We'd been friendly when we'd worked together a number of years back, his country and mine teaming us up to stop a Russian move in Afghanistan. Of course, what that would count for now, I wasn't real sure.

What I knew I could count on was Perreau being a snake. He was a big man, large-shouldered, round and sloppy. He didn't look particularly French, except in the face—around the eyes, especially. He was the soul of apology, "Forgive me this," "Pardon me that," always waiting for the right moment to make his move and plant his knife—just so—up to the hilt in your back. We'd worked on the same team once, and he'd lied about certain things that were going on and almost got half our team killed—did get two of his own people tagged. No one ever found out why, that I knew of. Officially he'd been retired in disgrace, but that was an old French trick. I didn't believe it the first time I heard it and, with Rice saying Perreau was a player working the Eiffel ticket, I wasn't buying it then, either.

That left Tai Sing, a real bad enemy of mine. I'd never met the man, but I knew of him well enough. More than one of my M.I. raids took me inside the golden triangle. On the last one, when our team pulled out, we'd left some six thousand acres of burning poppies. This action did not make us beloved by either Mr. Sing or his Tiger's Breath Triad. I didn't know if he actually knew who I was as a civilian individual, but I'd heard enough about his methods of dealing with his enemies that I was happy to wish that he didn't.

As Rice had said, there were certainly a lot of people and a lot more governments involved than one might have thought at first. The major and his people had obviously included every hint of an idea they had come across throughout their investigation—which, ultimately, was all right by me. I certainly was willing to have too much information rather than not enough. Pushing myself deep into my seat, struggling to find a way to fit my too-large frame into some sort of comfortable position, I closed my eyes, thinking of the hundreds of pages I had just skimmed and the hundreds more I had read in detail.

I set my mind to looking for all the questions Rice's files offered. Were these *all* the players? And, were all of these people *really* players, or were most of them just spectators—ready to run in and grab on if a quick strike looked possible, hiding behind their own weakness the rest of the time? How many of them just wanted the money? And of those, how many wanted the money for their governments and how many wanted it for themselves? How many wanted Kon Lu? How many of them wanted both? How many wanted Lu dead and how many wanted him alive? And, I suddenly wondered, how many had seen the photos Smiler had given us?

Wanting to prove my ability to still be a team player, I had shown them to Rice at the airport. He acknowledged being familiar with most of them. He also added his opinion, which was that whether they were real or not, they didn't count for anything. I found that interesting. As evidence they weighed pretty heavy against the wonder boy from Tian'anmen, but the major didn't seem to want to buy it. Of course, that was only his opinion. Rice, a man used to working within a strict code of beliefs, saw the photos as misleading from the truth. Smiler, a man with a somewhat different orientation from the major, saw them as proof positive.

What either of them thought, however, had to be pushed to the back. I was heading into dangerous water and couldn't afford to follow anyone's instincts but my own. I had other things to worry about—things like Slaner and Sil, Perreau and Cronberg and Sing and whether or not they were really the worst of all those involved. If they were, how was I going to find them? And, if they weren't, how was I going to find the ones I didn't know about?

The questions just kept piling up. How many of them knew about each other? How many knew about people I didn't know about? And, how many of them knew Peter and I were on our way? And, I added, the biggest question of all, which one of them had been so worried by that knowledge that once they'd received it they'd blown out the side of my home, trying to kill us before we could get there?

Yeah, I told myself, my fists balling of their own volition, crumpling Rice's papers, that was the big question, all right. In fact, as far as I was concerned, that was the only one.

CHAPTER 15

HONG KONG CUSTOMS officials weren't quite as much fun as I remembered them. Not nearly as much. In the old days the Royal HK had been a lot looser, more fast-paced operation. Their police, government offices, even their military personnel, could match anyone else's in the world for out-and-out corruption. Of course, it only made sense. After all, Hong Kong had as much money as anyone else, why shouldn't they have as many criminal opportunists as anyone else? That, however, was all changed.

In place of a customs staff that fifteen years earlier could be bribed to turn a blind eye at anything from a matched set of loaded .457s to a bowling bag full of children's skulls for nothing more than a price of a meal at a dim sum house, the modern international traveler now found a much changed beast. The higher-ups of HK customs had purged its bad eggs and replaced anyone whose vision wasn't twenty-twenty and then some. In fact, all of the Colony's governmental agencies, from the police to the Royal Department of Streets, Thoroughfares, and Corridors had been overhauled over the past few years.

There was no great mystery as to why, either. With their Chinese landlords ready to repossess everything in sight in 1997, a clean broom had become the only smart move. Despite all the bad things one can find to say about Communists, there's no denying their lack of love for criminals of all kinds—at least, the non-party card-carrying kinds, anyway. Wisely, nobody in any branch of any HK public service wanted to be seen as having their hands anywhere near the till. The word was special favors were out. All smugglers—from the jewel and gem market busters trying to get through the airport to the artifact pirates trying to slide through the harbors—had been put on very short notice.

Peter and I, along with the rest of our flight, were put through the slow crawl. We waited for almost twenty minutes while the two grimly serious bag checkers whose lane we'd drawn went through our things. I couldn't prove it, of course, but it seemed as if they were taking a longer time with us than any of the others were taking with our fellow passengers. Maybe they didn't like our luggage, or maybe they didn't like the thought of a Chinese and an American traveling together—two men, anyway—or maybe the look of us just set off their bells. Neither of us knew what it was . . . we just knew we were bone tired from our flight. All we wanted to do was get a cab, get to our hotel, fight over who got to use the shower first, and get some sleep. Such, however, was not to be the case.

"Hello, gentlemen," came a warm, accented voice from behind us. "And what could it be that would bring two fine men like yourselves to our shores?"

"Who wants to know?" I asked, eyeing the newcomer. Catching sight of him instantly made me glad that I'd ditched all of Rice's papers on the plane. I'd used an old gag, complaining about paperwork and ordering a drink to celebrate having "finished" it all. Following a stewardess happy to help someone get a little pleasure out of life, I dumped all the files we'd studied in the galley garbage, helping to clean trays, going on about what a relief it was to see the last of all that work the boss had stuck me with—watching out of the corner of my eye as we slopped the crap from about forty trays on them. I didn't realize just how glad I was not to have confidential government files in my luggage until I saw our new playmate.

He stood roughly five ten, 190, 200 pounds tops, most all of it looking fairly tight—hard. He had a slightly squared, slightly oval face, all of its features cut in stone and topped by a sharp bristle-cut. He was an island-born Chinese, Oriental in looks only, British everywhere else. Taking our passports from a completely deferential customs agent, he flipped Peter's open first, then mine, answering,

"To answer your question, Mr. Jack Ha . . . Hah . . . forgive me . . . how *do* you pronounce your surname?"

"That would be Hay-gie."

"Hay . . . gee?" he repeated.

"Yeah, right. Hay-gie. Gie-rhymes with lee. I'm not going too fast for you, am I?"

"Oh, heavens no," he replied with a wide smile. Pushing his accent over into a comedy rendition of the worst Charlie Chan impersonation I'd ever heard, he continued, saying,

"Mr. Jack Hagee and Mr. Peter Wei, both veelly good American citizen boys, both residents of regendary New Yolk City. We arr know Big Appre here—Browadway, the Statue of Riberty, the Empile State Building. Oh yes, hele in Hong Kong for preasurable sight-seeing, I am sure. Now let me think about it for one minute—where would you two veelly good American citizen boys most likely be off to first?"

I listened while he chatted at us, studying our passports, his eyes keeping track of each page, us, and the contents of our bags as the customs men kept going through them. Not an easy task. There was little doubt that he was an official of some sort. The question was what sort? He wasn't some petty bureaucrat. Someone like that just wouldn't bother. Someone like that wouldn't look like the guy hassling us, either. There were solid lines in his squared-off face—lines deep enough to match the silky growl running through his voice.

The longer he talked at us, the more his Charlie Chan bit wore off. He kept it up, though, the tone of each sentence getting just a bit nastier than the one before it.

"Maybe the Ocean Park Tour," he told us. "You'd like Ocean Park."

"You think so?" I asked him.

"Oh, yes," he answered. "It's a must for all the tourists in Hong Kong. Ocean Park's the most spectacular oceanarium in the world, with the largest marine theatre ever built by man."

"Is that a fact?"

"Oh, yes again. They have performances by dolphins and killer whales . . . three times every day. But the wise tourist can really get his money's worth. If you take the morning tour—that's tour code XT-01—you can see both Ocean Park and the fabulous Middle Kingdom."

"Sounds real exciting," I said.

"Oh, it is," he assured me. "The Middle Kingdom has full-size replicas of temples, shrines, street and public square scenes, pavilions, pagodas and palaces recreating the sights and sounds of China's thirteen magnificent dynasties."

"Must be hard to say that fast."

"What?"

"Pavilions . . . pagodas . . . and palaces," I told him. "Sounds like a real tongue twister. Not for a savvy guy like you, of course."

"No," he agreed. "Not for a savvy guy like me."

"Of course."

And then, suddenly, he handed our passports back to the customs man, making a short gesture with two fingers which seemed to mean he was through. As the bag checker hurried to shut our suitcases, our tour guide's phony smile faded. Pointing an index finger at us, he said,

"There are too many of you in Hong Kong now—way too many. There's going to be trouble and I don't like it."

"You're breakin' my heart, pal," I told him. "Give me a reason to care."

The hard face stared at me for a second, looking for something to hate. I thought hard about giving it to him just to be belligerent, but I stopped short, trying to remind myself that acting like a jerk just to get off a ripping good line was still acting like a jerk. I'm not sure what our tour guide might have found, but since he didn't come across what he had been looking for, he said,

"You know, instead of having you taken in for questioning for the next fifteen hours—something I'm sure you gentlemen would just love—I'm going to give you a break. And I'll even tell you why."

"That's so nice of you."

"I'm a nice guy."

"I know," I told him. "I could see it in your eyes."

"Oh, really? You saw it in my eyes, eh?"

"Uh-huh."

"You must be real perceptive."

"That's what they tell me."

"I could tell you something about yourself, too."

"Oh, please don't," I said.

"Why not?" he asked. "Afraid of the truth?"

"Oh no," I answered. "I'd just hate to have you tell me it was all over between us."

The stone face smiled again at that one. Not the phony, happy idiot grin he'd plastered on before, but an honest one, one that let me know we'd bought ourselves some time. As I wondered just what our tour guide was going to do next, a separate voice within my head made me take note of how easily Peter had kept his cool throughout the whole business. I had to admit that I was impressed.

Throughout our tour guide's little spiel he had let me field the team effort, not jeopardizing our futures for the sake of his ego. Some guys might have wanted to jump in and show what they were all about—a move that would probably have gotten us nothing more than that fifteen-hour pep talk our new pal had mentioned. Even in the short few minutes of our banter he had impressed me as the kind of guy who didn't like anyone in his face. Peter had kept out of his way, though, something I'm sure had impressed our tour guide as much as it had me. Finally getting to his point, our new pal told us,

"I'll tell you the truth, I'm giving you your biggest points for not trying to hand me some bullshit about why you're here. You two have got Kon Li Lu written all over you, but at least you're 'savvy' enough to know it." Reaching into his jacket pocket, our tour guide pulled out a worn black leather wallet, one holding his identification. It told us he was Ronald Lin, a captain in the Hong Kong police force.

"So now, just in case you two aren't savvy enough to understand what I'm telling you here, allow me to explain.

Your movements are going to be monitored as long as you are on British soil. You are both undesirables as far as I'm concerned—fortune hunters or bounty hunters, I don't care which. You don't have any jurisdiction here, Mr. Hagee, Mr. Wei. You're just two private guys from the home of the red, white, and blue, and you will be deported right back to your Uncle Sam's loving arms at the first opportunity you give me—do we understand each other?"

"I think we got it, Captain."

"How about you, brush-cut?" Lin asked Peter. "You bristling with righteous indignation?"

"I'm just fine, Captain Lin, sir," Peter answered calmly. "The most honorable high chief of detectives has proved that nothing escapes his notice."

"So," I asked, "we free to go, Captain?"

"Of course, gentlemen. Enjoy your hopefully brief stay in our fair colony."

Having been granted our exit we grabbed our bags, moving forward out of the customs area as fast as we could with our burdens. As we did, though, I called over my shoulder,

"Hey Captain, dolphin *and* killer whale performances three times—*every* day?"

"Every day, Mr. Hagee."

"Wow," I said, letting the word trail off into a whistle. "That really sounds great." Peter and I kept moving. My junior partner gave me a little smile, showing me he agreed with my sense of humor. Then, just to prove he had one of his own, he called out,

"Yeah—thanks, Captain," giving him a little wave as he did so.

What Lin said in return I couldn't hear.

CHAPTER 16

"SO HOW DID he know?"

"Good question."

"How about a good answer then?" Peter paced the floor in front of my bed, still disturbed by our run-in with Captain Lin. I didn't blame him. I was concerned with how he'd known to meet us myself. Putting down the copy of *The South China Morning Post* I'd picked up in the lobby, I said,

"Well, let me see. Fifteen, even ten years ago, the Hong Kong cops were all pretty bad. From what I hear, that's changed a lot now, though. With the Commies coming in soon, they've had to clean up their act. Of course, the military operation, being British, was always pretty regular. In the old days, a good cop could get cooperation from the military despite how corrupt the rest of the force was. Now—on top of that—the Hong Kong police are divided into two sections—enforcement and intelligence. I wouldn't doubt that they could have tumbled to the fact that we were coming into town all on their own."

"And if they didn't figure it out all on their own?" asked Peter, catching the note in my voice.

"Well, if that wasn't the case, then my best guess would be that we'd have to figure that if Rice has people on his end gathering information which he passed on to us, it's probably that someone tipped back a memo on the two of us . . . once again, most likely to the HK police intelligence division."

"You mean you think someone back in the States ratted us out?"

"'Ratted us out'?" I repeated, chuckling a little. "You're

112

getting awfully colorful. No, I don't think we were 'ratted out.' All I'm saying is if a couple of HK dicks were going to blow into New York to look into something Rice's people were connected to, their informants here would pass the word along. We stuck our heads into the pipeline to see what we could see. It's hard to do and not get seen by anyone else."

"Then who else knows about us being here?"

"Hard to say," I answered. Stretching my arms out, I worked at dislodging a kink that had settled in the middle of my back during the flight. "I was surprised at Lin knowing—more surprised at him being there to greet us."

Peter stopped pacing, sitting down heavily in the room's one chair. Pushing his legs out in front of him, he stretched them to their full length, doing his arms at the same time as he asked, "And what was his little show about, anyway?"

"I'm not sure," I answered truthfully, picking my paper up once more. "I grabbed the *Morning Post* because I wanted to look through it and see if anything had happened in town while we were in the air . . . anything that might sound like trouble between any of our players. If something had happened, knowing that more pieces were coming onto the board might have made Lin want to show us who's boss. He might have just wanted to show us anyway. Preemptive strike to get us under his thumb. He probably had us followed. One of his boys probably already has our room number."

"What do we do about that?"

"Nothing. This is Hong Kong, which means we're far from home. We're going to take the next few days and just act like a pair of rubes."

"You mean act like we're not here looking for Lu?"

"No, no. We don't want to insult our good buddy Captain Lin's intelligence. If we try to play it like we're just some kind of tourists they'll watch us twice as close. Uh-uh, we have to go about our business, but we just have to do a half-assed kind of job of it. We've got to leave Lin with the impression that we're just amateurs. Then once we've got some breathing room, we'll start making some real moves."

"Like what?"

"Well, we'll know that better after we've gotten some idea of the situation here. So look—you were going to take a shower, right? Well, go on, do it. Let me check out the paper and see what's going on in town these days."

Peter gave me a nod and then headed for the bathroom, leaving me to thumb my way through the *Post*. I didn't bother to do more than skim most of the headlines. No newspaper in any city in the world ever gives you much real information on the front page when you're trying to get the feel for a place. Twenty minutes with the local television news, even in one of the old eastern bloc dictatorships, lets you in on everything big that's happening in an area—at least, everything that you're going to get from *any* kind of official news source.

Newspapers, on the other hand, can give you a wealth of local information that the video newscasts just don't have the time for. One thing I noticed right off the bat was a half page ad for the Sotheby's Spring Auction. It only had one small photo and a couple of words in large print. The rest of the ad was all in tiny lettering, a massive list which seemed to only be a hint of what they had coming up on the block. The list of auction dates stretched on for weeks, offering hundreds of items—interestingly enough, the grand majority of them large, bulky pieces.

That told me that despite all of the Communists' assurances that they were going to leave the local economy untouched for the next half century, that it was possible nobody believed them. The local millionaires were putting all of their hard to move things up for sale, risking the fickleness of the gavel as opposed to being stuck with a lot of furniture, stone screens, and eight-foot-tall vases when it came time to make their break for some other part of the world. Couches are heavy . . . diamonds you can put in your pocket and run for the airport.

Other things caught my eye as well. The vast majority of the letters to the editor complained about things like TELA, the television and entertainment licensing commission, and their massive interference in Hong Kong's TV viewing habits due to their severely harsh monitors. Or warnings from the HK General Chamber of Commerce that Hongkongers would be better off putting their energies into the economy, and not into worrying about "so-called democracy." Scary stuff, to say the least.

Cricket scores took up less room than the baseball scores from America, or the results from the Hong Kong racetrack. That was telling, too. Things British being downplayed was another bad sign. Mainly because it was nothing that anyone wanted except the big boys in Beijing. The Chinese love to gamble, and as anyone who has spent even a little time in HK knows, cricket and the ponies are probably the two top things book is made on from one end of the Colony to the other. But Communists take a dim view of gambling so, once again, something had to give.

More than half the news in the *Business Post* dealt with the mainland as well—Chinese maneuverings in AsiaSat through their international investment arm, CITIC, letting the careful reader know that the Communists were making heavy demands on the space communications company for their own purposes . . . a report that the Hang Seng Market Index had finished another record-breaking week in which the index gained a remarkable 7.8 percent. And yet, the only thing the Chinese State Council's HK & Macau Affairs Office could do was issue a policy statement turning the positive sentiment into a pessimistic omen. There were plenty more articles, but I'd seen enough to get the idea.

Every section of the paper was the same—filled with the same kind of information. The freight and shipping appointments were crowded to the brim with reports showing people dismantling businesses and sending them overseas. The *Classified Post* was bigger than I ever remembered it, filled to overflowing with positions for top management people—a fact which made me guess that everyone with cash was getting out while the getting was good, leaving the big-money jobs open. Legal & General Notices was filled with court cases, lots of change of shares registrations and export licenses, but very few new business starts to be seen.

There was a lot of property for sale, also—commercial and industrial.

I folded the paper at that point, not needing to read any more. Throwing it on top of the nightstand, I folded my hands behind my head and closed my eyes, stretching out on the bed. Balancing what I had learned in the paper against what I could remember of Hong Kong from my old days in Southeast Asia, I could see that things were pretty much just as bad as I had imagined they would be.

The people were scared, the rich and powerful at the top of the ladder and everyone behind them on the lower rungs. In some ways I could see it making our job easier—in some harder. There would be a lot of people out there eager to help us for a cut of the profits, more so than in normal times. On the other hand, there would be a lot of people who would want Kon Li Lu and his cash to stay together and undiscovered, as long as he was still aiming it at the heart of the rapidly approaching Communists.

I, myself, had been hoping that the Commies could be trusted this time. It only seemed to me to be in their own vested self-interest to keep Hong Kong an open and capitalistic free market economy. China needed cash as much as every other Marxist outfit still limping along in the modern world. It was obvious that they were trying to change their economy over to a capitalist system from the special economic areas they were setting up all along their southern coast. That was why it seemed to me that to scare the British and their people and connections off the island with human rights edicts and the such as they had been for the past few years was just plain stupid. On the one hand, anyone could see that there were certainly enough Hongkongers sending signals that they were ready to cooperate with the least encouragement from the mainland. On the other, however, Beijing was playing its cards close to its vest, perhaps just to scare everyone—knowing that frightened people will do anything to get rid of their fear. Dictators never learn.

Letting everything jell in my head gave me a few ideas of what buttons I would start pushing once Peter and I got down to some serious work. As I lay there in the darkness, the weariness of the day finally started to catch up to me. I wondered what Elba and her brothers and sisters were up to. I wondered how Hubert was doing, and how Carmine's wife had taken the news. It hadn't even dawned on me as I hurried myself out of town that she was going to learn what had happened from someone else. That thought made me wonder about Francis. I didn't even know if he had any family—who they might be or where they were.

Well, I thought, what good could I do for any of them being there? Nothing. The only thing I had to offer any of them was vengeance, and I couldn't do anything about that in Brooklyn. For that I had to be where I was—stretched out on a hotel bed in Hong Kong. Then, the fact that I was stretched out there by myself made me remember Sally. That cut me off short. She didn't want vengeance for Carmine or Francis. She didn't want me there at all. What she wanted was me at home, in one piece, away from whatever was going to happen next.

Then why are you here? the little voice inside asked me. I wondered at what the answer might be, but couldn't think of one. So I told it to shut up and leave me alone. Before it could reply, however, Peter came out of the bathroom drying his hair, surrounded by a cloud of steam.

"All yours," he called, saving me from having to debate the point with myself any further. Slowly, I opened my eyes and dragged myself up off the bed, pushing myself toward the bathroom.

"Hope you left some hot water," I said, noting the amount of steam billowing into the room.

"I think you might find some," he answered back. Then, before I could get all the way past him, he dropped his towel down around his neck, letting it hang over his chest. Looking me in the eye, he said,

"You know that blundering around we're supposed to start with tomorrow . . . ?"

"Yeah?" I asked, not recognizing the tone in his voice. "What about it?"

"I don't think it's going to be all that hard on my part."

"Why's that?" I asked, suddenly getting an idea about what was coming next.

"Because you were half right without knowing it, I guess." I looked at him honestly, trying to let my expression say that I wasn't really sure what he was talking about. He understood.

"What I'm saying is that here . . . caught up in this game of spies and everything . . . well, I guess I *am* an amateur."

"So?" I asked. "So what? You telling me you're pulling out and going back home?"

"No, it's not that. I just . . ."

"Things too tough for you all of a sudden? We got leaned on a little by some HK slip-covered flatfoot and you want to resign the firm. Is that it?"

"No, Jack. That's not it."

"Then what is?" I asked, calm, trying to get him to the answer all on his own without any help from me.

"I don't know. I guess when you started talking about having partners and expanding your agency, I thought it would just be more of the same. You know, the kind of stuff both of us have always done. I wasn't expecting the first thing we did together to take us halfway around the world looking for treasure neck and neck with half the spies in the world."

"So what's your point?"

"Damn it, Jack. I'm trying to say I don't know how much help I'm going to be to you here. I'm the one who was making all the noise about 'four hundred and fifty million dollars' and now we're here looking for it. But I don't know anything about playing this kind of game. I guess . . ." He swallowed hard, afraid to say what he wanted to, but too much of a man not to come out with the truth. I knew where he was going—knew what he wanted to say—but I had to let him say it. After his pause, he did.

"I mean, I guess I'm just afraid that at the least you're going to be doing all the work and . . . and at the worst, I'm afraid I'm going to get us both killed."

"Well," I told him, "good. Glad we got that out of the

way. Now, let me say something. First, I didn't expect to be here doing this, either. Second, it is not your fault that we are here. I didn't do this to chase the money. At first I said I would do it for a very stupid reason. After that, there was Carmine and Francis, and I don't think I have to explain that one. They were both 'amateurs' too, you know. I was willing to hire them, just like you. They didn't make it. We did. And they're why we're here. Your chanting about four hundred and fifty million dollars didn't hypnotize me. I'm a big boy. I make all my own decisions. Just like you."

"Yeah, but . . ."

"But what?" Staring at Peter across the dimly lit room, I told him point-blank, "There's nothing else to bat around here. Nothing. All you have to do is tell me . . . you want out or you want in?"

"In," he answered, smiling with relief. "I want in."

"You know," I reminded him, "I'm not any kind of genius or James Bond or anything. Yeah, I played some games in this area a few years back and I may know a bit more about some of it than you do, but it's not much different than the usual stuff we do. People rob and kill each other for the same reasons, no matter how much they're stealing or how many people they're killing."

Standing up, I started to strip for my shower. As I threw my shirt on the bed, I told Peter,

"And that sums up the difference between street crimes and international crime—size. That's it. The senator who lies or the shadow agent who murders someone or any of it, despite all their fucking bullshit ideology, it all comes down to the same set of numbers over and over . . . whose wife did they want to fuck, how much money were they out to steal, who made them look bad so that they wanted to get back . . . et cetera, et cetera. It never ends, Peter—it just never ends. What big crime that you've ever heard of in your entire life ever came down to anything more than the motives of any regular curbside creep? The bad guys are all the same—some of them just enjoy a sense of scope." As I balled my socks up and threw them with my shirt, I said,

"You've got good, practical investigative skills. And

that's the reason why I offered you a slice of the agency. If I thought you were going to get me killed, I would have said something like, 'Well, you watch the office, Petey-boy, and I'll call when I get to Hong Kong.' I'm not stupid enough to partner up with a liability case just because I don't want to hurt somebody's feelings." Grabbing the shorts I planned to sleep in out of my bag, I finished, asking,

"Okay?"

"Okay," answered my partner, obviously relieved. Leaving him to his relief, I went into the bathroom so I could take my shower. I thought about what we had said while I let the steaming water soak away the eighteen hours we'd spent in the air. I didn't blame him for feeling the way he did, nor was I upset with him for telling me about it. If someone I was counting on to help keep me alive didn't think they were up to the job, I sure as hell wanted to know about it.

Finally finished in the bathroom, I came back out into our room to find Peter already sound asleep. I moved around as quietly as I could. Considering what we were probably in for over the next few days or weeks, I figured, let him get as much rest as he could. Then, just about ready to crawl into my bed, a sudden thought hit me. Considering once again what we either were, or at least *could* be in for, I took the chair from the room's wall desk and wedged it under the doorknob.

Sure, I thought, maybe Peter was right and maybe I was just getting old and a bit paranoid about things, but then again, why should he be the only one to get a good night's sleep?

CHAPTER 17

THREE DAYS LATER found Peter and me in our rental car, leaving our hotel bright and early. For two days we had hit the most obvious general information spots possible, even going to the police with questions, playing up our babes-in-the-woods images. Now we were heading out along the Harcourt Road for the tunnel to the Kowloon Peninsula, ready to finally start making some real moves.

Kowloon is the closest edge of the New Territories to Hong Kong island itself. Of course, all of it would soon once again just be known as China. At least that was the way of it according to some of the bored types we'd found while making the rounds of some of the local bars. As far as they were concerned, bothering with such specifics wasn't worth their time. Not quite ready to give up on a place that was home for so many years, I wasn't quite so bored.

We were headed for an establishment run by Felecia Morgan, a top-deal friend of mine from those old days. I hadn't heard from her in a number of years. Fair being fair, though, I had to admit that she hadn't heard from me, either. It was also apparent that if we didn't do something soon we wouldn't be the only people headed there. True to his word, Captain Lin had put a tail on us our first day. Or at the least, if the team following that morning as they had been the past two wasn't of the good captain's doing, there was little doubt that someone with a gray Saab was still interested in where we were going. As we finished paying our toll and headed into the tunnel, Peter said,

"Guy doesn't give up, does he?"

"Someone hasn't—I'll give you that much."

"You don't think it's Lin?"

"Oh no—it's probably his people, all right. But don't let it get under your skin or you'll be scratching the whole time you're here. Just think of him as another Fisher," I added. "You were on the force—you know the drill. Push a guy you think is up to something until he slips up and shows you what it is. Maybe not the oldest trick in the book, but I'm sure it's in the first chapter somewhere."

We came out of the tunnel and up into the early Kowloon morning, ready to see if the Hong Kong police were as easily scammed as their New York City brothers-in-blue. Taking a roundabout, we're-a-little-bit-lost-tourists route to Salisbury Road, we finally got on it fifteen minutes after leaving the tunnel with our tail still in sight. Moving at an even pace, I had Peter make it easy on our driving buddy, hoping for the always welcomed false sense of security to start entering into the picture. I wanted to turn around and take a peek at our friends to see how many they were, but I let Peter handle it with his mirrors, telling myself that if I was going to have a partner I'd better learn to trust him.

Peter was fairly sure there were two people in the Saab—pretty much what I had figured. When I saw the planetarium coming into view—a building I'd heard had been built but had never actually seen—I made a big production of unfolding a road map, telling Peter to slow down dramatically at the same time. Crawling along from that point all the way to the bus terminal, I made another big production of pointing out a right-hand turn to Peter on Canton Road. The Saab stayed with us.

Leading them down the road, we finally pulled over in front of the Royal Pacific Hotel. Getting out of the car, we spread our map out on its hood, gesturing angrily and animatedly, trying to get across the impression that we were now hopelessly lost tourists. We played our charade out for a full minute and then ended it with a pantomime intended to tell anyone watching closely that Peter should get back into the car and wait for me while I went into the Royal Pacific and asked directions. Then I stalked off, open map flapping in my hand, trying to look as frustrated and angry as possible.

Once I reached the front doors of the hotel, however, I ducked in and turned a corner, folding the map up and returning it to my inside jacket pocket, heading for the hotel's second floor at the same time. There I exited out onto the footbridge that extended from the hotel over the road and into Kowloon Park. Looking down at our car, I could see that Peter had not raised the radio aerial, the signal we had arranged in case anyone had exited from the Saab to follow me inside.

Confident that our plan had worked I moved forward toward Kowloon Park at the other end of the bridge. I knew that after another ten minutes Peter would just drive away, giving our pals in the Saab the choice of following him or trying to find me. Smiling down at our little friends, I gave them a short salute and then moved forward into the park.

My personal hope was that they would follow Peter just because our plan called for him to drive to Ocean Park. I was hoping Captain Lin might appreciate that little touch. I also knew we wouldn't lose his boys so easily the next time, but I had to see Felecia at least once without anyone knowing that I had any connection to her.

As I walked through the park I found it to be actually even nicer than I remembered it. It was hard to believe—so hard in fact I was forced to wonder if they could have actually improved it that much or if it was just the years I'd spent in New York City with its uniform lack of beauty that simply made it seem nicer. New York is such a miserable scumhole I was perfectly willing to accept the latter.

Knowing I had plenty of time, I took the longest route across the park possible, winding my way first through the ornamental circles, then heading for the water gardens. The weather was the kind I always prayed for when I was in the Orient, mild and warm with a light haze hiding the sun slightly. The Hong Kong humidity I'd always despised hadn't risen yet for the day, making the walk as pleasant a time as I'd had in quite a while. It being winter, I knew it was quite possible we wouldn't see much humidity the entire time I was there. The prospect was seductive—a job that took me out of freezing, rat-crack New York in the middle of winter and set me down in an Eden like Hong Kong was my kind of job. If it hadn't come with the price tag of two dead pals and half the world's trained killers I might have thought about letting the meter run a little extra.

Standing next to the main water fountain in Kowloon Park, however, I didn't think I'd have to tangle with too many of the others involved in the case. True, I was on the trail of Kon Li Lu just like they, but not for any of the same reasons. By that point my priorities had changed. I didn't expect to find the hero of Tian'anmen Square or his three billion. I didn't want to, either. All I wanted was whoever had killed Carmine and Francis. Period.

Knowing, however, that my ego and its desires didn't run the whole show, I decided to get moving again. Pushing off from the railing I'd been leaning against, I headed down the path through the sculpture walk and then, just to make sure no one was on my tail, I headed inside the maze garden. I wandered around for a good fifteen minutes inside, doubling back through the jumble of hedges over the same ground several times, half making sure no one had followed me inside, half enjoying the last of the morning before getting down to business. By the time I was finished I knew that if anyone was still behind me that they were a damn sight more professional in their work than I was and that I might as well give up trying to trick them. That decided, I exited the maze garden onto Nathan Road, and then headed up Granville for Felecia's.

Wedged in between the Grand Mark and the Kiu Yip Building, Felecia's place was one of the oldest original establishments on the peninsula. Forty years earlier the entire area had been hardly more than a collection of forests, fishing shacks, and bamboo huts. As soon as expansion had been allowed, however, capitalism changed all of that in its typical hurry. Now things were so overbuilt that Kowloon Park was practically the only green area in any direction for miles around.

Felecia's father, Clark Morgan, had built his place in

Kowloon with his pension from the British and the optimism of a fanatic. Like a handful of others with limited resources but high energy, he had seen the growth coming in the peninsula before a lot of others and managed to get the Five Great Grains built before the onslaught. Because of his foresight, his daughter had been left a legacy worth more than a few million Hong Kong dollars, and at least three million American ones.

Stepping up in front of the place I stopped for a moment, hesitant about going in. Not because Felecia and I had parted on bad terms or anything. It was just that suddenly I wondered if I had the right to involve her, to drag her into whatever would be coming next. On the one hand I knew that, sure, the Five Great Grains had seen more than its share of shady goings-on in the night. Felecia's old man had dealt in information—always ready to move it to the highest bidder—that's how we met. And when he'd bought the farm she'd been more than equipped to move in and take over that end of his operation as well as the restaurant.

I didn't want to know much, either. Peter and I had ruled out trying to computer search for the cash. With entire governments looking for the three billion, there was no way we were going to electronically stumble on to it before someone else was. Hu had called in the night before, letting me know that as far as Smiler's photos were concerned, there was no pinning them down. Some of his sources said Kon Lu had gone through all the money, the others said he was a saint. He apologized but had to admit he couldn't dig up anything positive one way or the other.

He did say that his best source in the area was laying high odds on the weapons being on Lantau, one of the larger islands that made up the Hong Kong colony. I thanked him for his efforts, telling him I'd keep him posted. After that I'd planned out Peter's and my little game for our friends in the Saab. So far, everything had worked. Now all I had to do was go into the Grains and ask Fel what she could tell me. Somehow, though, my reluctance kept me rooted to the spot.

I looked at my reflection in the place's big main window,

wondering where the guy I was looking at was getting all the morals all of a sudden. Felecia Morgan dealt in information. I needed some. What was so fucking hard? I asked myself. The little voice inside reminded me that two of my friends were already dead. It showed me Carmine's melted face and asked me how many more corpses I wanted on my hands. Growling under my breath, I told the little voice to go fuck itself and pushed open the front door. If the merchants inside didn't want to deal, they didn't have to—caveat emptor works both ways.

I stepped inside, out of the blinding morning sunlight and into cool darkness. Like most of Hong Kong, the cool breeze was supplied by the place's powerful air conditioners and dehumidifiers which kept the indoor conditions nearly perfect everywhere one went in the Colony—just as I remembered it. As I moved into a circle of light there in the main foyer, a high-pitched, semi-familiar voice announced from the far shadows across the restaurant,

"Too early. Not open yet. You too early. Lunch not for long time. No dim sum today. Too early."

"Hey, the way I remember it," I answered, wondering if the reference would be too many years out-of-date, "it's never too early for the five great grains." As I stared into the darkness, I made out the form of whomever it was I was talking to. The voice I had heard before answered me, sounding almost familiar. I wanted it to be who I thought it was so badly that I didn't trust my own ears. The voice called again,

"And what you know about five great grains?"

"I know that most wise Confucius believed that only a farmer can name them, and that a rich man, sitting all day in his palace, cannot."

As my eyes got used to the light again, I could see that the form I had been talking to was a male one. As I waited, he started moving toward me. He had a mop in one hand and a bucket in the other. As he neared the edge of the shadows, still a dozen yards away, I knew who it was and suddenly found myself fighting back tears I didn't know I had. His voice cracking with emotion, he challenged me, asking,

"And are you lazy, rich dog or honest farmer man?"

"Wheat, sesame, rice, beans, and barley."

"Bad Jack," he said, reaching the circle of light I had stayed in purposely. "Son of Trouble."

"Li Tsim, Father of Fun."

The old man stuffed his mop into his bucket and set them both aside, and then came forward with both hands extended, wrapping them around me.

"Bad Jack Hagee," he called, hugging me close, tears on his face to match my own. "You bad guy. No see in so long. No play poker so long, no play mah-jongg so long. Me think maybe you dead big time now." Then, suddenly, he broke his hold. Stepping back from me, his smile disappearing, he wiped at his eyes and then folded his arms across his chest, asking,

"How come no hear from you? No call. No letter. No send card on Chinese New Year. How come become so bad to poor old Hong Kong uncle?"

I had to answer. He was only the clean-up man, had been for at least twenty-five years, but I had to answer him. It wasn't just that having him happy would make it much easier for me to find out where Felecia was—the simple truth was I owed him. He was more than just a mop jockey. We had been pals when I'd been stationed in the East—best pals—Li Tsim had been the only civilian I trusted. I had been one of the few people outside of the Five Great Grains that had his trust. On top of that, I was the one that had disappeared. That made me the one who had to explain.

"I'm just a bad person," I told him. "You remember when I left the service, right?" He nodded his head quietly to show that he still thought of those days in the same way I did. "Well, it took a long time to shake that off. When I got back to America I thought it would be pretty easy to put that all behind me. I'd just leave the military at the gate and that would be the end of it." I stopped talking for a second, then added,

"It didn't quite work like that."

Li Tsim nodded his head again. He was old enough that he could tell just what I meant from the tone in my voice.

When I had first met him, feeling sorry for myself over the things I had had to deal with because of the service, he and I had sat up drinking, comparing evils we had witnessed in our time. I didn't win the contest. Li had escaped the Communists and come to Hong Kong over twenty years earlier. He'd seen every rotten aspect of the world and its people before I'd been born. Not letting it destroy him as it almost did me, however, he had married, raised a family, and apparently was still working every day—hard.

"But," I told him, "I'm a happier guy these days."

"That," said a voice from behind us that, once one heard it, one did not forget it, "would be a welcome change."

I turned sharply, happy to hear Felecia's voice, even happy for the chance to have her rub it in that I hadn't been in touch with anyone in so many years. What I was not happy about was the fact that anyone was with her. The man next to her moved into view, ready to introduce himself. There was no need. No one who's seen Bill Slaner's picture ever forgot his face.

CHAPTER 18

TO SAY THAT seeing Slaner with Felecia was not one of the things I'd been expecting would be to put it mildly. Felecia had never been a big friend of the C.I.A.'s. British by birth, she had chosen her friends carefully over the years, and not many of them had come from that particular organization's rank and file. Slaner was younger than me, not as broadly built, but he looked to be all muscle—hard and wiry, like a prizefighter who worked as a ballet star on the weekends.

Dressed in a lightweight, blue- and white-striped suit, he stood about five eleven, sporting short, brush-cut sandy brown hair atop chestnut brown eyes that seemed under their owner's complete control. He had a nose just a hair short of being too large for his face, sitting atop thin lips and a chin that looked like it could take dedicated hammer blows. Hoping I hadn't given away the fact that I'd recognized him, I decided to see how much he was willing to volunteer. Smiling, I threw all the joy I had into my voice, saying,

"Felecia. It's been a long time." Then, pretending to have just noticed her companion, I added, "I'm not interrupting anything, am I?"

"Nothing that can't wait," she said. Then, allowing the two of us to do our own dirty work, she suggested, "Why don't you boys introduce yourselves?"

I gave Slaner my real name. He gave me his in a voice that was cheerful and filled with the sounds of Manhattan. I did the best I could to mask any overt recognition of his name from my eyes, then added just for cover,

"Slaner. Bill Slaner. Maybe I'll just be looking silly here, but I'd swear I've heard your name somewhere before."

"Yeah. Well that was probably right here, just before you first left the islands," he answered coolly, letting me know pretty much exactly where he stood. He took a sip from the drink in his hand, but I noticed that his eyes never really left my face. His movements were slow, easy ones, his attitude friendly. Breaking out in a big, I'm-a-happy-kind-of-guy smile, the kind that really didn't fit with his New York accent, he set his drink on the bar and then continued, saying,

"When the Army was done waltzing you boys around in here is when Washington sent the first wave of us new undercovers in. I was here for about two months before you left. And that's spelled C . . . I . . . A—just in case you were thinking of keeping the ball in the air all morning."

"You been here ever since?"

"No, no," he answered. "I was only island-hopping the area for six years. The Company's moved me around a lot since then. I'm just back in town now looking for Kon Li Lu. Like you are, I would presume."

"You presume a lot," I told him.

"That's my job," he answered. "And, since the local badges were waiting for you to show up a few days back, I figure like them that you must be on the same trail the rest of us are." Raising a hand to keep me from making any denials, he said,

"Please, don't waste your breath. Let me just throw out my side of things and then you can do whatever you want." Reaching to the bar, he grabbed up his drink but didn't take another sip right away, telling me instead,

"I've got my contacts in the local station houses. As you might expect, they've been keeping track of those 'undesirables' entering the Colony. I knew the ever-determined Captain Lin was going to bust your hump the other night when you arrived. I knew you were a regular at the Five Great Grains in the old days, and I knew that if you had any brains at all you would first off, give the police the usual deuce to get bored and then second, you would probably start your search here. So, I came over early today to see how long it would take you to catch up to me."

Stretching his shoulder muscles a little beneath the light fabric of his jacket, he said, "As it was, you almost beat me." Finally taking another sip from his drink, the C.I.A. man leaned back against the bar, saying,

"So, now, why don't you tell the lovely owner here what you want, and then I'll make my pitch."

I looked over at Felecia. She looked back with a friendly but frozen expression that told me to do what I wanted. I ordered a chocolate coffee and then squared my own shoulders, turning back to Slaner, letting him know that any dealing I might do with Felecia would be between her and me. Then I leaned against the bar myself, waiting to hear what the C.I.A. had to say. It didn't keep me waiting.

"You don't trust me," he started. "Hey, old-timer, no skin off my teeth. I don't really care if you do or not. That's not what I need from you."

"Well," I said, not yet knowing how to read him, "that should make things easier."

"Yeah. Heck, since I can see you got a big day of being a tough guy all carved out for yourself, I'm going to do you a favor and keep things short and sweet."

"Well, that's damn nice of you."

"Kind of guy I am," said Slaner, his smile growing wider. "So listen, trailblazer. I figure you already suspect most of what I'm going to say, so let me do you a favor of verifying it. There's a lot of talent in town gunning for Lu. And some of it is merging up into some pretty odd teams—hard-core Commies sharing information with drug lords, the Germans working with the Israelis, you name it. I've noticed a pattern, though, that makes sense. Every time—it's some idealist working with some banker. I'm sure you can call the drill . . . you want his money, I want his body—let's work together. Now, I've got no friends because I want him to keep his body and his money and get both of them out of Hong Kong in one piece."

"That so?"

"Yes, my cynical friend, that's so. Your Uncle Sam is looking for Lu to throw his three billion at the Beijing regime and start it toppling. I'm sure you won't be surprised to find out three quarters of one of those billions came from the White House alone. There's only one viable Communist stronghold in the world anymore, and there isn't anyone outside of it that won't breathe easier once it's removed."

"So why all the interest in me?" I asked.

"Because I think we'd make one of those interesting teams. Like I said, I want him and his money safely together . . ."

"And what do I want?"

"You . . ." Slaner answered easily, his smile never breaking, "you want to get your hands on whoever deactivated your two friends back home. You do remember that little business of the winter wind coming through your living room wall, don't you?"

"Yeah," I told him, my lips tight, my voice bitter, "I remember."

"To me it says match made in heaven, Jack."

"News travels fast, huh?"

"It's a modern age, old-timer," he told me, downing the last of his drink. "Telephones, fax machines, satellite dishes . . . all that kind of stuff."

Putting his glass on the bar, the C.I.A. man reached inside his suit coat. Allowing his voice to trail off, he pulled out one of his business cards, one on which he had already written his current address along with three phone numbers. Handing it to me, he said,

"You can't stop progress, Jack. Anyway, the top number is my, shall we say, 'answering service.' The second is my car phone. The third is the local embassy—U.S., of course. If you finally decide you can trust me, or if anything else comes up where you feel like rekindling this conversation—then you just start punching the nearest touch pad. Any questions before I leave you to the lovely Ms. Morgan's gentle ministrations?"

"Yeah," I said. "Where does someone get a gun around here these days?"

"Why, Jack," answered Slaner, his smile cut with sharp edges. "Haven't you heard? Private ownership of a firearm is illegal in Hong Kong."

"Never hurts to ask," I told him.

"Some people it might," he said back. As Felecia approached with my coffee, Slaner put his hand to his forehead, throwing me a short salute as he said,

"But, be all that as it may, I'll be taking my leave of you now. The only thing I'll add is that your country wants Kon Li Lu out there fighting the good fight. And, I'd be willing to bet that ultimately that's what you want, too. If it is, and you need a friend . . . you do know where to find me."

And then, he disappeared out the door, waving good-bye to Felecia and shaking hands with Li as he did. Picking up the cup just set in front of me, I said,

"You're keeping new company these days."

"A girl's got to have someone to talk to," she answered as she sat down on the stool next to me. I was amazed to see how good she still looked. Although no one had ever been sure of her age, no one had ever doubted that Felecia Morgan was older than she looked. By that point she had to be well over fifty. But, despite what people may or may not have ever doubted, just looking at her she might as well have been my age. Her strawberry-blond hair still shone with the luster of a twenty-year-old. Her form had rounded out a bit since I'd last seen her, but her face and hands held no new wrinkles, her eyes and mouth no new lines. Curling her unlined mouth at me sarcastically, she said with innocence,

"After all, I know you'll find this hard to believe, but some people just waltz into your life and then back out again without so much as a 'fare thee well.' They'll disappear for ten years at a time—more some of them— and then, oh the gall of it—they'll show up again like nothing ever happened." She batted her still sturdy eyelashes at me coyly, finishing,

"Can you believe it?"

"Uuuuhhhh," I moaned, holding my chest melodramatically. "My blood flows as your wit cuts me to the quick. If you're that busted up about things I could just lie down on the floor and let you kick me."

"Don't go tempting me with holiday presents," she

answered. Her voice had an edge to it I couldn't quite make out. There had never been anything romantic between the two of us. She was twenty years my senior—minimum. The closest I ever came to being a member of the family had been bouncing Iris, her little nine-year-old, on my knee. But it was obvious that she was upset about something more than my disappearing out of her life, so I told her,

"Look, I know that you're mad about something and I hope I'm not making it worse by admitting that I don't know what it is. But all I can say is, Slaner was right. I *am* here looking for Kon Li Lu. He was also right about why I'm doing it. Two of my friends—one a really close one—they were burned up and turned into dog food the other night. I don't like losing friends, Fel. Don't tell me I've lost another."

Without turning to look at me, Felecia braided her fingers, saying, "You don't change much, do you, Jack?"

"No," I told her softly. "I guess not." My voice grew sad and faraway. I'd told myself before I came in that I wouldn't indulge in any maudlin scenes, knowing full well when I'd said it that it was a lie. Heading into my second indulgence of the morning, I sipped my cup of chocolate brew, one of the Five Great Grains' specialties, and then said,

"I didn't just come here to see what you knew about Lu, though. I could have just sent my partner in with cash in hand if that was all I wanted." Trying to get a smile into my voice—into hers as well, I said,

"I did want to see you, you know. You, and Li Tsim, and little Iris. Do you really think I could make my way back to Hong Kong and not pass through the doors of the Five Great Grains? Home of the best poker games in town—the best dim sum, the best floor shows . . ." Catching the faintest crack in her armor, I tried my trump card, hoping for the pot.

"Did you think I wouldn't come home?"

"Ohhhh," she answered in a whisper, her mouth moving closer to an actual smile. "And you think this is home, do you?"

"Yeah, as much of one as I've ever had. Better than most of them."

"You take a lot on faith, Jack."

"Oh, yeah?" I answered, trying to sound hurt. "Then tell me there isn't still a steel box in your desk with a .45 and a bottle of Gilbey's. Tell me you still don't hang my stocking on the bar every Christmas. Tell me there isn't an upside-down cup on the table on my birthday."

"Okay, okay," she answered, her hand slipping onto my wrist. "You win, you big jerk. We all still love you. Does that make you happy?"

"Yeah," I told her, breaking into my own lopsided half smile, surprised at how much memory our conversation was stirring up. "Yeah, it does." Putting every ounce of strength I had to keeping the waterworks from rolling again, feeling like an idiot for having lost it when I first came in, I put my other hand over hers, telling her,

"Fel, I've had a pretty rotten life since I left here. You know I had to get out. A soldier goes where he's sent, and since the government didn't want me dead . . . I guess they sent me back to the States. I couldn't keep it together, though. Things, I don't know, they just seemed to go from bad to worse. I tried, Fel. I really did, but somehow I just seemed to keep screwing things up as I went along."

"Kept telling the truth," she asked. "Didn't you?"

I pursed my lips, embarrassed by the memory. She'd always told me my inability to tell a decent lie would dog me. She'd been right. Li Tsim piped in,

"Me know it. Me say this guy never know to shut up—never know when to leave big dogs alone. Bet tong still mad like hell you and other U.S. boys burn fields. You never going to be good Chinese until learn tell good lie."

And then, just as I was beginning to think I was getting through to Felecia, she asked me,

"Have you, Jack? Have you learned how to lie, yet? Have you figured out yet how much pain comes from not being able to keep the truth behind your teeth?"

"No, not really, Fel," I told her. "I've seen too much go wrong in this world because of lies. There's been one at the root of every rotten thing I've ever dug up. No—I'm still not very good with them."

Her face softened as she looked at me, her eyes shifting to the focus I remembered. I'd always felt safe in the Five Great Grains—no matter how much trouble I was in or what I was running from—it had always seemed like home to me. Felecia had intervened with the HK police for me, gotten various embassy's staffers drunk for me, hidden me after the Suiciders and I had burned Tai Sing's poppies. Suddenly, seeing her face the way it was at that moment, I felt safe again, safer than I had in a long, long time. Disengaging her hand from mine, she said,

"Okay, Mr. Jack pain-in-the-ass Hagee—I'm feeling sorry enough for you to let you walk all over me again. You stay here and teach Li Tsim some more bad habits and I'll see what I might have on Kon Li Lu in the back." Turning to my old poker pal, she ordered,

"Go on. Set the bastard up. And see if you can keep him out of trouble."

Li Tsim got out a bottle of my favorite cognac to sweeten my chocolate coffee, pouring himself a tall one over ice. We sat at the bar for a long time without saying anything, just sitting and drinking with each other, staring into each other's faces, looking at the mileage. I thought about what had happened to me since the last time I'd seen him, filling my eyes with it, giving him the whole show. Try as I might, however, I could hardly find a decent moment to flash him.

Everything seemed to come attached with pain—the people I had killed, seen killed, or found myself unable to prevent from being killed—the broken men and ruined women and desperate children caught in between the thousand and one monsters all around us trying to swallow them up. I searched for golden moments but could only remember the hell of the cities I'd traveled through, one after another, each of them with their own finishing moment that had driven me from them.

I saw again that line of black men, tall and hungry, desperate and confused—wondering why their ultimatums were no longer being listened to—waiting for something to snap so they could charge the woeful line of police I was a part of. I remembered snapping my baton and crushing skulls while I watched ten of my fellow officers go down around me. I felt fights and relived their pain, saw friends die once more . . . remembered the beating to death of men carried out by my own hands and remembered those who had tried to beat me to death.

Li Tsim put up his palm to me, saying,

"You no have real good time since you leave Hong Kong."

"No," I admitted. "Not really."

"Then drink. Talk about time before leave. Forget the bad days. No sense to think of bad time. Only ruin tomorrow when no can let go yesterday."

I gave him a sour look, kidding him for his dime-store Confucius imitation. It got us talking, though, and remembering more than just the darkness. I was glad for that. It didn't feel bad to sit back and have a drink with an old friend and think back to a time when things didn't seem nearly so bad . . . when death was still a game that you believed could be won. We talked of picnics on the beach, betting days at the Jockey Club, trips to Macau to its gold and marble gambling dens. He told me how his birds had been doing. I told him about Balto. We talked for so long, I didn't actually notice the length of time we spent tied up together until the front door opened again.

While I watched, a fabulous brunette walked in, one who caught my eye and stopped my heart in the same moment. She paused to check herself in the large mirror by the front door, backlighting herself for us. I assumed she was one of Fel's new singers or dancers. She was young, but old enough—tall and long-legged and shaped like every woman they use to sell the best merchandise with. Her hair was dark and straight, hanging down about five inches below her strong but curved shoulders. It shone like fine leather in the light of the alcove, an alluring beacon that would attract any man.

All the rest of her inventory—her dress, heels, sunglasses, makeup, jewelry . . . all of it—everything fit together easily, marking her as a piece of merchandise I was sure had started more than one fight. Oh, yeah, I thought, way more than one. I was just about to make a comment to Li Tsim when she took her sunglasses off, and stopped me in my tracks again. Her eyes were a remarkable green, one I'd seen somewhere a long time ago—I couldn't place it exactly, but they made my heart break with memories of sweetness and love and feeling just, for lack of a better word, swell.

They were intelligent eyes, keen and sharp, and well made up. She was one of the most desirable women I'd ever seen in my life. No, I hadn't forgotten about Sally, nor did I plan on trying to—even for only a little while—just so I could make a fool out of myself with one of the Five Great Grains' show girls. But, I had to admit, that if we hadn't seen each other again before I'd left the States, I would have.

Then, suddenly she turned and noticed me at the bar. She looked me up and down the way any man would want her to, but for a reason I never expected. And then, as her face broke into a smile, she hurried over toward Li Tsim and me as fast as a grown woman can without dashing. She looked happier to see us than I could think she had any reason to be . . . until, that was, she threw her arms around me and shouted,

"Uncle Jack . . . oh, Uncle Jack. Mom knew you'd be back. She always told me you'd come back."

Patting her on the back, the way I did when my arms used to go a lot further around her, I said,

"Iris . . . eh, you got bigger."

CHAPTER 19

TO SAY I was stunned would have been putting it mildly. I was burning inside, wondering if my cheeks were giving me away, feeling like the worst kind of fool. On the one hand, part of my brain was telling me that there was no logical reason for me to feel embarrassed. After all, it reminded me, I hadn't seen Iris in over thirteen years. She had changed a lot since she was nine. A whole lot. And, it leered to me, it wasn't like we were really related or anything.

But, as much as some parts of me wished that information made some kind of difference, I had to disappoint it by saying it didn't. The woman I was hugging and who was hugging me back just wasn't a part of that game—not by a long shot. I might have started things out by giving her the hairy eyeball, but that was my mistake. This was a girl I used to tuck in and read fairy stories to—that had fallen asleep in my lap during the Chinese New Years' fireworks. I might as well have fantasies about waiting for Elba to grow up so I could go after her, too.

I felt stupid and mean, despite the fact that I really hadn't done anything wrong. I also knew that to admit to not recognizing her, to let her know I'd been thinking of the woman I'd seen as just another two-dimensional bit of cheap bang would be no compliment. In the split second I had, the back of my brain reminded me that although I might not know how to lie very well, there was nothing that said I had to open my big mouth and spill all the beans.

Trying to cover for my all too human nature, I pushed her back a few inches, far enough away so I could get a good look at her—far enough back so she could look into my eyes and see down past all the surface stuff to the truth of how glad I actually was to see her. Smiling across the two feet separating us, I did my best flying squirrel imitation, saying,

"Look, Bullwinkle, a message in a bottle." Without missing a beat, she came back at me in her deepest Moosylvanian accent, asking,

"Fan mail from some flounder?"

"No," I answered. "This is what I really call a message." Not wanting to let go of the gag or the memory, she kept on going.

"Hey, Rocky," she came back, her accent holding. "Watch me pull a rabbit out of my hat."

"Again?" I whined. "But that trick never works."

"This time for sure. Nuthin' up my sleeve," she answered, twisting her arm in the air with a flourish as if to prove her claim. Then, she shouted, "Presto!" following it with a growl, my cue to ask,

"Wrong hat?"

"I take a seven and a half."

And then we both laughed, ignoring Li Tsim's Chinese curses about stupid American cartoons. Looking at her with a more adult eye then, I said,

"Well, getting a good look at you, something tells me you don't spend much of your time watching cartoons today."

"No," came Felecia's voice from behind us. "It only took me thirteen years, but I have managed to eradicate most of the bad habits you left behind in this child."

"Mama," answered Iris, a laughing pout in her voice I recognized instantly. "How can you say that?"

"You're right, darling. Now that I think of it, I haven't gotten rid of very many of them at all."

Irish put her hands on her hips—partly to smooth her dress, partly to raise her shoulders at her mother—for the reason all women do it. She stared at Fel with a look that would have sent any man searching for an excuse to explain whatever he had done wrong, but which only made the owner of the Five Great Grains roll her eyes.

In a way I felt privy to one of the secrets of the ages at

that moment—suddenly I was the discoverer of the source of the lethal stares beautiful women give men—they simply learn to do it battling their mothers. Hiding behind my cup of cognac, all traces of chocolate or coffee long gone, I stared at the ceiling while Fel reminded her daughter of how long it had been since such looks had had any effect on her. Iris admitted it had been a long time. Then, the devil in her eyes, she said,

"It's also been a long time since I've had the chance to go walking in Kowloon Park with my favorite uncle." As she stared at me expectantly, I reacted like any man caught off guard by a beautiful woman—clumsily. Trying to set down my cup while taking a last drink from it at the same time, I managed to slosh some of its contents on the bar while spitting a few drops at the same time. The ladies both laughed—Iris softly behind her hand, Felecia, open-mouthed, slapping her chest. Once the laughter had passed, however, the youngster of the pair asked,

"Are we going?"

"What do you think, ma'am?" I said to Fel, joking as I did so, but asking her approval all the same. "Would it be proper for me to escort the young lady amongst the orchid trees and the casuarina?"

Fel looked at me with a mother's eyes for just a second, nature forcing her to examine the man she was going to entrust her baby to. I wondered how many times she had done it in the past—even when she'd been a tyke? I didn't blame her. She was a mother in a cruel and nasty world. If I'd been Iris's father, I wasn't sure I'd have trusted her with me. Having a higher opinion of my trustworthiness, however, Felecia gave us her blessing, telling me that she would go over the Kon Li Lu situation with me whenever we returned. I told her that I was more interested in tracking down a weapons shipment that had been hijacked from the Philippines that had been traced to the Colony. She said she'd look into both and see what she could find.

Then, before I could answer, Iris wrapped her arm around me, moving me toward the door. In less than five minutes we were back across Nathan Road, through the maze garden and headed for what appeared to still be Iris's favorite spot in the park—Bird Lake. We walked along the pathway bordering its northern shore, watching the hundreds of ducks and kingfishers and all manner of seabirds that skim its waters every day looking for fish and insects. We talked about the surroundings, how things hadn't changed. Finally we got on to how we had.

"You get hit a lot since I saw you last, Uncle Jack?"

"Oh, a bit. Why? Does it show?"

"A little. I don't remember you with so many scars." She put her hand to my face, one perfect nail tracing the cut over my left eye. It held the curve of that one long enough to remind me of the assassin who had broken my head open that time, then skipped across to follow the shallower cut that disappeared into my hair on the right side of my forehead—a much older injury.

"Those are new—I mean as far as you could know. I got both of those in the States. Well, the first one in the States, the second one I got here . . . but that was, oh, sort of close to the time I left . . ."

"You're still handsome enough," she said, smiling, starting us walking again—saving me from explaining how I'd gotten myself disassembled. "But you know that, I would imagine."

"Oh yeah." I chuckled. "I tell myself how good-looking I am every day when I see myself in the mirror."

"Don't tease me," she said back, defending me to myself. "You'd better be good-looking. I had a terrible crush on you, you know. And I don't just fall for anybody."

"You were nine," I reminded her. "And nine-year-olds do fall for anybody."

"Not like I fell for you," she said. "I cried a long time when you didn't come back again. I didn't have my first date until I was nineteen."

"You're kidding?" I said in surprise. "I would've thought the guys would be beating down the doors to get to you."

"They were," she said softly. "But I didn't care. I was waiting for you to come back to me."

Wondering if I was being told something that, no matter

how flattering it was, I certainly didn't want to hear, I steeled myself and then asked,

"Oh, Iris, can I assume this has all passed now?"

She stopped walking, leaning on the rail next to the lake. Her face turned out to look over the water, she asked,

"Why?"

I took a long breath before I tried to answer. Going with my long suit, I tried the truth first.

"Well, knowing women as well as I do, if you were expecting me to sweep you off your feet, you wouldn't be telling me about the crush stuff now—you'd be flirting instead. I figure you're just punishing me with guilt like your mom did before you came in to take over the second shift."

"And why wouldn't I be interested in you now?" she asked, her voice not giving me any clues as to why she was asking.

"My guess would be because now you're in your twenties and you're beautiful enough to have your pick of any man you meet." Her head turned just slightly toward me, letting me know I was on the right track. Pretending not to notice, I continued.

"And I figure your mom's taught you how to take care of yourself, and I can see in your eyes that you're intelligent enough to know what you're doing. Maybe I'm selling myself short, but I can't imagine you'd have much use for a beat-up old man like me. Not as anything except your favorite uncle, anyway."

"And that's all you see in me, your little niece?"

"All right," I said, knowing where we were headed. "If you're just fishing for compliments, then I'll admit that, until I heard your voice, I thought you were one of your mom's show girls. I was scoping you out like I would any other knockout babe, and I felt pretty stupid once I realized who you were."

"Did you?" she asked, turning toward me, staring into my eyes. "Do you really think I'm beautiful?"

"Sweetheart," I told her honestly, "I think you're one of the most beautiful women I've ever seen in my life. If I

didn't love you as much as I do, I could forget about being
a gentleman real easy. But, I mean, come on, you have to
know that you're a knockout. There must be guys barking
like dogs outside your window every night."

"Oh, I know. But they're just boys. It took Mom a long
time to finally get me to sing on stage. I've seen the way
men look at the singers. It didn't have a lot of appeal. People
have always told me I'm . . . that I'm good-looking and
all, but I guess, I just wanted to hear it from you."

Somehow knowing inside that we had crossed over into
safe territory, I asked her,

"Don't you have a boyfriend to tell you these things? I
mean, there must be some guy you trust enough to believe
when he whispers in your ear about what looking at you
does to him."

"There's one boy I see, but he's . . . I don't
know . . . he's always got other things on his mind."

"Does he love you?" I asked, wondering what any guy
could have on his mind except Iris if he was in her presence.
She nodded shyly, the way I figure a girl would if she were
having this conversation with her father. I asked the next
obvious question, and she admitted even more shyly that she
loved him, too.

"Well, then," I told her, "what's the problem? You've got
some nice guy you love who loves you back and who, I
guess, loves you for more than just your great legs. These
are all good things, right?"

"Yes, you're right, I suppose," she said, sounding terribly
British. "I guess I'm just being foolish. I just so want you to
like him, approve of him, I mean."

"Well, does your mom?"

"She likes him."

"Well, then—what's to worry?" Picking up a flat pebble
near the railing, I threw it at an angle, satisfied to get a triple
skim out of it. "You get him down to the Grains and I'll give
him the once-over and that'll be that."

Iris smiled at me for an instant, a dazzling look that would
bend any man I'd ever known to her will. But then, she went
suddenly serious, asking,

"You're in town because of Kon Li Lu?"

"Wow. Abrupt channel switch. Ah, yeah," I admitted. "I am. Why do you ask?"

"Do you think he stole the money?"

I looked at Iris with my head at a tilt, surprised that she would be interested in such things. Then, after stopping for a second to think, I realized I didn't actually have an answer for her question.

"To tell you the truth, sweetheart," I admitted, "I'm here because of Lu, but I'm not really looking for him." When she stared at me, waiting for more of an answer, I told her the whole story as briefly as possible. I told her about Sally, and my stupid reasons for taking the C.C.B.A.'s assignment, and then about what happened in my apartment. I left out Fisher and Rice, just telling her that,

"I have to admit that what I want to know is who killed Carmine and Francis. That's really the only reason why I'm looking for Lu."

"But what do you think about him? I mean, it is one of the biggest topics of discussion here. I know you want to find the people responsible for your friends' deaths, but you must have formulated some opinion about Lu . . . haven't you?"

It was certainly a reasonable assumption. As we began walking back toward the park's Nathan Road exit, I told her,

"Well, I have to admit that even with everything I've heard and read about the guy so far, I think he'd have to be okay. Now, God knows I've been wrong about people in my time before. Let's see what your mom and I can dig up on him." Iris went the tiniest bit stiff at my last sentence. Wondering if I'd hit some kind of nerve, I asked her,

"Are you nervous about your mom looking into things? Have I made a bad assumption here? Has she kept up her contacts over the years or am I getting her into something . . ."

She cut me off sharply, saying,

"No, no. Mom still serves all the top people. I've just been worried about this Lu situation. Every night—every single night there are people in the club, sometimes as many as a dozen, all whispering to each other, to Mama, to the bartenders and waiters, all looking for Kon Li Lu and his three billion dollars."

As we started to cross Nathan, I asked,

"What do you think? Do you think he took the money or that someone got to him or . . . or what?"

"I think he's the bravest man in the whole world," she told me. She said it with such conviction that I felt more like a father than ever, as if my little girl had suddenly come home to tell me about the man who was going to take her away from me. More convinced than ever that being a parent must be sheer hell, I listened quietly as she told me,

"I saw him at one of his early rallies, when he first came to Hong Kong to raise money. He's so young, Uncle Jack, so young to be so determined, to be so strong. I think he really does want to save China. I know he does."

"Well," I told her as we passed back into the cool darkness of the Five Great Grains, "your vote sure means a lot to me. If you trust him, that counts in my book."

I meant it, too. Sure, when she saw him she'd just been a girl of maybe twenty, twenty-one. A charismatic speaker can make a chump out of the best of us. But, I had to start building my opinion of the guy somewhere. If she liked what she saw back then, it gave me something to go on.

As we came back into the club, however, four men—three Orientals, one Caucasian—stood up from their tables, abandoning their drinks to move in on us from the shadows. I tried to put myself between them and Iris, but they came from all four corners. One of them put up his hand, however, announcing,

"We have no interest in the girl, Mr. Jack Hagee. We would like it most well if she would step away from you."

"Uncle Jack . . . ?" she asked, but I put my hand around her arm and pushed her toward the largest opening through the quartet, one they made even larger to let her pass through. Felecia came into view from around t   bar, the look on her face showing she was as confused as I was. She called for Li Tsim, but the leader of the four said,

"No need for shouting, Mrs. Morgan. We have what we came for. We shall be going now."

"We shall, shall we?" I asked.

"Yes," the leader said to me, the four of them coming in close. "You have been most foolish to return to Hong Kong, Mr. Jack Hagee. Now you must keep a long overdue appointment. Our employer is most anxious to meet you. He has been waiting for this day for some many years."

Fel asked me what she should do, but I told her that I'd have to handle this one on my own. Li Tsim came into the front area, ready to charge the quartet with nothing more than his mop, but I waved him back. The other early morning customers had already been given enough of a show. Dealing badly with the four men there in the club, even if I did manage to escape them somehow, would only bring reprisals against me or Fel or Iris or all of us together and I couldn't allow that.

I was the one who had set fire to Tai Sing's poppy fields. I'd always known that sooner or later I'd meet him. That moment seemed to be the time.

CHAPTER 20

THE DRIVE WAS a lot shorter than I'd anticipated. My first time in a Rolls Royce, I thought, and I only get to go two miles. I was surprised to find that Tai Sing would locate any of his Tiger's Breath Triad's operations anywhere near downtown Kowloon, but maybe it was just that kind of maneuvering that had kept him in operation for so many decades. Of course, I reminded myself, the file Rice had given me on him had implied that Sing had been carving out a very comfortable niche for himself on the respectability shelf.

As his men pulled into an underground garage off Moody Road, I found myself hoping that perhaps Sing had grown a little softer over the years. After all, I told myself, I hadn't been kept from seeing where I was being taken. Then I remembered that that wouldn't matter if no one expected me to be leaving.

As the driver pulled into what looked to be the Rolls' regular spot, my mind ran over exactly what was going to happen next. I had been kidnapped in broad daylight by men working for a drug warlord whose operation I'd once cost a number of millions. Now, on the one hand, I knew that a couple of million was chicken feed for a man like Sing. On the other, however, I knew that the action alone was an affront—a slap in the face. He had to have looked at it that way back then . . . the operation had been designed to embarrass him to the point where the smaller dogs in the business might be emboldened to make a stab at overthrowing him.

It hadn't worked that way, though. Enraged at the U.S. for

trying to depose him by remote control, he struck out at the only realistic targets he had—his competitors. Ruthlessly and efficiently, he had them slaughtered one after another until he had doubled his size and power. He would probably have never done such a thing, either, if not goaded into it by the clever bureaucrats back home. Foreign policy, I thought. Thanks a lot, assholes.

The two who had watched me in the backseat were both shorter than me, but cold and efficient as well. They moved a man in between them fairly well, not making any really stupid moves. As we all got out of the car, my new quartet of pals began herding me through the garage when a voice rang out from above us, calling a name I hadn't heard in a long time.

"Burger."

I looked up as slowly as I could. So far I hadn't reacted badly to my little band of captors. No sudden moves, no eye contact battles I didn't win—all my gestures had been open but neutral, neither threatening nor cooperative. The name had almost gotten me, though. It had been my old code name back when I was with the Suiciders. I had little doubt what I was being told by its use now.

I stared upward as calmly as I could, taking in the figure on the catwalk. After I was sure who it was above me, I lowered my eyes again, keeping my mouth in a straight line the whole time. He called out again in a happy tone,

"Hey, Burger . . . aren't you glad to see me?" Looking over at the thug to my immediate left, I asked,

"Is it all right if I respond?" He gave me a shrug that told me it was my life. Taking that as a yes, I lifted my head again slowly, shouting,

"Oh, yeah—I'm thrilled. Can't you tell?"

"You know who I am," he told me, calling back in a still jovial voice. Heading toward the end of the catwalk, he started down a spiral staircase, announcing,

"I had your rooms searched earlier. My people not find anything—nice work—playing things cagey, eh? No matter. So, tell me. You do know who I am . . . right, Burger?"

"Oh, yeah," I admitted. I knew the face staring at me. I remembered it from the picture in Rice's files. And, even if I didn't . . . he was right again. A guy in my position at that moment would have had to be a fool not to know who it was that was walking across the garage toward me. Another thug met him halfway, waiting there to hand him the leash to a ferocious-looking boxer. I was surprised to see how short Sing was—no more than five feet tall. He was lean and well-manicured, though, without any fat or jewelry to slow him down. I made a short bow, saying,

"There aren't many players in this area who don't know the name of Tai Sing."

"And," he answered, walking toward me, the dog straining to get closer and take my scent. "What do you think that name means, Burger?"

"Well, in all honesty I'd have to say that it means many things throughout the Orient—and far beyond. It tells the tale of a man who came from nothing to become one of the most feared warlords in history. Many have tried to break that name, to throw it in the dirt. Some small and weak, some more powerful than any could imagine. But that name has never been diminished. Every time it has been challenged, it has prevailed. Every time it has been attacked, it has conquered. It means invincibility. It means power."

I watched Sing expand as his men listened to me talk. I spoke slowly, giving myself time to choose every word carefully. I had to be able to believe what I was saying because I knew Sing didn't get to the position he was in by falling for flattery. Whatever he planned to do to me, I didn't see any reason to make it easy on him or hard on me. Besides, he'd earned my little speech. America had used Tai Sing like it has a lot of petty, backwater thugs in its time, then tried to dismiss him when he became too big. But it didn't work and he'd slapped America's face when it didn't and made himself a king in the bargain. Now I had to wonder how much of my hide was going to have to make up for that.

"Very good answer," he told me. Looking me straight in

the eye, daring me to blink, or worse, look away, he continued, saying,

"Very good, indeed. I can feel your passion in your voice. Strong, honest. I am sure you left out few things. Probably you are not big fan of my merchandise—probably think Tai Sing is small of soul for dealing in drugs and women—in arms and assassination. But that's okay. It was good speech. Well thought out for 'off cuff,' as Americans say. But, anyway, I would like you to do favor for me."

So far we hadn't broken eye contact—his digging into mine, watching for any change in reaction to each word he said. I allowed him one when he said he wanted a favor, though. In truth, I'd have had trouble stopping it. My eyes narrowed then, cutting us off from each other. He jerked back then, having to hold his dog in place. Even the mutt had caught my reaction. Chastising the boxer in Chinese too fast for me to follow, he relaxed as the dog sat down at his feet. Then, returning his attention to me, he said,

"So, you are suspicious of granting the disreputable bandit favor, eh? That is oh kay. I am Tai Sing. I understand. Perhaps I should first explain favor. Would that be good?"

"It couldn't hurt," I admitted.

"I would like you to demonstrate to my men that they are too lax in their duties. Show them what you would have done to escape them—what you could do now, even—if you so desired."

I looked at Sing a bit confused. When I asked if he wanted me to explain how I might have gotten away from them, he told me that no, he wanted me to show them— physically. Not at all sure what he was up to, but knowing I had no choice other than to play along, I said,

"You will hold onto the dog, won't you?"

"You are afraid of my Gigi?"

"No," I told him. "I just hate to hurt animals."

With a large smile, the mightiest drug lord in all the Far East told me,

"Do not worry. She will remain here with me."

"Well, then," I said, turning slowly, a set of stumbling hesitations built into the action. Giving his men a look designed to be as disarming and confused as possible, I answered, "Gee, I don't know. First . . . I guess, I would probably have—"

And then I struck. Throwing my upper torso down and to the side, I brought my leg up, kicking the man to my left away and into the Rolls. With the only obviously armed man down, before coming back up I stretched my fingers as far to the right as I could, just managing to catch the pant leg of the first guy's opposite number. Jerking hard, I pulled his feet out from under him, dropping him on his back and skull.

I tried to get myself out of the way of the guy in front of me, but I just didn't have the time. Knowing I would have to take his first blow I tried to compensate by throwing myself back and away from him, risking taking another hit from the man behind me as well. The thug in front of me went for a body kick, managing to connect at at least half power. The impact added to my backward speed, propelling me into the man behind me. I threw my arms behind me as I hit, grabbing for any hold I could get on my unseen playmate.

Managing to get my hands around his left arm, I pulled as hard as I could, jerking him sideways—keeping him off balance and myself from falling. Then, almost climbing up his body, I slammed my fists mallet-style against his chest to get myself upright and send him crashing. The one that had given me the chest kick had pulled a wickedly long butterfly knife, one he had already flicked open and locked in place. Not bothering to think about what he might be able to do with it, I turned my back on him and leapt for my first target, who had just picked himself off the Rolls and gone for his gun.

He should have gone on the defensive, but like most gunmen, his only thought was to get to his weapon. He didn't have the time, however, and I caught him with his hand still trying to pull it free. I hit him a meat-solid, open-palmed blow to the throat with one hand while I tore his jacket open with the other, pulling his gun hand into the open. The tussle pulled us down to our knees, threatening to

give those behind me enough time to get to us. Then, getting
my fingers around the 10 mm he'd been going for, I
managed to get it out of his hand and into mine, aiming it for
the knife-wielder's midsection just a fraction of an inch
before he could close with me.

Breathing just a little bit hard, I managed to calm my
voice enough to say clearly,

"Have to, have to, ah . . . do something like this." I
stood up from my crouching position, flipping the gun in the
air so that I caught it by its barrel. Handing the gun back to
the thug I'd taken it away from, I steeled myself for
whatever was coming, saying,

"Was that what you had in mind?"

I stepped away from Sing's men toward the approaching
drug lord, awaiting him, his dog, and his pleasure. I knew
I'd had no chance to shoot my way out of the place. I'd seen
men with machine pistols on both ends of the catwalk
watching me. I also knew that even if I did escape I'd be
leaving Fel and Iris to whatever revenge Sing wanted. My
only hope was that whatever he wanted out of my little
show he'd gotten it and that he'd now focus his attention on
me and me alone.

Maybe he's mellowed, I thought. Yeah, maybe.

Whatever the case, I was sure to know in a moment.
Closing the gap between us, the drug lord came as close as
he could without allowing his dog a closing distance and
then he made a full bow in my direction. Knowing I had
nothing to lose, I followed suit, hoping for the best. After
that, much to my surprise, Tai Sing broke into a big smile
and began clapping his hands furiously. This action started
the boxer jumping and barking—not toward me, just
toward the garage in general. The drug lord calmed his pet,
then said,

"Wonderful. Wonderful to watch. You haven't been M.I.
for some time now, have you?"

"A lot of years, to tell the truth."

"And still, so quick, so smooth. Not just fighter, not just
soldier—warrior. Rice—he make good warriors. What I
would not give to have had ten such as you in old days."

Sing's eyes took on a faraway look. As I watched, my four pals picked themselves up and headed away from us, walking toward an exit. I could tell from the looks they gave me that nothing we had done had been staged for my benefit. They had been as surprised as I had at their boss's request—even more surprised at the results. Suddenly, however, the drug lord snapped back to the present, saying,

"So, shall we go get something to eat?"

"Eat?" I asked with surprise, having been expecting many different possibilities but not that one.

"Eat—yes," he answered slyly, enjoying throwing me off balance once again. "What did you think?"

"Considering the circumstances, I didn't know what to think," I answered honestly, desperate to figure out what the game was. Wondering if the direct approach might work as well as always, I asked,

"No offense, but why exactly would you want to eat with me?"

"Because," he answered, looking me in the eye again, clearly amused, "no man would come to Hong Kong to thwart Tai Sing twice. Therefore, I know we are to be partners. And partners were meant to share all things. Yes?"

"Well," I admitted, liking anything better than just being shot and dumped in the Tolo Channel, "it *sounds* pretty good to me."

"Then," answered Sing, his boxer leading the way, "let us eat."

CHAPTER 21

THE CART GIRL had just left an order of still sizzling, fried stuffed taro horn on our table. Tai Sing had had me brought to a restaurant—more specifically, his restaurant. He alluded to owning several others throughout the Colony, but it was clear that Green Leaves By the Door was his personal favorite. It was also clear the place was indeed a headquarters for him. Obvious sentries had met us at a half-dozen points as we'd moved from the basement garage up through to the restaurant proper. At every turn, in every hall, no one who saw Sing did not greet him with a warm smile or some other, pleasing, deferential gesture. People are right—it *is* good to be the king.

Sing had stopped a dozen times in the kitchen, busying himself with looking over the cook's shoulders as we walked in between the massive, Chinese-style stoves with their extra-high, extra-hot burners. To some he gave instructions, to others warm compliments and friendly pats on the back. Everyone made time for the boss. I was impressed by his dog. On television, every dog you see will give up his job instantly for any hunk of meat the hero feels like throwing to it. Obviously the people in Hollywood don't know much about real dogs. Gigi sat at her master's side wherever he stopped, not interested in the least by the bowls of pork, hanging ducks, sides of ribs, or any of the other treats available. No one tried to curry favor by slipping her any scraps, either. I'd have been more impressed if I hadn't still been wondering when Sing might tell her to use my ankle for dinner.

Once we left the kitchen area, the first waiter to see us

moved to the drug king's side immediately. He took us to the best available table, snapping his fingers for a busboy as he moved. Chairs were pulled out for the two of us while the rest were removed at the same time. No crowding, freedom of movement, and nowhere for someone else to sit if they came up to the table. Tai Sing obviously knew how he liked things.

Gigi curled up on the floor under her master's chair while he got himself a cigarette. The drug lord offered me one, which I accepted. Wondering when the blindfold would follow, I told him,

"I'm impressed with your dog."

"Isn't she magnificent? Have you ever seen a better dog in your entire life?"

"Well, I've got one of my own that I think could hold his weight in a competition, but I wouldn't give him better than even money. She a good fighter?"

"What do you think?" he asked, honestly interested in my assessment. Telling him the truth, I said,

"She's got the weight to be a good scrapper. I like the way she holds her ground, and her tongue. She's got solid legs and a good chest and she's not stupid. I'd certainly want a club if I had to go up against her."

"Most kind words, but let us hope it does not come to that." Despite the constant mention of her, Gigi never moved from her spot. I was more impressed with each minute. Sensing that in the way any dog lover can read it in another, the drug lord told me,

"But, I will admit that your enthusiasm for Gigi's abilities is not unwarranted. She is a terror when confronted. My little sweetheart has killed four men for me since we came together. What more could a man ask, eh?"

I myself was wanting to ask just what was happening, but I knew better. Such was not the way to conduct business in the Orient. And I was quite sure that Tai Sing wasn't an idiot. There was no doubting that he had me in an uncomfortable situation. In the same place in America, though, I could ask what was going on and get down to business. To ask in Hong Kong, however, was to admit to fear and to curiosity and to thus give Sing the upper hand.

Everyone has heard of the concept of "Face," but few westerners seem to know how it actually works. Every facet of Oriental life has a thousand customs—minute bits of ritual that must be observed at all times. Even in the position of kidnapper and kidnapee, if Sing were to not offer to refill my teacup every time I drained it below the halfway mark, he would be mortified. Whatever he hoped to gain by his little game would be set back immeasurably simply because he would have failed to follow the rules of society.

Not that he could have possibly cared deep down what I thought about him, but if others were to find out, then word would spread. Soon everyone would know that Tai Sing was rude to his guests. And who would want to go to the table of a man who was rude to his guests? Who would want to deal with a man in a business manner when he couldn't even be counted on to keep his guest's cup filled?

Like anything in life, the whole thing is a lot more complicated than that, but the example gets the idea across. Having decided not to worry about it, however, I sat back and waited for the first of the dim sum carts to arrive. For those that have never had the chance to try it, I can only express my pity. If the meal I was sharing with Tai Sing was indeed meant to be my last, dim sum was the way to go.

The best way to describe dim sum is to call it China's answer to brunch. Restaurants begin serving it as early as nine in the morning. Some will keep it up as late as four, five in the afternoon. The major difference between dim sum and all other forms of restaurant dining, however, is in the choosing of one's meal. Rather than ordering from a menu and then waiting for your food, dim sum customers just sit and chat with each other while carts of food are wheeled in between the tables. Some carts carry desserts, some vegetables, some meats. Some come equipped with their own grills. Each usually has only one type of dish on it, never more than three.

One's time is spent at dim sum basically talking to friends and waiting for carts. It is a social experience more than a daily meal, with people moving from table to table, visiting with their neighbors, doing business, meeting with family. Everyone takes from any plate set in the center of the table, which explains why everything is served in one or two bite sizes.

As the meal goes on, whenever a customer sees something they like, they call the cart in question over to their table. The woman pushing the car will stop and give them as many orders of what she has as they want and then will add their purchase to a bill kept on their table. Up until a few years ago, the bill was tallied at the end of the meal from both the number of dishes on the table and their sizes. It has only been in recent years that too many people have taken advantage of the custom, hiding plates in their pockets or bags.

Unable to afford the loss not only in daily revenues but in dishes as well, sadly almost every dim sum house in the world has had to abandon the thousands of years old practice of trusting their customers—replacing it with the more practical one of treating them like the potential criminals too many of them are. Not worried about those things I couldn't change, I took one of the fried taros balls out of its paper cup and up off the serving dish with my chopsticks. Dipping it in the small bowl of black sauce provided by the cart girl, I took a big bite, savoring both the fine dusting of yam coating and the heavy taste of the taro inside.

As time went on and the carts continued to pass by, Sing and I both ordered different dishes, picking from each other's selections like brothers meeting for the holidays. I also found myself commending the drug lord on his kitchen's fare with each new choice. The pork dumplings were thick with the texture of meat, not jelly, like so many places in New York. The paper-wrapped chicken was so steaming hot and tender that I got two extra plates.

Between us we crammed down orders of stuffed crab claw, quail egg dumplings, water chestnut cakes, and green peppers stuffed with shrimp as if we hadn't eaten in days. Even considering that each dish taken only held six or seven bites of food—some only two or three—we were still both happily stuffed by that point.

Which, of course, to a good host like Sing, meant it was time to bring out the house specialties. The drug lord insisted I at least sample each of them. Following the form of a good guest, I smiled extravagantly, promising to try to fit in a bite of each. Shark fin dumplings came out then, followed by Peking-style spareribs, shredded chicken in vermicelli, and finally the sweetest, most perfectly spiced sata beef sticks I'd ever had. Not wanting to explode there in the dining room, I told Sing,

"No more. If this is an execution, I've got to admit that it's better than I deserve, but I just can't eat another bite." Drawing my hand across my forehead, I added,

"Really . . . I'm full up to here."

"It does my heart good to see a man eat. I mean really *eat*." He said the word with a joyous intensity, putting all the power he had into it. Sitting back in his chair, pushing his spine against its back, he said,

"So few people today understand how to enjoy themselves . . . how to make every experience a real one—a memory worth having. You are one of special few . . . Jack. May I permit myself the privilege of calling you by such?"

"It's your place," I told him. "You make the rules."

"You have such marvelous attitude, Jack—you understand so much of life. It makes everything so . . . uncomplicated. Most Americans, even Europeans, tend to—need to, even— try and bend every situation to their own advantage, as if looking at cards in one's hand from a different angle could change their value. You cut right to heart, you do the . . . proper . . . yes, that's the word I wanted . . . proper thing every time."

Pulling his cigarettes from his pocket, the mightiest drug lord in all the Far East shook two free from his pack—one for each of us. I lit his with my Zippo. Then, as I lit my own, he asked me,

"Tell me, Jack. Why did you burn my poppy fields?"

"Well," I said, slowly, giving myself two seconds to let

my brain search for the truth, "I could try to just say I did it because I had my orders, but you already know that much. So, I guess what you really want to know is why did I follow those orders?"

The light in Sing's eyes intensified. Underneath his chair, Gigi stirred uneasily, making small noises, showing that she sensed her master's sudden interest. Telling myself *here goes nothing*, I said aloud,

"You were the enemy. Our team was presented with what you did and what our country wanted you to stop doing. We were presented with a mission and told to get it done. Nothing in what they said presented me or anyone else with any challenges, so we did it."

"You did not remain with military intelligence much after that, did you?"

"No," I admitted. "Not really."

"Because they began to present you with challenges, yes?"

Biting my lip, remembering the last few months of my last hitch, I nodded my head, saying,

"Yes—you could say that."

Sing looked back again, looking pleased but thoughtful. Then, sitting forward again, his elbows on the table, he said,

"I do not fault you for the past. I certainly do not fault soldiers for action of generals. Do you know that men in your state department—ones who ordered that I be cut from influence loop—do you know what happened to them?" When I admitted that I didn't, Sing told me,

"They were killed. All of them. In most painful manners that could be arranged. And, now that you know this, I have most important question of all for you." I cocked my head to one side, ready for the worst. As I stared forward, unblinking, the drug lord asked me,

"What do you think of that?"

"Well," I said, stalling out my two seconds again, "if they were just murders committed because the American government was trying to clean up the trade coming in, I'd say you were a fucking lowlife. But that's not what it was. The government'd make deals with you and then tried to have their cake and eat it, too. I wouldn't be surprised if it hadn't even been a policy matter—just three smart guys pushing some political angle of their own. Now, don't get me wrong," I said, gesturing with my hands for emphasis.

"There are drugs I approve of and drugs I don't. Your kind—heroin, opium, cocaine, hash, crack, ice, all the stupefiers, the debilitators—they're ultimately killers. They're the kind I don't like. Somebody pays me to burn poppy fields—I don't have a whole lot of problems with that. But, someone gets me to do it just to further some rotten agenda of their own, I don't care much what happens to them, either." Sucking down a long drag of my cigarette, I let it out in a large cloud, then finished, saying,

"Does that answer your question?"

"Yes," said Sing, nodding his head, smiling. "Yes, completely."

"Then you mind answering one of mine?"

"I will not only answer it, I will tell it to you. You wish to know what is happening. Why you are here, what I want from you, what you receive for cooperating."

"Besides lunch," I added.

"Yes," he agreed, smiling even wider. "Besides lunch. First, what is happening? You are here to search for Kon Li Lu. Second—why are you here? We have been brought together because, between us, we have many contacts. Between us, we can find him. And when we do, we will have the answer to the riddle . . . what did he do with the money? Which brings us to the third point . . . what will you get out of it?"

Sing exhaled a great cloud of his own, then finished, saying,

"That, of course, will depend on how much money we find."

Looking Sing straight in the eye, wondering if there was any way to determine how much of what he was saying was straightforward and how much I should take with a dump truck full of salt, he surprised me by saying,

"Do not believe me simply because I have words to

speak. I do not mind you require some form of proof. I certainly would."

"Thank you for understanding that."

The drug lord made a pass in the air with his hand dismissing the thought that I might not trust him as nothing. Reaching into his pocket, he pulled out one of his business cards. Scribbling an address on the back, he said,

"This is the location of the Hong Kong Cultural Centre. It is here in Kowloon. Meet me there tonight with your partner." As my eyes went up at his mention of Peter, he waved his hand again, dismissing my thoughts, saying,

"Please, do not fill yourself with worries. If you do not come tonight, I will know you are not interested and will not bother you further. I hold you no grudges for the past. It is a forgotten time. In truth, if your government had not burned me out, I might have remained a minor player for all my days. Now . . . I am no such thing. Come tonight, Jack." As he stood to leave the table, I asked,

"Where would I meet you?"

"In the parking lot."

And then he walked away from me, Gigi quietly following his heels. I shouted out abruptly,

"But how would we find you?"

"If you want to," he said over his shoulder, paying me no more attention, "you will."

And then he was gone.

CHAPTER 22

I ALMOST JUMPED the first cab I saw back to the Five Great Grains, hoping to get there before things got out of hand. The little voice inside stayed my hand, however, suggesting I call instead. Following that advice, I got Felecia on the second ring. After she gave out with the name of the place and her best business "hello," I said,

"Pretend it's just a routine call—okay? And 'hello' yourself."

"Jack!" she answered in a startled whisper. "Where the hell are you? What happened to you? Are you still in one piece? Do you need help?"

"Whoa, whhhhhoooooa," I told her, hoping the tone in my voice might calm her down. "Take it easy—I'm fine . . . I'm fine. Absolutely. All right?"

"For the moment. Jack, what was all that? Those were Tiger's Breath Triad members—Tai Sing's men. I was afraid you were going to be feeding the fish in Junktown. How did you get away from them?"

"It's a long story. I didn't *get* away—let's just say for the moment that I was released on my own recognizance. First, tell me what's going on there."

"This place is a bloody wet rooster," answered Fel, her whisper growing even fainter. "First off, after they put the snatch on you—I rang Uncle Robert . . . and I'm sorry if you didn't want the police involved, but I didn't know what else to do." I smiled at her name for the police, sort of a Hong Kong "John Q. Law" . . . the kind of term even the most civil Americans wouldn't use for the cops anymore. Trying to keep her at ease, I said,

"That's all right. What happened?"

"They must have transferred your name over to Lin's department. He and a boatful of his people were here in no time. We gave them all the facts, everything that happened. But they didn't go away."

"Did Peter show up?" I asked, hoping against hope.

"Yes, Jack. A second carful of Lin's people arrived with him after. He's not quite in chains, but it seems as if they'd like to have him fitted for some."

"Hey," I cut her off, not needing her any more upset. "It's fine. There's nothing you could have done. Just tell me . . . is Lin still there?"

"Yes, all of them."

"Then Peter is still there, too?" When she gave me an affirmative, I said, "Good. All right. You just pretend you haven't heard from me. I'm going to get a cab. I'll be there as fast as traffic lets me—a few minutes—I'm not that far. Don't say anything unless they make to leave. Tell them whatever you have to to keep them there—just don't let them leave."

"Even the truth?" she asked.

"The truth is fine," I told her. "I'd use it as a last resort if I were you, just to keep yourself uninvolved. I'll get there as soon as I can, though, to try and keep you from having to make any major decisions over a new career in police snitching." Before I could break off, however, Fel hissed at me to wait, saying,

"There's more."

"Well, go for it," I told her, wondering what else could have happened besides Lin getting something on us as well as getting his hands on Peter. Still whispering, Felecia gave me the rest.

"Slaner certainly must have those contacts he says he has. He was back in here twenty minutes after I called Lin. He hasn't left, either. And, there are some other types greasing up the place you might want to know about."

"Such as . . . ?"

"There is a Mossad agent here—Saul Cronberg. He came in after Slaner. Same as another . . . I don't recall his name, but he's a 'known' from the old days—used to work for the Frog Kingdom . . . no one's certain if he still does or not. Soft body, greasy hair—heavy, very un-French glasses. Dazed eyes, like he could be harmless, but his smile . . . his lips just can't help but put the lie to what his eyes are selling. Do you have any ideas about him?"

Yeah, I told her, and none of them much good. I had no doubt she was describing Louis Perreau. Thanking her for being a good pal, I assured her once more that she had done all the right things and then told her again to keep Lin and Peter there and that I would be there myself as quick as I could.

Hanging up the phone, I looked around for the nearest taxi row. Unlike New York, Hong Kong doesn't allow its cabs to run rampant, any more than it does its citizens. Fairly high metal railings—sometimes extending for ten, twenty blocks or more—divide the streets throughout the city, discouraging jaywalkers.

As luck would have it, the only designated taxi pickup spot in sight was almost directly across the street. And, following the same path, the railing outside Sing's restaurant seemed to go on to infinity in both directions. Not having the time to run up and around and back, I jumped the curb and dashed through the oncoming traffic, hurdled the railing two-handed style, and then zigged my way through the cars coming in the opposite direction, jumping into the backseat of the first cab in line.

"You big hurry? Right talk?" asked the cabbie, gunning his motor.

"Right talk and a half," I told him. "Do you know the Five Great Grains?" He hit his meter and then pulled away from the curb, saying,

"You bet. No problem. You there fine as rain. No problem. Smoke?"

I laughed as I took one of the unfiltered Camels he was offering me, both at getting one of my own brand of cigarettes from him and at the thought of a place where smoking in a taxi was not only legal but encouraged. I lit up, thanking him profusely, sitting back to try and think things out before I threw myself into Lin's clutches.

What, I asked myself, could Slaner, Cronberg, and Perreau want? It was no accident they were all there. Were they working together—any two of them, perhaps? It was bad enough trying to figure out what Sing wanted . . . to have the three of them on my tail was three more than I needed.

It complicated things in ways I couldn't even begin to unravel. If Lin was willing to give a pair of minor players like Peter and me trouble, then he had to be aware of who my trio of new pals were. He had to know them by face as well. Why would they come there and expose themselves to someone as openly hostile to Kon Li Lu hunters as Lin? What was in it for them . . . that I could supply?

Suddenly I was very concerned. I had taken the offer Smiler and his people had made because I was mad . . . mad and stupid. I knew, however, that I had nothing to offer the C.C.B.A. Sure, maybe I might be able to stumble over something—*maybe*. But this was looking as if people were seeing me as some kind of tiebreaker. Like I was supposed to have some kind of answers that no one else did.

And, I asked myself—wondering if I might possibly have any kind of an answer—what did all that add up to? What would make the intelligence network of at least two countries, possibly three, as well as that of the area's chief gangster, think that I knew more than they did? Anyone who could crack Lin's security would stand a good chance at Rice's . . . no information is secure anymore.

Why? I asked again, almost out loud. *Why?*

Not surprisingly, I had no answers for myself. That was all right, considering that I hadn't expected any. What I had been trying to do was to remind myself to stay on my guard. Riding in the back of what appeared to be the fastest cab in Hong Kong, it suddenly dawned on me that everything I had told Peter was coming true. We had been sucked into the same old dirty game, the one I'd grown to hate so long ago, the one that had killed almost every friend I'd ever had and that had almost killed me. Something was going on I didn't understand, something that I knew I'd better figure out soon if I wanted to keep on breathing.

Then, the cabbie turned us onto Granville Road. Knowing we'd be at the Five Great Grains in just a moment, I peeled off fifty Hong Kong dollars—not nearly as much money as it sounded, but enough to award my driver his best tip of the day. As he pulled up to the curb, I asked,

"Tell me, is there anything going on at the Cultural Centre tonight?"

"Centre, Centre, Centre . . ." he said to himself, finally answering, "no. Nothing go at Centre tonight. No. Not in Centre. Why ask? Can help what? Why?"

"Probably nothing," I told him. "Someone asked me to meet him in the Centre parking lot tonight and . . ."

"Ohhhh," he exclaimed as if the heavens had suddenly opened. "Parking lot. Sure thing. Big time. People's fair, every night no thing inside, people outside. Sell many thing—every thing. Good time, good thing buys, very much good best place fun."

"Okay, I get the idea." I told him. Handing him the fifty along with one of the desk cards from my hotel on which I'd written my name, I asked, "Listen . . . think you can pick me up at this address at seven-thirty tonight?"

Seeing the fifty, he stared into my eyes immediately, looking to see if I was expecting any change. As soon as he verified that I wasn't, he put on his biggest smile and then told me in no uncertain terms,

"No worry no problem. Seven-thirty out front in line no problem. You no worry, no problem. Me number one driver, Jimmy Wing, move you best fine. No problem."

I thanked him as I started to get out of the cab, and then I turned back quickly, warning him,

"Hey, I just remembered . . . I actually might be in the lockup at seven-thirty tonight." When he looked at me with a pained expression, trying to tell me he was willing to do whatever it took to keep getting my kind of tips, but that he didn't know what I was talking about, I switched to my limited Chinese. Then, once I'd finally gotten across what I meant, he told me,

"No problem, number one boss." Pointing to my handwritten name on the back of the card, he asked, "This you?" When I told him it was, he answered,

"Then no worry. No problem. You not hotel, I find. You get bash, Jimmy find, make big noise. You no stay bash. I get you fix. Get you out. No worry."

"No problem," I told him, stepping up onto the curb and away from the cab. I gave him a short wave as he drove away, admitting to myself that it felt pretty good to have someone else on my side, even if they were only there for mercenary reasons. Then, I moved across the sidewalk and into the Five Great Grains, ready to confront Lin and to find out just how hard Jimmy was going to have to work that night to earn his tip.

CHAPTER 23

"HEY EVERYBODY," I shouted as I came through the front door, curious to see just what such an entrance would prompt, "the party man is back!"

Customers turned to see who the big mouth was. Felecia came from around the bar, heading toward me just two steps ahead of Peter, Lin, and a pair of his men. A wave of relief washed through me to see that Peter was still both there and not in cuffs. That meant that perhaps we had a chance to keep this from getting too ugly.

I spotted Slaner seated out in plain view at the bar. He stared right at me, amusement and approval mixed on his face. Cronberg and Perreau had either left or taken up positions hidden from my vantage point. Oh well, I thought, there was always time to deal with them later. Right then, I had other things to deal with. Putting on my number one best why-whatever-could-you-mean smile, I made obvious note of the approaching Lin and said,

"Captain, fancy running into you today. You come here often?"

"Mr. Hagee, so good to see you again. Tell me, can I get everything out of you that I want, sitting here comfortably, in what I would imagine are surroundings that are to your liking, or will we have to switch to something with more glass and gray metal . . . and bars?"

Pointing toward the curved mahogany behind Lin, I said,

"A place with just one bar suits me fine, Captain. Why don't we find a place at it and discuss whatever seems to be on your mind?"

"The bar's a little crowded at the moment," said Fel in a

voice implying hopefully only to me that she wanted us to do something different for a reason. "Why don't I get you a nice table toward the back? I mean, it is usually fairly hard to get five seats together. And since you and your men won't be drinking . . . couldn't we leave the bar open for the paying customers?"

Lin acquiesced, either without noticing that Fel had some alterior motive for moving us or being as cool about it as I was. Following Felecia to the back, I caught on to the purpose behind her act, although I had no way of knowing if Lin did as well. She had wanted me to see my other two playmates. I was glad she had. What I found most interesting was that Cronberg and Perreau were sharing a table. The three of us all pretended not to notice each other as our group went by, however, leading me to believe that whatever those two wanted could be thrashed out later.

At the table Fel led us to, Peter and I took the seats which put our backs to the wall—fairly indicative of how we were feeling—while Lin and his men took the ones surrounding us. As we all got comfortable, Fel asked everyone,

"So, what'll it be, gentlemen?"

"Privacy," responded Lin in a manner which allowed for no argument. Fel gave me a meaningful shrug of her eyebrows and then backed away, letting me know she had done all she could and that I was on my own. It wasn't a new feeling. Deciding to see if there was any room for rocking the boat, I quoted Fel just to see what the reaction would be.

"So," I said in her same chipper voice, "what'll it be, gentlemen?"

"Let me get a line drawn between us," answered Lin, his voice filled with a dark thin edge that didn't promise anything nice. "I'm only going to draw it once, so please, if you can't see it, or if you suspect that there is anything wrong with your vision . . . if you see two lines, perhaps, or can't tell where the line I've drawn starts, or finishes, let me know. Because I want to be sure you understand me."

"Go for it, Captain."

"I will not tolerate any games here—especially those

being played at my expense. Do you understand?" After
Peter and I assured Lin that we understood, he said,

"We shall see. There will be a number of tests of this
understanding of yours. The first test of this will be your
answer to my first question. Why did you stage your
elaborate charade this morning to lose my men?"

The eyes of the man to the captain's right narrowed,
letting me know he had been one of those men—probably
the one in charge. I could see it was my day for making
friends with powerful people's subordinates. Peter fielded
the question before I could answer, however, saying,

"Those were your men, Captain Lin, sir? Oh, we're so
sorry we dumped them so easily with such a childishly
simple trick." I watched the subordinate's eyes thin down to
mere slits. Peter had just taken his face and jumped up and
down on it. The act didn't bother me—just its possible
repercussions. Not having the time to worry about them
then, however, I merely continued to listen as Peter said,

"Why, we would have been happy to provide you with an
itinerary of our travel plans. You should have told us you
were so interested in what we were doing. Heck, I mean,
maybe if a few of your boys had been hiding in the palms
out in front of the restaurant earlier, Jack wouldn't have
gotten himself kidnapped. Or maybe the upcoming end of
British rule has made anti-Caucasian crime something that
doesn't interest you very much anymore."

"Nice speech, tourist," answered Lin, his tone telling us
he was not our friend. "We'll get to you consorting with
known felons later. First off, though . . ."

"Consorting with known felons?" I repeated. "Come on,
now, Captain. Let's give this tough guy stuff a rest, shall
we? I'll answer the questions here since it's apparent if I let
you and Peter waltz around we'll be here all day. First—
yeah, we thought it might be your people following us this
morning, but we weren't sure. Do you understand
that . . . we . . . weren't . . . sure. All I wanted to do
was visit my old friends here without involving them in
some sort of bad business . . . the kind they're now
involved in somehow, anyway. So, big mistake, I guess, but

it's done. If you hadn't been acting so cute, we wouldn't have, either."

"I'm sure," snorted Lin.

"Be sure," I told him, forcing the point. "I don't give two shits about you, your Kon Li Lu or his goddamned money. I'll tell you what I want, and all that I want—the people who killed my friends—period. If I have to find Lu to find them, then I'll find him. And I'll work with the police when I know something. But I won't call you."

"And why not?" asked Lin.

"Because," I answered, pointing back toward the table where Cronberg and Perreau were sitting, "it appears your phone lines aren't trustworthy. If you think those two are here for the sugar noodle balls, guess again."

I give Lin credit. I watched as his eyes followed the direction of my hand, stared at the pair sitting at the table in question, and then turned back to me. They were filled with more than embarrassment. Their suddenly down-turned edges told me that their owner was just as sure as I was that Cronberg and Perreau had gotten the information that I had been spotted at the Five Great Grains from his office. But, they also told me that he wished it was different. I had stopped him in his tracks and caused the captain a severe loss of face by taking the high moral ground for myself.

Cronberg and Perreau, to their collective credit as operatives, did not react to being singled out or discussed. The pair made no reaction whatsoever to the fact that they had suddenly become the objects of police scrutiny. While they continued to sip at their drinks—beer for Cronberg, tea for Perreau—Lin returned his attention to me, saying,

"And so, Mr. Hagee, how exactly do you propose to work with the police if you will not speak to us?" Lowering my voice, I told him,

"I'm sure we can come up with something that will work for both of us. However, do you think we could get out of earshot of our pals over there before we do?"

"You do not trust foreign nationals?" asked Lin with a trace of humor. "Hong Kong is a free port, after all."

"Yeah," I agreed, "so's New York City, and look at what a shithole that's turned into."

The captain gave me a smile at that crack, one that told me I hadn't lost him. Continuing to keep my voice low, amusing myself by watching the pair at the far table trying to catch what they could of our conversation, I answered Lin's smile, saying,

"You've got a few choices . . . roust the two of them, or have your boys keep them here while we leave, or we set a meeting time for later and get back together."

"And which would you prefer?"

"Well, if it were up to me, I'd say keep them confused. You and your men roust Peter and me, drag us off . . ."

And then, before I could continue, Lin slapped his hand against the table, saying angrily,

"No! I do not have to listen to any more of this. I've tried diplomacy. Now we must act like people in bad movies." Turning to one of his men, the captain ordered,

"Check everyone here—find me witnesses. I want the truth." Pointing at Cronberg and Perreau, he said, "Start with them and cover everyone in the place. Now."

The detective gave his boss a conspiratorial blink and then moved in on the pair of operatives before they could flee the restaurant. Then, Lin and his remaining man marched Peter and me to the street, all of it looking official enough to fool Fel and everyone else in the place which, after all, was the point. Once outside, he hustled us into an unmarked police car, detailing his man to bring ours along behind. Seconds later, with Lin at the wheel, we were cruising the Hong Kong traffic and I was telling him my story.

I told him everything that had happened between myself and Sing . . . both today and fifteen years ago. When I asked him what he thought Sing might be up to, he had no ideas. When I asked him why Sing might want me to meet him at the street fair that night, he drew another blank. After a few moments of silence, as he slowed the car for an approaching red light, the captain finally said,

"Why is it I get this feeling I should trust you, Mr. Hagee?"

"Because I remind you of your kindly grandfather?"

"No, I don't think that is it. Have you any other thoughts on the subject?"

"How about because deep down you know I'm telling the truth and you've got nothing to lose by letting me play out the crummy few little leads I've got?"

"I will give you half credit for that answer," said Lin as he pulled forward into the newly moving traffic. "Yes, 'deep down' as you say, I do think you have been telling me the truth. Not that nonsense about not knowing it was my men following you this morning, but given that the arrival of my men has brought undesirables into the lives of you and your friends, perhaps we can forgive one such action."

"You're too kind," I told him.

"Yes, I know," he answered, throwing my humor back at me. "It is a grievous failing. But, as to my having nothing to lose by letting you run around my city doing as you please . . . you might want to think that part over again." And then, Lin pulled over to the curb. As he did, he fished in his pocket for one of his business cards. Scribbling an address on the back of it, he said,

"Tonight, after you have seen Sing and discovered what it is that he wants, you will come to this address and continue to cooperate fully with the local officials. Correct?"

"I'll do my best," I told him honestly.

Lin turned and looked over the seat at Peter and myself. Staring mainly at me, but including my partner in his scolding look just for good measure, he said,

"Let us hope your best is very . . . *very* good. Do you understand me, Mr. Hagee? Mr. Wei?" After we agreed that we did, the captain stared at us for one long moment. His eyes weren't what I would call cold. To tell the truth, I was at a loss to describe them at all. He was searching us for something, but what it was, I wasn't sure. Then, all of a sudden, he pointed to the street and said,

"Get out. Take your car."

As we clambered out to the sidewalk, we started an

involved shuffling of seats—us leaving, Lin's man taking the driver's seat, Lin taking the back. Peter accepted the keys to our rental from Lin's driver, neither one of them saying anything to the other. Then, just before they could drive away, I told the captain,

"Thank you for having some faith in us, Captain." Looking out of his window, Lin answered me, saying,

"I have no faith in you. I have faith in my own ability to determine a situation. This one seems as if it will determine favorably. Do not do anything that would shake my opinion of myself, Mr. Hagee. It would not make me any friendlier toward you."

And then, Lin tapped his man on the shoulder, signaling him to get going. Peter and I watched their car pull off into the traffic. Trying to figure out what to make of the captain, I said,

"Too Zen for me." Peter simply looked back at me blankly, saying,

"The word you're looking for is 'inscrutable.'" I eyed him for a second, wondering what kind of joke he was making and at exactly whose expense. Finally, deciding that it really wasn't worth knowing, I just said,

"Get in the car, will you?"

"Oh, yes, western running dog."

Of course, then, I knew at exactly whose expense it was.

CHAPTER 24

THAT NIGHT, JIMMY Wing picked me up at the hotel. Peter, following in our car, trailed the two of us to the fair. I figured that Sing's not knowing Peter was around would be our only advantage. Jimmy made record time, at least as best I could figure how long the trip should take. As he parked his cab, I started to tell him what time to pick me up, but he wasn't hearing any of it.

"No way. Not let number one boss get bad turn. No way. You pay Jimmy good. Jimmy take good care number one boss. No problem."

I tried to convince him that while he was losing the chance to grab a few more fares I could take care of myself. He told me back that he was already on his own time. He also said that maybe I could take care of myself in America, but I wasn't in America anymore . . . I was in Hong Kong and what I knew didn't matter. Figuring that, who knew, maybe he was right, I surrendered and let him lead me off into the bowels of the bazaar.

The people's fair turned out to be an amazing collection of goods and services being offered for a staggering array of prices. As we walked up and down the lanes made up artificially by the placement of the different booths and tables and roped-off areas, I found myself being sucked into the tourist end of things, no matter how hard I tried to keep my mind on finding Sing. Fighting my way through the crowds, I began to wonder if there was any way Peter would be able to keep track of me.

No matter where I looked, everything I could imagine was for sale—everything. There were marketers selling jackets and skirts, belts, pants, ties, shoes, hats, and underwear—in every shape and style and size you might need. There were those selling kitchen utensils—bowls, chopsticks, tea balls and woks right next to the rice steamers, hot-water machines, and refrigerators. Others sold toys for children, some dealt in antiquities, the rest had playing cards and whistles, fireworks, potted plants, cigarettes, pen and pencil sets, watches, cans of motor oil, vegetables, writing paper, rugs and curtains and chairs and lazy Susans, earrings—or more to the point I was making before—everything.

Fortune-tellers could be found at every turn—card readers, palm readers, tea leaves readers. Some claimed to be able to just look into your face, others wanted to feel the bumps on your head. Some specialized in the next day's race winners. Others could be rented to pray for you—supplicants for hire. I thought about hiring one of those, myself. I wasn't sure what exactly I'd have them pray for, but it was certainly beginning to seem as if I should have some kind of prayers in the air trying to do something for me.

As I threaded along through the crowds, hoping Peter could keep me in sight, I tried to put everything together in my head with which we had to work. Nothing added up, and I didn't know where to turn for any answers. The police are waiting for Peter and me when we land and dog us everywhere we go, giving us the hairy eye as if we were the bad guys. My old playmate Sing tracks me down and instead of having me killed takes me to lunch and makes nice. Hu goes over the "evidence" that both Smiler and Rice had given me and drops the answers in my lap . . . they were both absolutely right. Yes—Kon Li Lu spent the money on whores and cars and general all-around high living, and yes again—Kon Li Lu was a saint who never touched a dime of what he collected. Put on top of that that someone had felt worried enough about me to blow a hole in my apartment and kill two of my friends and nothing made sense at all.

Why try to kill me? What did I matter? What did anyone

think I could do that the rest of the hired guns in town
couldn't? It didn't make sense. Was Lu a thief or wasn't he?
Why did the police have their eye on us, and who told them
we were coming in the first place? And then there was Sing
and whatever he was up to. Which was . . . what? That
thought entered my head just as I focused on the crowd
ahead.

A large knot of people had gathered around an area in
front of us. I asked Jimmy what was going on.

"Kids. For kids. Puppet show. Shadow puppets. Big
favorite for kids." Not having much luck tracking down
Sing, I said,

"What the hell. Let's look at the puppets."

The stage arrangement turned out to be a lot like the old
Punch-and-Judy setups—a big box with a cutout stage at
the top. Unlike the hand puppets westerners would expect,
however, the entertainment here came from delicately
cutout pieces of paper attached to sticks which the puppe-
teers manipulated from below. Light was shown through
the paper from behind, casting shadows on the curtain at the
front of the box. A little man sitting to the right side of the
box played on a stringed instrument something like a zither.
He never seemed to look up at the stage, but somehow his
music always matched the action on stage. As I watched the
show I could see that Jimmy was getting bored so I gave
him an American ten-spot and told him to get us a couple of
bowls of noodles and to keep the change. It was a hell of a
tip, but what the hell, I thought. The show was free—I felt
like I should be paying for something.

As the show unfolded, the laughter from the audience just
got louder and louder, including my own, as well. Even with
my substandard Chinese I found myself getting two out of
every three jokes. A lot of them weren't half bad, either.
True, a lot of it was Three Stooges level humor, but then, I
never claimed to be on a much higher level than the Howard
brothers and their partner, Mr. Fine.

As I continued to listen and laugh, my eyes started to
wander through the crowd, over their heads, up and down the
booths, hoping for a glimpse of Sing. Hell, I thought . . .

Sing? I couldn't even spot Peter or Jimmy. Then, however, suddenly I saw a flash in between two of the people next to me too familiar not to rivet my attention. Someone with a gun in hand was moving through the crowd. I wondered if I could have possibly seen right. A gun? In public? In Hong Kong? This was not a New York City street with a gunman or three on every corner—this was one of the most heavily controlled areas in the world as far as such things went, with penalties higher than any other free country.

My radar went out, searching for the handful of metal. Hell, for all I knew, it was someone scouting the crowd for me. Why not—the back of my mind reminded me edgily—it hadn't been so long since someone had fired a rocket into my living room. A simple thing like a handgun would be a relaxing change of pace.

People next to me began to notice my sudden lack of enthusiasm for the puppets. As the long seconds ticked by, several of those standing next to me began to back off—some just giving me more room, others leaving the area entirely. I had started generating a field they could sense, filling the air around me with concern, apprehension, anxiety. Where was the gun? Where was its owner? All I'd seen through the crowd had been a hand holding a gun—no, I thought, I'd seen an arm, too. What had I seen—anything?

Trying to remember, I kept scanning the crowd physically while trying to dig through my memory. What had been happening on stage? I asked myself. What had the puppets been doing? Faces and heads passed before my eyes— hundreds of them, some the same, unmoving, watching the show, others pushing by us in both directions, simply trying to move through the fair. At the same time, the back of my mind focused on the recent past. I saw the stage in my head, heard the laughs, watched the puppet dancing as it had been a moment earlier when I'd seen the gun . . . *yes* . . . *the puppets had been doing their dance.* . . .

One memory brings back the other; I forgot the puppets, concentrating on holding the image of the gun, the hand holding it, the arm attached—hairless—the rolled-up sleeve, dark red shirt . . . *yes, again* . . . I thought. *Dark red shirt*. Now I know what to look for.

Scanning the crowd, I stopped wasting time looking for the gun—looking for what was being hidden—and concentrated on finding that same shirt again. I turned in a circle, studying those around me, searching for a dark red, rolled-up sleeve. Seconds later I spotted it—a man, ten bodies forward and to the left, moving away from me. I studied his movements while I tried to worm my way toward him. He stopped—I kept moving. And then, his hand began to come up, slowly, carefully. Looking at what he was doing, I was stunned. He was lining up the puppet theater. Without thinking, without knowing why I was doing what I was doing, I surged forward, pushing people to both sides, heading straight for the dark red shoulders.

People started screaming—some injured, some just mad. I couldn't afford to worry about them. I had to cover distance, close with the target before he knew I was coming. No chance. With still two people between us I could see he had heard the commotion, knew that it somehow had something to do with him, was already turning toward me. Slamming my arm in between the last two bodies separating us, I wedged the man and woman in my way to the left and the right, my fingers closing on the arm of my target. The arm without the gun.

Jerking him off balance, I pulled him forward as best I could. His gun hand was already up. The only problem he had was getting a clear shot at me. As I shoved the man and woman aside he got his chance. He tried to aim as I dragged him toward me. The gun came close to my neck. My other hand connected with his face, an open-palmed punch that closed over his eye. The impact shook him, throwing off his aim. The chamber cleared, powder burning my cheek. The bullet missed me by inches, streaking above the stunned crowd and off into the night.

I hit him again and again—once with each hand, both body blows. The gun hit the pavement. All around us the crowd pushed away, trampling each other in their haste to clear the area. Women covered their children's bodies, grown sons shielded their mothers and fathers. I put my foot on top of the gun to keep it from disappearing and then grabbed the shooter again. He was too dazed to defend himself, but I didn't care. He had been ready to gun down a puppeteer. I saw every thug with a gun that had robbed a grandmother or shot a child, and I drove my fist into his already bruised face.

The blood poured as his nose broke. The little voice inside reminded me that the worse he looked the worse I'd look when the cops arrived. I punched him again, not caring—rage driving me. I was hoping for damage . . . expecting it. Peter finally managed to clear the crowd and reach my side just as I hit him again.

"What's going on?" he asked, just as the shooter cried out,

"Stop, please! Leave me alone. Lemme go. I've got rights. Stop it. Stop it."

Peter and I looked at each other. The thought in both our heads was clear on our faces. English. The Chinese man decked out in typical HK Chinese street wear was begging us in his voice of first instinct—English. I was just about to comment on that when suddenly the puppeteer came out from behind his theater, his dog bouncing about at his heels, looking for whatever it was that had caused so much excitement around her master.

"Burger," he cried, somewhat surprised.

"Sing?" I answered, extremely confused. I wondered if everything that had just happened had been another of the drug lord's elaborate setups for a moment, but the look on his face convinced me it wasn't. I wanted to ask his opinion of the situation, but before anyone could do anything, we were suddenly surrounded by five Hong Kong foot patrolmen, and casual conversation with anyone but them became a thing of the past.

CHAPTER 25

"NOW, LET ME see if I have this in proper flow. . . ." The speaker was Captain Lin. Back at the people's fair the cops had been on us like shrink-wrap plastic. I got a kick out of the radios built into the shoulders of their uniform jackets. Like something out of a science fiction movie, they pulled the mikes out on a retractable cord and got the lowdown on us all from their central command in minutes. After that, it only took a few more minutes before ambulances and patrol cars showed up to take everyone away. And I do mean everyone.

The shooter had disappeared into an ambulance. The word was they had to take him to the hospital before they could get anything out of him. I wasn't very upset at that particular piece of news. Sing and Peter and I got taken downtown, of course, along with about fifteen members of the surrounding crowd who had all been tapped to be witnesses. Gigi had remained behind with Sing's people—to me a remarkable act of faith on behalf of both the dog and the master.

We all told our stories to Lin and his people—several times—after which they pulled all our tales together. Since none of the three of us had anything to hide, everything seemed to match up. After repeating everything we had told him and his people back to us, Lin asked,

"Would you care to agree that that is pretty much what happened?"

"Yes," I told him, tired and bored of the whole thing. "Yes, yes. Absolutely. Now, can we call it a night and go get some dinner, or is it time for breakfast already?"

"Find it within your heart to indulge a poor, hardworking man of the law." Indicating Sing with a wave of his hand, the captain continued, saying,

"Be like your wise friend here. Here is the head of the Tiger's Breath Triad, straight from an evening of working hard at both being a puppeteer and an almost murder victim. You don't see him straining at the gate, do you?"

"He's got more to worry about."

"Like what?"

"He's the one people are shooting at—not me."

"You interfered. Which means you could be next. So," said Lin, small upturns forming in the corners of his mouth, telling me just how much he was enjoying the situation, "please go ahead and, as they might say on American TV, 'get attached to you chair.' For the moment you and your partner are not going anywhere."

"No chance, huh?"

"Sadly," answered the captain, his eyes giving away the smile he was trying to hide, "I must insist."

"What about me?" asked Sing. "Am I prisoner here, as well?"

"No, not at all. Mr. Hagee is not a prisoner, Mr. Wei is not a prisoner. You are not a prisoner. I would merely like to look into who is trying to murder you and whether or not they will now try to murder Mr. Hagee and even possibly Mr. Wei, as well. Now, understand. I do not care if any of the three of you are murdered . . ." He repeated the sentiment in a lower voice just to make sure we got it,

"Not any of you. But, I do have the peace to maintain. People firing off illegal handguns—very nasty business— very hard on the peace. So, if we could begin with a few questions . . . Mr. Sing?"

"Yes?" answered the drug lord wearily, bored with the game already, his tone indicating that he had more faith in his own resources than in the police.

"Can you tell me what such a famous citizen is doing at the people's fair working a shadow puppet box?"

"Yes, I can. I do it because I like to do it. Did you know I was most popular entertainer as boy? Do you know reason? Do not guess—I will tell you. Because I cared about my audience's enjoyment. I wanted them to be happy. Not just for coins they would throw, but because I wanted to give back equal to what I was getting. I still do. I like for people to be happy, Captain Lin, unlike you of the police force." I caught a flashing in Lin's eyes at Sing's crack—caught one in Sing's as well. Neither man forced the issue as the drug lord continued.

"I still do . . . want people be happy, that is . . . especially children. So, as many nights as I can—at least once a week—I go out and perform—all the great stories, all the tales they need to hear to have some idea of how they should order their lives. Tales of moral strength and individual courage. The kinds of words they need in our repressive, *modern* world."

"You think Hong Kong is a repressive society, Sing?" asked Lin with a mocking tone.

"Ask me again in '97," answered the drug lord, his tone grim as stone.

"I'll try to remember to do that. Meanwhile, can you provide us with a list of people who knew about your benevolent activities?"

"Not one that would include who send man you have locked up somewhere. You do remember him, don't you? Man with gun? Man who shot at me? Man who would have most likely killed me if not for the kind intervention of Mr. Hagee here."

"And," piped in Peter suddenly, "what makes you think this guy gives a rat's ass about that?" As all attention shifted to my partner, he continued, saying,

"Captain Lin here is part of the 'Intelligence' division. In case everyone forgot, he isn't interested in maintaining the peace. That's not his job."

I had to give Peter a mental slap on the back for that one. Even I'd forgotten that fact for the moment. Lin, not happy to have his game plan upset, directed himself at Peter, asking,

"And what do you think my job is, then?"

"So far you've shown that you don't care that Sing almost

got murdered, or that Jack prevented it. You're treating my partner and me as if we were as big a threat to Hong Kong as Sing. Since I'm willing to give you the benefit of the doubt and not just assume that you're just another dumb cop, then I have to figure that your job is humping the leg of everybody involved with Kon Li Lu. That's all you give a damn about," answered Peter, pushing himself back into his chair. Crossing his legs, folding his arms across his chest, he closed himself off from Lin as best he could and then fired off his last comment, telling the captain,

"Either because that's all you've been assigned to do these days . . . or because you're looking to put the nab on the money yourself."

I almost hesitated before looking into Lin's eyes. I did, though, not liking what I found. The cold anger that I'd been seeing there ever since our first meeting heated up dramatically. I saw his shoulders shaking, his hands make fists he couldn't unclench. Peter had hit more than a nerve—he had tapped into something that struck the captain like a pot of water flung in his face—water so hot that he could barely stand it—water so hot that just another degree and he would have had no choice other than to scream aloud. Getting control of himself, however, Lin choked his anger down without letting any steam escape, then answered,

"Out of the choices offered . . . because it is my job. Just as it is your job to crawl through the filth of other people's lives, breathing their farts and drinking whatever swill they call water. Your job," continued the captain, the edge in his voice getting red and mean, "thug for hire, garbageman, peeper, nuisance, shit raker, thief . . ."

"*Captain*," I blurted, not needing to see how far he could go, knowing he didn't need to see either. "Maybe we could get back to the point?"

"The point?" he asked, absently and yet filled with rage at the same time. "The point? And what would that be? You tell me what the point is here, Mr. Hagee. You come into my country filled with arrogance, strutting across the land on your mission of vengeance. You do not impress me—not you nor your money-hungry lackey nor your old friend the puppet-loving gangster. None of you know what is going on here and none of you care past your own miserable self-importance."

"And," asked Sing quietly, "you do?"

"Do?" asked the captain, coming up out of his seat. He whipped his head around so fast to stare at the drug lord that the sweat in his hair flew toward Sing in a speeding arc. As half the droplets splashed against the drug lord's suit, Lin demanded,

"Do what? Do *I* know what is going on here?"

"Do you *care*?" asked Sing.

The detective captain stopped in his tracks then, frozen by his inability to answer the drug lord's question. Sitting back down, he used his feet to push his wheeled chair back toward his desk. He stopped when it bumped against his open drawer, lifting his head to look at each of us. Finally, after reviewing each of our faces for his own private reasons, he answered Sing's question.

"Yes. I care. Possibly not about the same things you do, but I still care."

"We all do, Lin," I told him. "So, what do you say we pool our information and start working together? Let's all be up-front and tell each other what we're looking for and see if we can't get some of this solved."

It was a dangerous proposition. I had no guarantees that any of us wanted anything similar from what was going on. I had no idea of what Sing was after, nor even Lin for that matter. After my own recent experience, I couldn't say that cops and gangsters can't ever work together—on either side of the tracks—but that was New York, and a couple of different sets of gangsters and cops.

Lin crossed his eyes for a long moment, obviously thinking about what I had just said. No one said anything. There was no one to dispute that he had more to think about than anyone else present. Finally, however, the captain opened his eyes with a sigh and then said,

"Who goes first?"

CHAPTER 26

WISELY—OR AT least, so it seemed to me—we adjourned our meeting and left police headquarters, returning to the Five Great Grains. Unbelievably, we found Jimmy waiting outside police headquarters to take us wherever we needed to go. Sing's men, of course, were waiting as well. I passed on both Lin's and Sing's offers of a ride, not wanting to leave Jimmy out in the cold. I'd told him where to wait—he'd waited—he deserved the fare. Besides, I didn't want to show any favoritism between the other two sides, and until I knew why people were shooting at Sing, I didn't think I'd be sharing any cars with him.

Once we arrived, I paid Jimmy off for the night, telling him we'd make it home on our own. I told him he could call the hotel in the morning and check to see if we needed him. That, along with his tip, seemed to make him happy enough. After that, Sing told his men to wait outside, taking only Gigi in with him. Lin parked his vehicle in an official's only zone and then joined the rest of us.

Fel gave us a private room in the back—the back that most people didn't know about, including the police. Lin made the kind of noises that we were all off duty and that whatever he heard or saw or did until we parted company was off-the-record. I let Fel decide whether or not she believed him. I'm a good judge of character, but I know my betters. Besides, it was her secret room that was being offered up, not mine.

In the end she decided she could trust him, though, so back we went. She let us in, got us comfortable, took our orders, treating us like any other bunch of tourists. A few minutes later she returned with our drinks—two to a man. Peter had asked for a Budweiser, Sing for an iced tea. I'd ordered my usual gin on the rocks with a twist. Lin had asked for Sanliangye, a Chinese grain drink made from rice, wheat, and sorghum. It goes down smooth but packs a devastating kick. Gigi contented herself with curling up under her master's chair. To each their own. Fel set our drinks in front of us, saying,

"If you need anything, there's a buzzer under the table in between Jack and Peter. Feel around—you'll find it. And that does mean anything. You want out for any reason, including to go to the priv, use the buzzer to call someone to open the door. That's the only way out."

So saying, she closed the false door on us—locking us in and leaving us to our own devices. We all settled into our chairs around the table. Lin slid a black, soft leather case down out of sight next to his chair. Everyone took a sip of their drinks. Long sips. Eyes flitted from person to person. It was fairly clear that no one wanted to go first. It made sense. We were all caught up in a runaway game with stakes higher than just life and death. Trust was not something that was going to come easy to anyone at the table. Having just been in the situation of mediating an uneasy truce between gangsters and the police the last time people were throwing lead around in my vicinity, I figured I had more experience than anyone else in such games, so I went first.

"Well, we going to get our cards up on the table or not?"

"What would you suggest?" asked Sing.

"First off, I think we'd better clear the air about Kon Li Lu. And as long as I'm talking, I'll be happy to go first."

"No," interrupted Sing. "Allow me. I think it would be all for best if I were to, as you say, show my hand first." The drug lord took another sip from his iced tea, cleared his throat, and then started.

"I'm looking for Lu because I want to get to truth of what he do. Like many others, I gave him—for his cause—a considerable sum of money. Now, I have received evidence perhaps he is not man I thought he was. There are rumors of him spending his collected riches on women and horse races. Although I have been known to spend money on such things myself, I have never placed a bet on a two-year-old thinking such thing could stop Communist tank. I am not man to be made fool of. If Lu has attempted to do so, then I will know about it." Taking another sip of his iced tea, Sing sat back in his chair, saying,

"And that is all there is to it."

The drug lord looked over at me, letting me know I could start my tale. Knocking back a long slug of gin, I obliged him, saying,

"Myself, I don't care if Lu is on the Riviera spending his billions or facedown in some gutter somewhere. I'm here because two friends of mine were killed. Someone tried to stop me from coming here with a rocket. I don't know who and I don't know why, but I figure if I keep looking for Lu, I'll come across whoever murdered Francis . . . whoever made a widow out of Carmine's wife and orphans of his kids." Taking another belt, I continued, saying,

"Peter here, he's—"

"No," interrupted Lin. "Let him talk. He can tell us why he's here."

The captain had a point. Each man should be telling his own tale. I didn't argue. Neither did Peter.

"I'm here because it's a job. Okay? I knew Francis and Carmine, but not like Jack. For me—the chance to become Jack's partner is a big move. He's got the better situation and it was just good business sense to link my wagon to his. I'll give you the point that I didn't expect this kind of case right out of the gate, but hey . . . if we solve it, we're rich."

"You could solve it and become dead, as well," added Lin.

"You could become dead even before that," suggested Sing.

"Then," answered Peter, taking a defiant swig from his beer, "I'll get a chance to become better acquainted with Carmine and Francis."

"Brave boy," said Sing back, seeming very pleased with Peter's answer. "Brave and honest. You have chosen your associate very carefully, Jack." When Lin looked at both Sing and I with narrowed eyes, I asked,

"So, what's with you, Captain? What's your interest here? And I say this to both you and Sing—I don't give a good goddamn, okay? I don't care what either one of you is in this for. I just want to know what's going on and whether or not we can help each other."

Lin lifted his glass to his lips, finishing off his first drink in one full-mouthed gulp. Putting it back down, he started to talk.

"It's a job," he said, his voice calmer than it had been all night. "But it is a job with many facets. Kon Li Lu . . ." The captain hesitated for a long moment, then finally plunged forward, saying,

"The man is a bomb—one with the ability to throw our entire world into chaos. The Chinese, everyone knows, will take over the affairs of the Royal Colony of Hong Kong in 1997. Not very far away. For the government of our islands, however, '97 came quite some time ago. Did you know that since 1980 the Communists have been sending people here, insisting they be given key positions of authority in all levels of our life? They are in the police force, the banking houses, all forms of transportation, commerce, whathave-you. They want to make sure the British don't loot the Colony before they run away with their tails between their legs." Lin took a pull on his second drink and kept going.

"Did you know that cross-border crime is not only tolerated by the Chinese authorities, but oftentimes being orchestrated by them? Smugglers—we don't allow their speedboats to exist in Hong Kong. No one can own one. How do you account for the over five hundred sightings of their high-powered *tai feis* a month? How do you account for the fact that when we ask the Chinese Public Security Bureau for help, none of the cases we report are recorded? Mercedes-Benzs and other luxury cars are disappearing at a rate of several thousand a year from Hong Kong. Where do you think they are going?"

The captain puffed out a weary breath, his hand lifting his

glass once more. Throwing back half of his remaining drink, he said,

"Two years back, Crown Motors launched a massive advertising campaign across the border. They were warning potential receivers of stolen cars that spare parts would be unobtainable. Why buy a stolen car if you won't be able to get it repaired? Makes sense—right? Certainly. Care to guess what we catch one smuggler in three with these days?"

"My assumption is spare parts for luxury cars."

"You assume very well, Mr. Hagee."

"Yeah, great," I told him. "But what's the point? And I'm not saying you don't have one, I'm just trying to get you to it."

"My point?" answered Lin absently, looking around the room with distracted eyes. "My point, gentlemen, is that each of you know exactly what you want . . . what you are supposed to be doing. Everything is so simple for you. But me? Tell me, what is my job, Mr. Hagee? What exactly am I supposed to be doing about Kon Li Lu? Do you have any answers, Mr. Wei? Mr. Sing? Who are my masters in this? What are my orders? Who am I supposed to be pleasing? The Royal Hong Kong government? The Communists? And, can I trust what either one wants—or *says* they want? Can I?"

The captain finished off his drink, replacing his glass on the table with an unsteady hand. Staring at it, watching a last drop slide down its lip, over its edge toward the table below, he said,

"Let me tell you a story. Years ago, when I was still with the Army, the British Army . . . I was a sergeant, working border duty. You know, keeping the Chinese from getting over the border." The captain laughed for a moment. Then, his eyes focusing on the wall somewhere behind me, he let us in on the joke.

"Me—keeping the Chinese out of Hong Kong. Of course, sir, whatever you say, sir." Lin's words were bitter, filled with an angry sarcasm that seemed mainly directed at himself. Eyeing his two empty glasses, he accepted the fact they were empty and continued.

"One night, two brothers tried to come over. We caught the younger one. We used the usual plastic strip tabs to secure him to a tree and then some of us went looking for his older brother while some of us hid near our captive. The whole time we waited, the younger one kept screaming to his brother, 'Run, run. Don't come back. Don't come back.' As you can guess, the older brother tried to rescue his brother from us." Lin paused again, his eyes drifting to his empty glasses once more. The edge in his voice dropped, replaced by a building sorrow as he told us,

"We knew he would. They always did. That's why we didn't gag them, you know . . . so they could give their relatives, their friends—whoever they tried to come over with—something to home in on. That night, though, these two brothers . . . the older one crying—so thankful his brother was unharmed, the younger one cursing him at first for not going on without him, then agreeing that they were better off." The captain started moving his head then, his eyes no longer unfocused. Looking into the eyes of each of us at the table in turn, Lin told us,

"They thought it better to be returned to the Communists together than to face the world without each other's support." And then, his eyes stopped at mine and his voice began to again fill with anger.

"That is what it means to be Chinese, Mr. Hagee. Support for the family, for the group, the nation. I stopped doing border patrol that night. Those brothers were the last I could look at, the last I wanted to hear in my sleep. But what good was my gesture? Now, the Communists are poised to loot my home. Already they are sending their agents forth to begin the stripping of Hong Kong. And who will stand against it? Will the British protect us? Having already caved in—even where they were not asked to—I do not think so. The Americans? Will they intervene? Sadly, again . . . I do not think so."

Shoving the empty glasses before him to the center of the

table, the captain leaned back in his chair, some of his intensity fading. In a quieter voice, he said,

"Those in charge now tell me my job is to maintain order against those who disrupt Hong Kong. But those doing the most disrupting are soon to be in charge. Those in charge now are not Chinese. Those who will be soon are—but they do not believe in the world I believe in. So, tell me, any of you . . . what is my job, and why should I trust any of you?"

After a long moment of silence, Sing offered,

"Your job is to help protect Kon Li Lu, because he believes in the world you believe in more than any man. You asked who will protect Hong Kong. I believe that if anyone will, it will be him, simply by getting all Chinese everywhere to resist, as he has resisted."

And then Lin began to laugh. It was a mirthless chuckle that grew from deep within him—one that did not stop as he reached below the table for the leather case he had brought in with him. Still laughing, he pulled forth a series of color photographs—pictures of Kon Li Lu bent over the gaming tables of the Riviera, drinking from cut crystal under the dazzling chandeliers of the gambling palaces of Macau . . . all copies of the same photos Jackson In had given me.

"This man?" asked Lin, bitterness making his words a curse. Obviously agreeing more with Smiler's assessment of the situation than Rice's, he said,

"This man will teach us to resist? What, Sing? What exactly will this man teach us to resist?"

The drug lord's face grew ashen as he went through the pictures, letting everyone else in the room know that he must have been pinning a lot of hope on the young fund-raiser. He looked at the entire series once, then again. Then again. The third time through a puddle started to form around each of his eyes. Not wanting to embarrass Sing by staring at his sudden loss of control, I picked up the first of the photos he had dropped onto the table and started going through them myself.

And then, suddenly I found my hand reaching for my

half-finished first drink. Without conscious thought I raised it to my mouth and threw it back, draining it in a gulp. It took conscious thought to keep myself from going for the full one still before me.

One toss off, I knew, would be interpreted by those around me as shock akin to Sing's, a giving in to the notion that Lu was as corrupt as the Communists he was supposed to be trying to destroy. Taking up the second drink and doing it some damage would have been noticed, however, so I forced myself not to . . . forced myself to simply flip through the pictures as Sing had, keeping what I had seen in them this time which I had not noticed before—which I could not have noticed before—to myself.

I did, however, press the buzzer that would summon Fel. I knew we were going to be needing more drinks soon. As soon as I heard the door opening, I picked up my second, wanting it more than I had wanted a drink in a long time. If anyone noticed how badly my hand was shaking, they didn't comment.

CHAPTER 27

OUR MEETING WENT fairly quickly after that. Suddenly, none of us was studying percentages anymore. Sing admitted that he and his people were solid supporters of Kon Li Lu and his organization. The drug lord and his compatriots had made massive donations to the cause, never losing faith in their investments . . . at least, none of Sing's friends had. Sing himself had started to feel a little uneasy in the stomach a few moments after Lin had thrown out his copies of the damning photos.

Peter and I admitted to having seen variations of the pictures already. For what it was worth, I added Major Rice's positive interpretation of the same evidence. Somehow it didn't seem to be worth enough to cheer anyone up very much. At least, I thought, it looked as if Lin were finally on our side, which sat just fine with me. I'd never been sure Peter and I were going to be able to find Lu or his money on our own. However, I'd certainly been able to figure out that having Tai Sing and Captain Lin on our side was a hell of a lot better than having them against us.

Fel came in with our second round. I could see the surprise in her eyes that I had knocked off both my drinks. She didn't know Lin and didn't care much about Sing, but she did know me. I could tell from the look in her eyes that she was warning me not to lose my head. I gave her one back telling her that I knew exactly where my head was.

Then, after she left we finally got down to discussing the murder attempt. Sing told us he had no specific ideas as to why anyone would try to kill him. Lin put a call in to his office, checking to see if anyone had been able to get anything out of the shooter. His answer was that they weren't even close. So far they hadn't even been able to establish who he was or where he was from. The captain gave us the bad news, though, with the assurance that it was still early in the prisoner's interrogation.

"Sooner or later," said Lin with confidence, "we shall get our answers from him."

"Hopefully," responded the drug lord, "before anyone else tries to finish his work for him."

After that, we continued to talk, each faction seeming to give up everything they knew. I wondered if Lin and Sing were no more trustworthy than me. After all, I reminded myself, I had a new piece of the puzzle all of a sudden that I wasn't sharing with anyone else. What were they holding back because, like myself, they had their reasons?

Sing seemed incredibly open, answering questions without holding back. The captain seemed to be doing the same. But then, I had to remember, hopefully so did I. We worked on our drinks and each other, finally coming to the conclusion that none of us really had any leads. Sitting back in his chair, feeling calmer than he had earlier, Lin took a short sip of his drink, then said,

"Mr. Hagee, can I ask you one last question?"

"Sure," I told him. "What the hell. Shoot."

"What directed you to Hong Kong? What made you come to look for Lu here?"

"What's brought in the other ones?" I asked.

"Various things. Some have followed the photographs. Context clues within them establish that the ones taken in Macau postdate the ones from the Riviera. Others have heard rumors of him being hidden by family here in Hong Kong. We have no intelligence that places any of Lu's family outside China except for some cousins in Canada and San Francisco, neither of which is Hong Kong.

"Then, of course," he added, taking another sip of his drink, "there are the weapons." Catching the look in my eye I allowed to slip, he asked,

"This means something to you?"

"Could be. My main information contact back home, that

major I told you about, he's pretty certain that a shipment of
U.S. government weapons that was stolen a while back was
earmarked for Lu and his movement.''

"And where were these weapons supposed to have been
shipped?" asked the captain.

"Lantau Island," I told him.

"Huuummm. Interesting," answered Lin, setting his drink
down. I could see he was trying to throw off the effects of
too much alcohol, working at clearing his mind before he
tried to pull anything more from me to add to the mix he
already had. Before he could, however, Peter suddenly
jumped in at that point, asking,

"Question—when did the weapons get stolen and when
did the pictures get taken?" Lin and I both looked at Peter,
wondering where he was headed. He told us.

"Answer—about three weeks apart, right?" Trying to
remember the dates in my head, it seemed close enough a
guess for me. A confirming grunt added the captain's
agreement. Keeping the stage, Peter put forth his theory.

"Jack's Major Rice wasn't real clear, but he made it sound
as if a lot of people died when they were taken. What if,
after all his talk about arming the people and bringing down
the Communists and all that, when he saw what happens when
you start pumping money into revolutions . . . innocent
people ending up dead . . . what if that got to him?"

The three of us sat in silence, listening to my junior
partner, half-amazed at how simple the answer seemed,
half-shocked we hadn't thought of it ourselves. As we all
reached for our drinks at the same time, Peter continued.

"What if the blood and all that comes with war—even
after seeing everything that happened at Tian'anmen—
didn't actually mean anything to him until he had a hand in
spilling it? I mean . . . if he *did* arrange for the weapons to
be stolen, and then found out that a lot of soldiers got
murdered so he could get his guns . . . I don't know . . ."
Peter's voice faded out for a moment, then returned, filled
with a faraway quality suggesting that he was thinking as
hard about what he was saying as he felt Lu might have.

"If he were to have thought about how many more people

might have to die just so they could collect up the weapons they needed just so they could *start* the killing—innocent people—I don't know . . . a few weeks of brooding, maybe he just said the hell with it and ran off with the cash. Better guys than him have lost it when they came up against the consequences of their actions."

I was impressed with Peter's logic. Suddenly pieces were beginning to fit one up against another. Having trouble with just one rough edge dragging against his theory, I asked the group,

"But why does a man with three billion dollars have to cause so much trouble the first time he tries to buy something? There are plenty of arms dealers in the world. No muss, no fuss. Just pay your money and take delivery. Why get involved with murder and theft if you've got a squeamish stomach in the first place?"

"Perhaps," offered Sing, "he was approached by a person who did not have a squeamish stomach. Perhaps a middle-man with access to Lu told him it was a good time to acquire weapons—made it sound like an easy thing. Perhaps Lu only discovered the blood his money had purchased after the fact."

I can't say what it was, but suddenly the air in the room changed. All of us looked at Sing, somehow aware that he was not reciting a theory as had Peter. Even Gigi, troubled by the shift in the atmosphere, came out from under her chair, staring up at her master, waiting for orders. The drug lord merely patted his knee, summoning the loyal dog to him. She rested her powerful jaw against his leg, making only the tiniest of sounds to let Sing know that she was troubled.

"Something you want to tell us, Sing?" asked the captain.

"Yes," admitted the drug lord, his voice sounding hurt. "I will tell you now, I was not the seller—I knew nothing of weapons being bought until Kon Li asked me to store them for him once he took delivery. Also, I never heard from him again after that time. It has not been until this moment that all has been made clear to me. If I had been able to piece this together as had our young Mr. Wei, I would have already acted upon it, I assure you."

And then suddenly Peter wasn't the only guy piecing things together. These were the weapons that had blown the hell out of my apartment. These were the weapons that had killed two guys I liked, one of them one of my best friends. Whoever Sing's mysterious seller was . . . I knew that was who had tried to kill me. My hands shaking slightly on the table before me, my cheek twitching past where I could stop it, I tried to speak, tried to ask Sing who the seller was. My mouth opened but nothing came out. Rage at the killer, fear that Sing might not know who he was, anxiety over needing to know—the three emotions tangled over each other, freezing in my throat. Finally, though, the moment passed and I was able to ask,

"Who was the seller, Sing?"

"He is an American . . . from your home, actually, Jack."

Making a fist out of my jumping right hand, keeping myself under control, I asked for the seller's name. Sing told me.

"Jackson In," he said. And then, I understood.

CHAPTER 28

IT WASN'T LONG before we had everything out in the open. Rice's weapons were in one of Sing's warehouses tucked away on Lantau, the largest of the Hong Kong islands. The drug lord gave us as much of the story as he knew. To the best of Sing's knowledge, when Kon Li Lu had come to New York City to give his speeches and gather in the cash, Smiler had approached him with a deal. As the leader of Mother's Blood Flowing, he said he could lay his hands on some very nice revolution-starting equipment. He had made the deal sound as if the weapons were sitting on a dock somewhere, waiting to be shipped out.

Lu had agreed on a price, arranging for Sing to take delivery. Sing did not know In at the time as anything other than a C.C.B.A. board member and an up-and-comer in the NYC drug trade and thus welcomed the connection. What he had not realized was that Smiler thought stealing a trainful of weapons from the United States Army using gang members as his strike force would be as easy as it looks in the movies. It turned out he was wrong. By the time his ill-fated robbery attempt was over, he and his survivors had escaped with the weapons, but eight of his people had to be left behind dead, along with twenty-seven servicemen in the same condition.

The weapons had been delivered as promised. Sing had taken care of payment out of funds transferred to him by Lu. But Lu had disappeared shortly after that, starting the entire controversy. Given that to work with, along with Peter's theory, the rest was easy. Sure, we figured, Lu heard of the slaughter caused by his purchase and it affected him bad.

Suddenly he saw money in a different light, as a weapon that could kill without even intending to do so. To think of someone getting hit with what he did going off the deep end into some wild throw-it-away spree was not all that hard.

The question was, what had happened to him after that? Where had he disappeared to? Or, more importantly to most people, where had his money disappeared to? Hoping to find out, Smiler had stirred up the C.C.B.A. and gotten them to approach me. Then, knowing me as well as he did, he decided to insure their investment by lighting a fire under my tail. I had no doubt that it was Jackson In that had ordered my apartment blown to bits. At first, Lin had rejected my logic.

"Doesn't make sense. In couldn't be the one who got the C.C.B.A. rolling. He wouldn't want Lu found. Lu would be the only one to connect him with the weapons' heist. Besides, why blow up your place? To kill you so you can't come to Hong Kong? Why send you in the first place?"

"For the same reason he said—to get his hands on three billion dollars. Remember, Captain, I didn't get killed. Someone sat waiting a long time for me to leave my apartment so they could make it look as if someone was trying to kill me." I laughed at myself for a moment, the bile of my stupidity threatening to choke me.

"What a lucky break that I stepped outside, huh?" I said, my voice hard and bitter. "How fortunate the triggerman chose to fire during the minute I chose to dump the trash, right? Yeah—right. At last, fate finally cuts Jack Hagee a break. Fuck."

I let it all sink in, sitting there thinking of what a chump I'd been . . . cursing myself for being the fortunate one while Carmine bought the farm. And all the time, it had been planned from the start. I thought of the different operations I'd been involved with when I was in the military, the "random" bombings we'd planned down to the second. I could see Smiler's men, binoculars raised, could feel their relief when they'd spotted me heading for the door, trash in hand, reliving it through the memory of having been them in the past.

Then I reminded myself not to get too carried away . . .
I'd never been one of them. I'd been trying to do my bit for
God and country. It hadn't been murder on consignment, not
just for profits and good times . . . maybe to some, but not to
me, anyway. Then the back of my mind started to remind me
of other things from those days, prompting me to just tell it to
shut up and stick with the present. Getting back to Sing and
Lin, I told them,

"In did it because it was the easiest way for him to keep
me focused. Remember, Captain, crooks think like crooks.
A dishonest person thinks everyone is dishonest. He didn't
want me hanging out at the horse track or taking the day off
to go antique hunting in Aberdeen. He wanted me on the
case twenty-four hours a day. If I found the weapons I'd
come as close to Lu's trail as anyone could. And, since
there'd be little chance I could find them and not find out
that they were Lu's, my guess is he hoped that I'd become
convinced Lu ordered the termination attempt."

"Meaning," suggested the captain dryly, "that his gamble
was he hoped to use your thirst for revenge to motivate you
to somehow find Kon Li Lu where the rest of the world
could not."

"Yeah," I said, feeling my confused anger starting to
focus, shifting from blaming me for Carmine's death toward
blaming his killer. "Something like that."

"Mr. In must be highly impressed with your abilities."

"At least, Captain Lin," added Sing, "with his tenacity."

"So then," asked Lin as I reached for my glass, "granting
all of this, what do you suggest we do next?"

I took another pull on my drink as he voiced his question,
letting the cold chill of the watery gin numb the back of my
throat. I let it last, feeling my teeth start to hurt from the ice.
Finally, however, I stopped short of finishing it and set my
glass back on the table, saying,

"Call him." When my suggestion met with universal
surprise, I repeated,

"Call him. We call him and tell him that we found the
weapons, that we have Lu . . . the whole nine yards. We
get him to come here and we nail him."

"Not to disrupt your revenge, Mr. Hagee," answered the captain, "I understand your emotions. But if I could remind you . . . we're supposed to be meeting here to decide what we can or should do about Kon Li Lu."

He let the statement hang in the air, but I knew what he meant. I also knew what I had to do next. Knocking back the last of my gin, I said,

"You and Sing and Peter, you three go to Sing's and give In a call." Pointing at the drug lord, I told him,

"You make the call. Tell him Lu finally surfaced. Said he was coming in for the weapons. Say he left you holding the bag and you're pissed off. Tell him the Americans are breathing down your neck and you just want out of the whole mess. Tell him you're ready to put the nab on Lu and you're willing to split the three billion with In if he gets rid of the weapons and Lu."

"But why would Sing have to call anyone in to help him?" asked Peter.

"Ahhh, because American gangster can kill Lu and it not be nearly as bad for him as for Hong Konger," said Sing, warming to the game. Playing his part as if he were already on the phone, he said,

"If I am caught with weapons, it is international incident. I already have fortune—ten fortunes. But what good they do me if American government is breathing down my neck? I not want to spend remaining days hounded around globe by C.I.A. . . . I have enough to worry about from Communists. I am old man . . . people are trying to kill me. I want out of this." Then, switching back to his regular voice, he added,

"He will believe it. Young dogs always willing to believe old dogs no longer have teeth."

"But," interrupted Lin, "although this is nicely balanced for pleasing the American government and easing your burdened conscience, Mr. Hagee, it does little for our main concern—finding Kon Li Lu."

Now it was my turn to look down at my empty glasses, licking the inside of my mouth, wishing I had at least one swallow of gin left. Making do with the memory of those I'd already had, I told the others,

"Okay—here it comes. I'm going to have to ask you all to trust me. This is going to sound like grandstanding, and well, hell, maybe it is, but that's the way it's got to be." I paused to suck in a deep breath, trying to force a little oxygen to my brain. Hoping some made it I continued, saying,

"I think I know how to find Kon Li Lu. I can't tell you what it is I know—not now. Not yet." Turning to Lin, staring into his eyes, I told him,

"I know it's asking a lot and that you don't have to go along with this, but I'm asking—no, let me go straight to the edge—I'm begging you . . . for reasons that . . ."

And then I stopped, taking another breath, not certain how to proceed, finding the need within me so important I couldn't figure how to express it. Taking pity on me, Lin held up his hand to stop me, asking at the same time,

"This is something very important to you, isn't it?"

I pursed my lips, nodding my head, half meeting his eyes, half not. Understanding, the captain dropped his own head for a moment, then looked up again, asking,

"Tell me, Mr. Hagee, if you had to choose between keeping whatever secret you seem to have suddenly discovered and avenging the death of your friends . . . which would you take? Which of these is more important?"

Without hesitating, realizing I might be selling Carmine's memory down the river, I told Lin,

"I really need to handle this my own way." The captain stared at me, considering my answer. Peter and Sing stared as well, not knowing what to make of my sudden tactics. Making up his mind what he thought, Lin asked,

"How much time do you need?"

"I can't say for sure, but probably only an hour or two."

"And you can do whatever it is you need to do without any assistance?"

"I'd prefer it that way."

"And you will be able to do this without getting killed?"

"Well," I told the captain, "I hope so." When he reminded

me that Sing's almost assassination might have been engineered by Smiler, I nodded, letting him know that that thought had crossed my mind. Waiting just a beat, Lin pushed his chair away from the table, his head nodding up and down as he did so. Standing, he said,

"I hope so, as well, Mr. Hagee." Then, looking at the others, he asked, "Mr. Sing, Mr. Wei, are we ready?"

Peter and the drug lord stood up, acknowledging that they were indeed ready. Both gave me curious looks, but neither asked what I was up to. I pushed the buzzer under the table, signaling Fel that we were ready to leave. She was there in a handful of seconds, unbolting the exit. As she did, the others stretched out their kinks, preparing to reenter the known world. As I kept my seat, suddenly Gigi crawled out from under the table and came over to me, placing her head on my leg. She stared up at me with her sad eyes, telling me how she felt with her honest dog face. Reaching down, I cupped the back of her head in my hand, scratching her ears, letting her know I appreciated her advice.

"You know, Jack," said Sing in a soft voice, tinged with his amazement, "if I didn't trust you before, I do now."

And then, he turned to follow Lin out into the hallway. Peter stopped long enough to give me a look that asked if there was anything he should know. I shook my head, trying to let him know I was sorry, but that there were just some things a man has to do on his own.

He gave me a little nod, then turned to follow Sing. Gigi jumped away from me then as well, running the few paces she needed to close the gap between her and her master. And then, Felecia stuck her head in, asking,

"You coming?"

"Yeah," I told her, standing slowly, not wanting to move. "Yeah. Let's get this over with."

CHAPTER 29

FEL AND I walked through the Five Great Grains, out from the hidden back rooms into the side dining area. Making our way around to the front, I noted that the place seemed pretty filled up for so late at night. Curious, I asked,

"What's the big draw?"

"It's showtime, Jack."

"You still singing headline?" She laughed at the question, from the back of her throat, deeply, but quietly. Shaking her head as we walked, she told me,

"Not for a long time . . . a very long time. No, Iris headlines." When I stopped in my tracks for a moment, Felecia, not understanding, turned with a smile and said,

"She's not your tiny little knee-bouncing baby girl anymore, 'Uncle Jack.' In case you hadn't noticed, she's grown up in a big way. . . ."

"Oh," I admitted, giving my voice enough of a leer to make a mother proud, but not enough to worry her, "don't worry. I noticed."

"And, I might add, she has her mother's voice, if not more so," added Fel, her pride overflowing. Moving us a few yards further into the club, she pushed me gently into a seat at the bar, saying,

"This is about the best seat left in the house. I don't care what intrigues you and your runabout playmates have brewing at the moment . . . you've got time to sit and watch your favorite niece do one song." She stopped for a moment, then locked her eyes into mine, asking,

"*One* song?"

Smiling back at her, I said,

"At least one, Fel."

Then I settled into my seat as the bartender came up to me and Fel went off to tend to whatever backstage duties she had. Feeling the effects of the amount of gin I'd already poured into my system, I decided to give myself a little breathing space. I asked the bar girl for a pot of chrysanthemum tea and then just folded my arms on the bar, waiting for the show. Straight ahead of me was the Grains' fairly standard arrangement of oversized mirror and liquor bottles. Staring at its center, however, I studied the bar's centerpiece, a stuffed alligator, roughly a yard long from tip to tip, with a baby crocodile riding its back. The alligator was done up with saddle, bit, and bridle, and the crocodile wore a miniature representation of the shirts the riders wore down at the Jockey Club. It had been a conversation piece in the bar for over thirty years. And, although no one was talking about it at that moment, it had my attention.

I stared at the pair, both sharp-toothed, both savage-looking, both cold-blooded monsters when one got right down to it. Two creatures from a species hated and feared by an overwhelmingly large part of our population, which was all right, I supposed. After all, they didn't think much of us except as food. I continued to look at the pair, fascinated by them. Two killers—one riding the other, directing it forward—both with their guts torn out, replaced with cotton and sand, mounted and put out on display for the amusement of the general public.

I didn't know what to make of it all in any higher sense, nor did I draw any conclusions from staring at the pair. I merely found myself wondering, looking at my own face reflected in the mirror behind them, which one I was. Was I the killer in charge, driving forth the slow-witted one, or was that me—the brute without even sense enough to know it was being wheeled about the landscape? And, I thought, if I was either one of them, who was the other—and who was it that set the two of us up to be laughed at in the first place?

Then, deciding that maybe it was just a stuffed alligator and crocodile after all, and that perhaps I had had enough gin for the night, I thanked the returning bartender for her promptness and poured myself a much needed cup of warm caffeine. Three sips into it, Felecia's voice came at all assembled through the club's sound system. With a minimum of fanfare, she introduced Iris to the crowd, her mother's pride coming across to those not in the know as press agent admiration. When the curtains parted and the headliner stepped out, however, the audience paid attention. Being a part of the audience, I was no different.

Iris walked up to the microphone at center stage slowly, as if she were almost hesitant. The extra moment gave the crowd time to soak in her looks, her costume, her attitude. The three went together very well.

Her looks were as dazzling as they had been earlier in the day, but more so. Before it had just been her street look, the makeup of a girl going out looking her best in the early morning. This, however, was the look of an attractive woman—not one who desired to be attractive, but one who, no matter what she wanted, would be attractive. Her costume didn't hurt, either. The skirt was long and flowing, ebony black covered with golden rosebuds, just like her jacket—the edges of each as well as her cuffs heavily embroidered in a golden pattern of full roses growing in and around each other. It was her attitude, however, that made it all come together.

The looks spoke of a younger woman than the costume was designed for. Her hair was cut for a young woman— her hips and breasts were still those of a young woman— but her attitude . . . that was what justified the sweeping skirt and the smocked waist, the jeweled neck jacket and the mid-calf length skirt. Her attitude said that she was of an age to wear the costume—that she had seen enough of life, tasted enough joy and pain to understand sorrow, to know what love was, and to do any damn thing she pleased.

As her hands reached for the microphone, I suddenly found myself wondering exactly what she was going to sing. I was intrigued. Before I'd run into her that morning, she had been just a kid I'd tucked in at night and made Bullwinkle jokes with. After this morning she suddenly transformed into a dazzlingly beautiful woman, one who was young and happy and in love. Now, she was suddenly a force of nature. As her fingers closed on the mike, I realized I didn't have the slightest clue as to what she was going to sing. Deciding I didn't mind being surprised, I sat back to listen. As I sipped my tea, she told me,

> "Have you ever met him?
> Have you ever seen his face?
> And if you met him?
> Did you find a trace . . .
>
> "Of what I meet, of what I see . . .
> In him."

It was a bad boy song, one of those slow, mournful nobody-understands-Johnny-like-I-do ballads. In this one, however, unlike the majority of the genre, it didn't seem as if the singer was deluding herself. "Johnny" here came across as truly misunderstood—not as a guy with a cluelessly naive girlfriend. I wondered if it were really the writing in the song or the strength of the conviction in Iris's voice that was doing that particular selling job.

> "There are those who want to hurt him,
> Those that cannot play fair,
> Those that don't understand him,
> And those that just don't care.
>
> "There are people everywhere,
> Who want to see my baby dead,
> Not because of what he's done,
> Or because of anything he's said."

I sipped my tea as she launched into the chorus again, deciding it was a little of each. Iris's Johnny had to have done something to stir up so many people against him. On the other hand, however, when a woman as perfect as the one singing said that her man was innocent, there was something that stirred inside, wanting to give her the benefit of the doubt.

I found myself wondering if any entertainment types had come around with a contract yet—any silk-suited piranhas nibbling at the door, looking to cart off the green-eyed beauty on the stage with the great voice and the overwhelming capacity to maintain faith in her man. There had to have been, I told myself. Hong Kong was too small a place with too many deal-makers, too many hotshots—too many people looking to put their money to work, to try something fresh, to shake up the world with their hot new discovery. There had to be a record contract or two sitting on Iris's desk. Someone, somewhere had to be trying to shove her into some other type of music, something hotter, hipper, some watered-down pabulum for the youth of the world to suck on.

> "I will never leave him,
> No matter what they say,
> When they tell me their lies,
> All that I can pray . . . is,
>
> "Have you ever met him?
> Have you ever seen his face?
> And if you met him?
> Did you find a trace . . ."
>
> "Of what I meet, of what I see . . .
> In him."

The punch Iris put into her ending brought the house down. Men and women throughout the audience were putting their hands together violently, filling the air with applause. Some of them had tears in their eyes. I looked over at the bar girl watching Iris accept her tribute, adoration in her eyes for the woman in black and gold on the stage. As the next number and the one after that came and went, I watched everyone in the place, just to see their reactions as well.

It was interesting. When someone we know does well in an entertainment career—dancing, stand-up comedy, painting, writing, singing, whathaveyou—it's always hard to understand how someone we know, just another person in our lives, could be special to other people. But Iris had become very special, and listening to her act, I had to wonder why she hadn't become even more famous than she was.

She finished her set as I finished my tea. Thanking the audience for its enthusiastic response, she left the stage headed for my spot at the bar. I didn't know if Fel had told her I was part of the audience or if she had spotted me on her own, but I thought, what did it matter? As she approached, I held my hands out in front of me, giving her a little fatherly applause, answering the question in her eyes. Her smile widened at the sight, making what I had to do next all the harder. As she positioned herself on the stool next to me, I figured it was best to just dive in, so I said,

"I don't want to look like a creep who's trying to catch you off guard . . . so I'll just come out and ask you. Where is he, Iris?" When she just stared at me, her look letting me know that I was going to have to go the extra step, I didn't wait for her to ask "who?" I just told her.

"Kon Li Lu, sweetheart. Where's your boyfriend?"

CHAPTER 30

FOR A MOMENT it looked as if she was going to embarrass both of us with a lie. She thought about it. I could see it on her face. She knew I knew, though, and spared us both the bother of arguing. Rather than say anything further, she took my arm and led me into the back corridors of the Five Great Grains. For no particular reason we took over her mother's office. She sat in one of the chairs in front of Fel's desk, I took the other. Then, once we were settled and there was nothing else left to keep us from getting down to things, she asked,

"How did you know?"

"There are photos of Lu circulating," I told her. "Gambling on the Riviera, in Macau. You're in the same photos. It took me a while to notice you in them. The first time I studied them, of course, I wasn't looking for you. Even if I had been, I would have probably forgotten that you might go ahead and grow up on me. I saw them again tonight, though. There was no missing you, then. I'm surprised no one else has made the connection."

"I'm not sure no one has," she told me cryptically. As I stared, waiting for an explanation, she said,

"I know about the photos. And yes, they've got me worried, all right. Luckily there are no extremely clear shots of my face. Mom didn't think anyone who didn't know me personally would be able to tell. Of course, neither of us thought we'd be seeing you over this." When I stiffened slightly, involuntarily reacting to what sounded like a wish I'd never showed up, Iris sensed my discomfort immediately, telling me,

"Oh, no, Uncle Jack—that didn't come out right. I mean, it is true . . . we didn't think you'd show up in Hong Kong looking for Kon. It doesn't mean I'm sorry you're here." Not wanting to argue with her at that point, I just nodded and smiled, listening as she continued.

"Anyway, I've been keeping a low profile ever since the pictures surfaced. I've turned down a couple of very tempting offers over the past few months—tours, a record contract, that kind of thing—to keep people from getting the chance to make the connection." Looking up at me then, finally making clear eye contact, she told me,

"I've been trying to keep myself from looking like I do in the photos. Nothing obvious, like dying my hair—I thought that would just attract attention. Mom said the easiest way to throw people off would be to change my attitude, instead. Since I look pretty college-brat in the pictures, I decided to keep the show girl image up in public."

When she had first mentioned her mother it had come as no surprise to me that Felecia was in on everything, too. Iris's mentioning her again, however, got me to thinking. How about Li Tsim? Was he in on everything as well? Was everyone in the Grains working together to keep me in the dark? Iris's protestations to the side, did the people there distrust me or not? Keeping my wounded feelings at bay, reminding them that a fifteen-year absence can have a legitimate effect on people's judgments, I asked,

"But you're not sure it's working?"

"No. There have been a lot of people in the Grains that Mom is sure are looking for Kon. She's spotted running shifts. A couple of the groups have kept people in here every minute we're open for weeks now."

I nodded, feeling something of the chump. I'd seen Slaner and the others and assumed that if they were there they had to be revolving around me. Sometimes my ego gets a bit out of control. It also dawned on me that I was in an even bigger mess than I'd thought. Was I supposed to go chasing after Iris's man now? And even if I caught him, what was I supposed to do with him?

As questions began to fill my head, a voice from the back

of my brain told me that perhaps it would be best if I started asking some of Iris. Figuring it best to take that advice, I reached over and took one of Iris's hands in mine. She accepted the gesture, a fact that improved my feelings over the whole situation intensely.

If she'd reacted with fear or tension I'd have been worried, wondering if she and Fel were setting me up as well. She didn't, however, and suddenly the little girl I'd known and loved back when the whole rest of the world around us had seemed a nightmare was in the chair across from me. Patting the hand I was holding with my free one, I asked her,

"Iris, I'm sorry, but I've got to ask you this—do you still trust me?"

"Uncle Jack, I . . . ah . . ." She wanted to resist, wanted to stop herself and do something—I didn't know what—that was somehow against her nature. She didn't, however, instead telling me, "Yes. Yes I do. I'm tired of being afraid and scared of everyone."

She looked into my face, past the scars she'd noted earlier, down to the oversized playmate she remembered from her childhood. "If I can't trust you," she declared in a voice that made it sound as if she had just made the decision, "then I can't trust anybody."

"Good," I told her, knowing that if she could still feel something that honest that she had to still be honest herself. Now all I had to do was find out why she and Kon Li Lu had been spending money that wasn't theirs. Wanting to start at the beginning, however, I asked her,

"Sweetheart, do you love this guy?"

"Yes," she said, strong and proud and happy to do so, "I do. He's just the best man I've ever known—when I first heard him speak, heard him talk about what he wanted to do, he was so different from anyone I'd ever met. He wanted to change things, lots of things—big things."

She went on for a while in the same vein, telling me about how important Lu's work was, how she had gotten involved in his cause, how they had come together, how things had gone beyond crusader and crusadee. By the time she started telling me about Lu the boyfriend and lover as opposed to Lu the champion of the oppressed, I was beginning to get a fairly good picture.

I was sure Iris was in love, but on top of that I was also fairly sure that she wasn't having the wool pulled over her eyes. All along the way, some of it with a lot of prompting from Fel, she seemed to have asked the right questions, doubted things when an intelligent person would. She'd had a number of sour relationships before Lu, including a father-figure kind of thing in college that had cured her of taking too much at face value. On top of those revelations, she put a sad smile on her face as she reminded me,

"And it's not hero worship, either. I got that out of my system waiting for you to come back to Hong Kong."

Knowing I was being teased, at least a little, I pulled at my collar in an exaggerated manner, saying,

"Fine—go ahead, torture me—drag me over the coals. Jeez'o Pete . . . and to think that you used to be such a sweet little girl."

We traded our quips back and forth for another moment, but then Iris changed the feel of things for us. Maybe she wanted to save me the discomfort of asking. Maybe she just wanted to get it off her chest. Whatever the case, her tone got very serious suddenly as she asked,

"I know you're being nice about things, but truthfully, you need to know why we spent the money—don't you?"

Taken somewhat aback by her abruptness, but grateful for the chance to get down to the facts, I told her,

"Well, yes, actually—now that you bring it up. When you come right down to it, a lot really does hinge on the answer to that question."

And then, before anything more could be said, the door to Felicia's office banged open. I spun around in my chair, too slow to be able to do anything except watch Saul Cronberg and Louis Perreau come through the door, preceded by two others I could only assume to be working for them. Their thugs were both packing heat, one of them openly. Ignoring me, which considering the circumstances did not seem to be very much of a mistake, Perreau, wearing a lightweight set of extremely sophisticated headphones, looked down at Iris, telling me,

"Yes—our Mr. Jack is most correct. That is indeed a most important question. So, if you would please, tell us why you spent the money—won't you? And then," he added, a sneer filling his round, pasty face,

"Tell us where it is."

CHAPTER 31

"YOU FUCKING IDIOTS," I yelled, filling my voice with the depressed snarl of a gym teacher whose class just can't get up the rope. "Now? You break in . . . now?"

"What are you jabbering about, Mr. Jack?" asked Perreau, his face drawn into a puzzled expression. "Perhaps you think we hold some kind regard for you after all these years?"

"Oh, and who could care? You pack of jerks. I spend all this time priming this stupid, empty-headed bitch and you jokers come in and . . ." After that I simply threw my hands in the air, trying to convey as great a feeling of hopelessness as I could. Cronberg narrowed his always suspicious eyes more so than usual. Staring at me, he said to his partner,

"Do not listen to him."

"Why?" asked Perreau. Amusement playing in his eyes, both at having the drop on me and at his partner's concern, he said in a laughing voice, "Are you afraid of our poor, helpless Mr. Jack?"

"I am afraid of you being too stupid to see through his little game here."

"Oh?" responded Perreau. Looking at Cronberg, he pointed toward Iris, saying, "And is our little flower here playing a game as well? Look at her face. She is entertaining the notion now that her sweet Uncle Jack is just another money-hungry bastard, and she is crestfallen." When Cronberg failed to respond, Perreau prodded him, saying,

"You Jews are so serious. You know nothing of women. Look at her, I tell you. Give our Mr. Jack what credit you

217

will, but I say . . . look at that girl." Crossing over to Iris's chair, he ran his index finger under her chin. The action made her close her eyes as her whole body shuddered, seemingly proving the Frenchman's point as he said,

"You see? Look at the embarrassment, look at the hurt." Grabbing her chin, he turned her face toward Cronberg, telling him,

"Look into her eyes. Whatever our Mr. Jack is up to, *she* is believing it." Unhanding Iris, Perreau turned back to me, saying,

"Now, it is up to us to see whether or not we believe him as well. So, please, Mr. Jack, talk to us. Make *us* believe."

"What?" I answered. "You think I'm cutting you clowns in on this? Fuck that. I've worked too hard on this one to give it away now."

"Please, do not bluff with me, Mr. Jack. I am giving you an opportunity to stay in the game. Do understand, I am as intrigued as always with your flare for the theatre of the moment. You have a rare talent for turning events on a instant's notice. But, if you are trying to play an empty hand, I must warn you that this is not the table for such things." Pointing to his headset, he announced,

"We have heard every word of your conversation. We know all about our poor dear one here and her passion for the fiery young Mr. Kon. So, weave your tale very finely, very quickly, and also, very soon. Entertain and inform, otherwise we shall be forced to kill you and begin working on our little Miss Iris." Then he sat in another of the room's chairs, giving me a flourish of his hand to signal that he was ready for my performance. Taking an involuntary deep breath, I leaned forward in my chair to give him one.

"First off," I said, "you don't have to work on her. Hell, I know where the money is."

"Oh, shut him up," spat Cronberg, moving forward. Perreau put up a hand, however, signaling the man without a drawn weapon. The second thug moved slightly into the path between Cronberg and myself, subtly indicating that perhaps the Israeli should calm down. Undisturbed, Perreau turned back to me, saying,

"So, Mr. Jack . . . you know where the money is. Then why is it you have not gone and taken it and retired from this place to one less dangerous and more . . . stimulating?"

"Because it's not the money I'm after." Perreau's smile grew wider, breaking into a toothy affair that filled his face. Sitting back in his chair, looking as if he were almost ready to break into applause, he said,

"Ah, Cronberg, and you would have us miss all of this. You are a fine man to work such a thing with . . . we have made a splendid team and as you can see we shall soon be rewarded. But let us take the fun with the profit." Then, turning back to me, he said with a flourish,

"And now, oh please, Mr. Jack, tell us why you do not wish to confiscate Mr. Lu's billions. Tell us what could be more important to you."

I did. I gave them the straight truth, telling them about Sally, about getting drunk, about Carmine and Francis and Rice. By the time I was telling them about the major's files listing them as two of the most dangerous people who might be in my way, even Cronberg was listening without impatience. I kept playing to the crowd, working on getting them to understand that all I wanted was Carmine's killer. Then, seeing that the quartet was growing relaxed enough for me to try something, I played the last bit I had, hoping it was enough.

"That's why I don't appreciate your interference. I don't need to know where the money is. Just Lu. He's the one that blew my place to bits . . . had it done, anyway."

"That's not true!" shouted Iris, indignant and hurt, unbelieving that I could have turned out to be such a total shit. Not daring to show her anything like the truth in my eyes, I wheeled on her—raising my arm as if to slap her—growling,

"Shut up. Get it through your head you little bitch that I don't give a good goddamn what you think. I know what happened . . . hell, your own mother knows what happened." That stunned her. That she had no answer for me was obvious to the entire room. I hated watching her flinch away from me almost as much as our audience seemed to enjoy it. Using the moment for what good I could get out of it, I took her pain as my cue, saying,

"Don't believe me? Well, what a surprise. I didn't think you would, but you'll believe this." Getting up out of my chair, I circled Fel's desk, ignoring Iris, telling the quartet holding us,

"Wait 'til you see this. Her mother's got a stack of papers locked up on Lu, I've been through them. Looks like even Mom wants the little fuck's blood money. Wonder when she was going to get around to using them against you?"

Perreau was completely entranced by the show, sitting by hungrily, waiting for more details. Cronberg I'd interested when I'd started to treat Iris badly. European and Middle Eastern men have come to believe that an American couldn't possibly raise his voice to a woman, let alone play them for a fool. That takes their own special brand of sophistication. Hoping I could count on them to stay sophisticated for just another minute, I opened Felecia's bottom drawer, digging through the papers in the front for the box I hoped was still in the back.

"You're going to love this, you stupid cunt. Everything you've told her, every secret the two of you had . . . it's right here." As my fingers touched metal, I pulled the box forward, my fingers trying to determine its contents from its weight alone. As I got it out from the back, I rested it on the edge of the drawer, saying,

"Here's the kind of person your mother is, bitch."

Cracking the box's combination, the same left-right-left that had opened it fifteen years ago, I blessed Fel's name. There was my service .45, in exactly the same place I'd put it a decade and a half earlier when I swore I'd never handle a gun again. Fat lot of good that vow'd done me, I thought sourly. Pushing the notion from my head, however, I threw out a few more lines of my phony tirade, preparing to take my chance.

I could see that the clip was still in it. Of course, I reminded the portion of my brain trying to plan things, it could have been an empty clip, it could have been that fifteen years might be too long to not clean a weapon, let alone fire it. And even then the damn thing might blow up in my hand. But, it was also the only chance Iris and I had. Deciding an only chance was better than no chance, I pulled it out of the box and then straightened up and came out shooting.

I put the first bullets into the thug with the drawn weapon—the first slug plowing through his head, the second through his throat. The other got two in the upper chest before he could clear his own weapon. He went down in a gurgling pile, slamming into Cronberg as he spung around, a spray of hot scarlet blasting half the room as he fought to keep his balance, coating the floor when he lost it.

Not knowing whether Cronberg was carrying or not—not caring—I put one through his side and then another through his head. He had launched himself across the room at me, would have gotten his arms around my throat if I hadn't managed to send him flying backwards with my first shot. After that, I saw little choice other than to give him another.

First off, of course, he was the type who might have been armed, anyway. Second, not only was he the type that no one would ever want to avenge, but he was also the type who would have come after me twenty years later if he had to—to extract whatever kind of revenge he would have felt his dignity demanded after having been made a fool of. Third, he was the only one that had wanted me dead—regardless.

Perreau, on the other hand, never went armed, and had at least seemed to be willing to let me live. On a personal level I disliked him much more than I did Cronberg, but letting personalities interfere with work like ours is always dangerous. I shook my head for a moment, trying to shake the vicious ringing all the gunfire had started within it. I knew Iris and Perreau would be the same—guns in enclosed spaces always create the instantly hard-of-hearing. Not worrying about that for the moment, though, I moved in on Perreau.

Knowing I had him where I wanted him, I came around the desk, pointing my .45 at him, smiling as I growled loudly in my best gangster movie voice,

"Now, fat boy. Youse and mes is gonna talk."

CHAPTER 32

"INDEED," ASKED THE Frenchman, raising his own voice to be heard over the ringing in his ears, "and what is it that you want to talk about, eh, Mr. Jack?"

Perreau was one cool number . . . even I had to give him that much. Keeping my .45 aligned with his face, knowing he simply wasn't the type to give me any trouble when there were still percentages to be played, I called Iris over to my side, asking her,

"Are you all right, sweetheart?"

"Yes, yes, I'm . . . Uncle Jack . . . is everything, I mean, what you said . . ."

"Iris," I said in the softest voice I had that she would be able to hear, "everything's fine. Don't worry. No, I don't know where the money is and I don't think your Kon had my friends killed. I do want to know where he is and I do want to talk to him, but those are things better attended to after we've taken care of our friend here." Then, turning back to Perreau, I asked him,

"Don't you agree?"

"Let us say, Mr. Jack, that I do not disagree. Not too strenuously, anyway."

"Good to hear that you can be so cooperative, Louie. Now, spill it . . . what do you know that you can give me that will get you out of here alive?"

But then, before Perreau could begin to answer, Felecia burst through the door with half the help in the place. I looked at her, almost sheepishly, saying,

"I thought you had this place soundproofed?"

"Against street noise, you idiot. Even over the band I

could hear that something was going on back here." Seeing that things seemed to be under control, Fel dismissed all but two of her people, then shut the door. After getting the guns up off the floor and making sure Iris was all right, she asked,

"Now, just what the hell have you been doing?"

"I know about Iris and Lu." Indicating the bodies strewn about the office, with a wave of my hand, I added,

"So did these gentlemen—including chubby, here. They forced the issue—I played my hand. Now it's just me and Louie. He was about to tell me how he plans to keep the floor clean by convincing me not to shoot him, too."

"Don't even bother," answered Fel, her voice a bitter sneer. Indicating Perreau with an accusing hand and a hard stare, she said,

"This piece of crap was threatening Iris? You were threatening *my* daughter, you sack of shit? Why should he even get to live? These other sons of bitches had guns, right? Let's just kill him with one of those guns. We'll put your gun in his hand and let Uncle Robert sort it out."

The Frenchman looked into Fel's eyes and was chilled by the sight. He knew she wasn't kidding. As far as she was concerned, the difference between killing three or four people in her office was too negligible a concern. Turning to me, he could see that the years had no more improved his standing in my eyes than had his performance of a few minutes earlier. But, he also knew that mine was the deciding vote. His smile fading, he asked me in a humbler, almost halting voice,

"Mr. Jack, this is not . . . a thing we must take to, how to put it—extremes? Yes, no? I was not your enemy earlier. It was not me calling to execute you. No. That was my . . . can we say 'former' partner? That could change. I could be your partner . . . I could help you get what you want. You could help me get what I want."

Saul Cronberg I had gunned down. I was mad and scared and knew he wanted me dead. That wasn't the case with Perreau, though. He was different than Cronberg. And, truth to tell, I had to admit that I wasn't up for killing anyone in blood that cold. Intrigued by the Frenchman's offer, wondering what he might have that I might want, I asked,

"And what is it that I want, Perreau?"

"You want to avenge your dead friends. I heard you before. Yes, your little trick fooled me very well, *c'est la vie, c'est la guerre* . . . what is done is done, no?"

Not daring to smile yet, nor to turn his eyes away from mine, he continued on, saying,

"It was a trick that worked because that much of it was true. You want to make the killers who took the lives of your two friends pay. I believe that you are really not interested in Mr. Lu or his billions. I do not like you for several reasons, Mr. Jack, the foremost of them the fact that you can only be hired—never bought. You and your type with your stone-etched ethics . . . you are all too hard to deal with." Perreau broke eye contact then. It was an involuntary reaction, a blink and a shudder that showed his distaste for the subject at hand. He recovered instantly, however, saying,

"But, there is one good thing about such behavior. If I cannot employ it, at least I can predict it. If we were to, as you Americans say, cut a deal . . . then I know that if you were to promise me what I wanted for my cooperation with you, I know you would move the heavens themselves—or at least attempt it—to keep your word. In my current circumstances . . . what more could I ask?"

I thought about what he was saying, wondering how far I could trust him. Not very far, I was sure. Still, as long as I didn't promise him anything I would regret delivering, what was the harm? Seeing that I was at least willing to listen to the Frenchman, Fel advised,

"Easier to kill him, Jack. Why even listen?"

I gave Iris's mother a look, trying to get across to her that I had enough to wrestle with for the moment. Looking over at Iris, I asked,

"How about it, little sweetheart? What do you think of your mom's plan? Do *you* want me to blow our pal here away? And if I do, do you want to be in the room when it's done?" When she didn't answer, I reminded her,

"Think about it. Perreau is the only person we know of

standing between you and Lu and whatever you've got planned. He could cause you a lot of trouble."

"Please," interrupted the Frenchman, showing a side of him I would have never expected, but probably should have. Looking back and forth from Fel to me to Iris, he said, "Do not put this poor young one through such as this. What you will do you will do. It is not fair to involve her vote as if you would listen—and please . . . let us not argue." Staring at me at that point, he added,

"You are not one to kill me in cold blood, Mr. Jack. It is not your way. And, although I am sure our lovely proprietess might be happy to do it for you, I do not even think you would allow that. The game we are playing now is over how much discomfort you are going to put me through, and for how long, before I am finally released by you. It is over whether or not the police will be brought in to the picture. We all know this, except possibly our young Iris here." Turning toward her, he said,

"They will not harm me, little one, unless of course my behavior toward you calls you to join your mother in wishing for my head to be served up à la carte. You have seen enough of that side of life within this affair. You do not need to see any more."

Setting the .45 down on Felecia's desk, I clapped my hands together, applauding Perreau's performance. He was correct and he knew it, which made some ways of working harder, but others easier. Always willing to go the easy way, I turned to Fel and said,

"Have your boys take care of the bodies. Do you still use . . . ?" She cut me off, saying,

"We don't have to discuss it. I don't want a pile of corpses leaking all over my office any more than you do." She directed her people to get started on removing the dead, then turned to her daughter, asking her,

"Iris . . . what do you want, honey?" She looked from her mother to me, then from me to Perreau. Looking back to her mother, she said,

"I just want to get Kon and myself out of all this. If we could . . . be *happy*? Is that too much to ask?"

Her voice was so sweet, so naive, so tender in its strained pleading that she broke every heart in the room. Turning to Perreau, I caught him wiping at his eye. It was a quick wipe—secretive and embarrassed—but I believed it all the same. Looking down at him, I asked,

"So, now we come to you."

"*Oui . . . ?*"

"Yeah, you. You told me what I wanted out of this. So, now let's hear it. What do you want?"

"Of course, Mr. Jack. If I were to state my desire directly, I do not think you would believe me. So, permit me to explain a bit. I think that if you could righteously claim Mr. Kon's billions that you would be happy to do so. Avenging your friends is not the only thing you want . . . it is the thing you want most. In this context, I do not wish Mr. Kon's billions, either."

"No?" I asked, curious, almost ready to trust his tone. "Okay. For the sake of argument, I'll bite. What is it that you want most?"

"My freedom. To be allowed to live, to avoid police and deportation and ugly embarrassments and having my hands strapped behind my back. I am old and such things are wearisome. If I could get out of this affair losing no more than I already have, at this point I would consider that almost a victory."

I thought about it for a moment, wondering what would happen if I agreed. I was sure the Frenchman had something to offer me, which if I did things his way he seemed ready to give over. My instincts told me he was being up-front. The problem with untrustworthy people is that they can be up-front one minute and then stab you in the back the next.

The biggest problem I had was that Perreau wasn't the only one feeling old and weary. I was starting to lose my focus. Things hadn't shaped up in any way as I thought they might and suddenly I just wanted things to be over. Also knowing that I was still the one with the guns, I figured what the hell . . . I wanted to see his cards. Calling for an end of the game, I threw my last chips in, saying,

"All right, you have anything I need, at the very least I

won't bother the police with our little differences. Now, what do you have that would interest me?"

"I have been working many ends against each other here. I knew it was foolish, but at my age . . . I don't know . . . perhaps I was hoping to be able to make a grand sweep of the board and disappear with the riches. Who knows? Anyway, to be honest I am almost grateful you killed Cronberg. As I was playing off against my employer, he was his. We teamed to try and turn against them both, but . . ." The Frenchman made a futile gesture with his arms, rolling his world-weary eyes at me as he shrugged off his folly. I asked,

"And who were you working for?"

"Sil Hung Yee."

I stopped short, frozen on the edge of the desk. Rice had been right again . . . the Communists were involved, and using the best of their agents. Perreau explained that he had been contacted by her operatives and paid to turn over all information he could find on Lu. So far, his healthy respect for the legends surrounding Yee's skill as someone who could make life unpleasant had forced him to turn over everything he had found. Which meant that she knew everything he had learned up until his listening in on my various conversations that day. Not a pleasant thing to discover. The next thing he had to offer was more useful.

"Fine," I said, obviously not meaning it. "Well, it's better I know such things, I guess. But you said you and Cronberg were both working for different people. Who was he working for?"

"Ahhh," answered Perreau with a smile, knowing he was giving me the kicker, "like yourself, Mr. Jack, his employer was Jackson In." The Frenchman let his words sink in, then added,

"Small world, *n'est-ce pas?*"

CHAPTER 33

I FLICKED A butt over the railing as the hydrofoil glided smoothly across the top of the thick green sea at high speed. Its engines kicked up a great deal of spray, boiling the ocean behind us and filling the air with a thick metal din. The police's fast assault vehicle was incredibly noisy and almost as uncomfortable, but it was the fastest thing available and thus the best bet we had.

Things had come together and fallen apart in equal measure when Perreau had named Jackson In as Cronberg's employer. From there he went on to tell me that Smiler was in Hong Kong at that moment, wanting to direct his search for the three billion personally and up close. At that point things began to make sense. The only problem was what to do about them.

I went to my meeting with Sing, Lin, and Peter with Perreau, Fel, and Iris in tow. I brought the others up to speed as quickly as possible. I told them about everything, including the shooting in the Grains, and then tried to get everyone to agree on what should be done next. Seized by a sudden inspiration, Lin led us to interrogation. Taking Perreau to the room with the shooter who had tried to kill Sing, he asked the Frenchman if he knew the man. Perreau identified him as one of Cronberg's contacts.

Armed with that information, the captain joined his interrogating detective, asking the shooter if the death of Cronberg meant anything to him. Within a half hour we knew that Smiler had commissioned Sing's attempted murder. Now both Sing and I wanted Smiler to go down. Of course, what we needed to do then was convince Captain Lin.

"We're coming up on the beach, Jack."

I thanked Peter for the information, pulling myself out of my trance. Without thinking I fired another Camel, taking a long drag. After another, just as tasty as the first, I pulled my .45 from the shoulder holster the captain had loaned me, checking the smoothness of the draw.

Lin had called upon an old Royal Colony law, giving himself the power to deputize Peter and myself. Of course, with my typical luck, the law only allowed him to grant us limited legal status, meaning we had to bring our own guns. Thus, while the men prepared to disembark, all of them weighted down with automatic weapons, shields, truncheons, tear gas, and God knew what else, Peter and I had to make due—me with my old service .45, him with the gun we'd taken from the downed thug in Fel's office.

"So, Mr. Hagee, do you think this is all going to come off without a hitch?"

"Nothing comes off without any hitches, Captain," I told Lin. "If you want guarantees, shop at Sears." He smiled at me, an action that threw me so far off it got him to smile even wider. When I questioned his sudden cheerfulness, he told me,

"Things have changed now—so I have with them. We are about to dispatch fearsome criminals, so the Crown is happy. Since they are fearsome capitalist criminals, China is also happy. I am also about to clear my home of great bins of trouble. Finishing off this Kon Li Lu affair will drive a great number of undesirables from our shore . . ."

"Like myself?"

"You . . . ?" he said with a question, as if he had forgotten that I was a part of that list. Looking at me, giving me a smile that curled only one side of his mouth, he answered,

"You I could tolerate . . . if you stopped finding guns in drawers and killing people with them."

"Self-defense . . . cleaning up the streets . . . protecting innocent women . . . averting ugly headlines . . . doing my citizen's duty . . . ahhh, let me think—I'm sure I can come up with a few more."

"Unnecessary," he said, waving a hand before me. "The fact that everything you just said is true, and that you have cooperated in every way is why you are here with me on this launch instead of behind bars." Swallowing hard, as if trying to keep down an ugly truth, the captain said,

"I'll needle it for you, Hagee—three billion American dollars is a big pie. The Hong Kong force is an exceptional group these days, but . . ." He let his voice trail off, then finished, saying,

"You're both here, you and your partner, because I need bodies, period. Understand?"

"Why, loud and clear, Captain," I offered innocently. Trying to break the tension with a little fuck-you humor, I told Lin in a conspiratorial tone,

"But, you know, I was thinking. We've got to retire too, right? Maybe we could skim just a little off the top—what the heck? Just a couple million a piece . . . heck, beer money. What do you say?"

And then, the captain simply threw his head back and laughed. It was short but loud, and satisfying to hear. Reining himself back in, Lin said,

"You do not act like a typical American private eye."

"Sure I do," I told him. "I'm as typical as they come. Nobody does that 'Hawaii 5-0' shit. That's just for the movies and the rubes that don't know any better."

And then, the hydrofoil began to convert itself back into a regular boat. Minutes later we were in the harbor, Lin and his men thundering down the deck while the ship crew was still tying up. Four vehicles were waiting for us—one bus, two private cars, and one truck—as the captain had expected. None of them bore any official markings.

As we climbed aboard our assigned transports, I felt the itch climbing my back—the itch that said we were still a long way from target, but that I wanted to start doing something violent right away. I hadn't felt that way for a long time, more years than I could count. Then again, no one had killed a good friend of mine in a long time. Images began flooding my brain—the sight of Carmine's burning skull came back to me, the look on Balto's face, Francis's crumpled body, the blood and smoke and fire-tossed shadows—the helpless feeling that had run through me at that moment was finally being replaced, but not by anything particularly better or even helpful.

I could feel my temper rising, felt my ability to control myself slipping, being taken over by a beast that wanted nothing more than to kill Jackson In. Noticing the look on my face, Peter asked quietly,

"You okay, Jack?"

"Yeah, sure," I told him. Then I explained by asking, "You ever kill anyone, Peter?"

"Um, no—actually."

"Well," I said, "it's an ugly thing. It changes you forever and each time you run into someone you'd like to kill it just makes it easier."

"You thinking that you might want to, ah, run into Jackson In tonight?"

"Yeah, I'd like to run into him tonight, right. Right now, that would be about the easiest thing in the world."

Peter didn't say anything else. Neither did I. We merely sat in our car, watching Lin direct his men into the other vehicles, waiting for everyone to have a seat so we could move out. Everything was going to be over in the next few hours, one way or the other. After Lin's people had confirmed that Smiler had put the X on Sing's head, we'd had to turn to Fel and Iris. It was up to them.

They told us that Lu had been hiding out in the Five Great Grains for quite a while, secreted in one of the place's hidden rooms. After I had arrived, however, they had been afraid I might sniff him out at the Grains, so he had moved on to Lantau Island, taking refuge at the monastery there. The island was a weekend vacation spot for locals as well as a tourist attraction. The locals went for the beaches and the little day apartments. Tourists came for the Po Lin Monastery, home of the world's largest outdoor Buddha.

Hide in plain sight, Poe had said. Kon Li Lu's problem now, however, was that his plain sight was the same as

Smiler's. Sing's warehouses—the ones housing Lu's weapons—were on property owned by the Po Lin monks. To make a long story short, when we finally had all the pieces of the puzzle in one place, we found that Smiler had taken a large group of his local drug pirates to get the weapons.

Jackson In, according to his man, was making his big move. He had sent Perreau and Cronberg on a wild-goose chase to lead people away while he stormed Sing's warehouses, armed his men, and then went after Lu, himself. According to the timetable we got out of the thug in Lin's detention, we were already three hours behind Smiler when we started.

Thus the captain's acceptance of Peter and myself as crew . . . thus his turning over of Perreau to Sing to keep him quiet until we returned . . . thus his release of Felecia and Iris. If Kon Li Lu was to be kept alive and his billions out of the hands of the man most of us wanted dead, Lin had to act and act fast. Ten minutes after we had put the whole puzzle together, the captain and the rest of us had been speeding toward the harbor.

Lin had hoped to be able to press some of the local Lantau police into service. His radio message to them had been purposely vague. When we had arrived, however, there were four of them waiting, eager for something more exciting than keeping tourists from climbing into the lap of the Buddha for snapshots. That brought our total number to twenty-seven. A seemingly powerful force, but I knew how Smiler liked to operate. I wasn't so sure it would be enough.

After Lin had gotten all of us into our four vehicles he waved the bus and truck on, telling the drivers to head for the monastery. The road up and down through the mountains to Po Lin was a treacherous one, a winding affair that allowed most vehicles only one speed—slow. The commandeered work truck and tourist bus would need the head start. There was no reason for us not to go with them, however, nor for Lin to have positioned himself outside our car, unless he were waiting for something. Getting out of the car, I called,

"What's the stall, Captain?"

"We are waiting for one more person," he answered, even as the lights of another boat showed themselves out in the harbor. I lit another cigarette, sucking down the thick, good taste of it, waiting for our mystery guest. I could have just asked Lin what was up, but he didn't seem like he wanted to talk and I didn't care enough to ask. By the time I was grinding the butt of my Camel out on the pavement, two figures were hurrying across the dock's open drive-through to join us. From a distance they seemed male and female, the male looking to be the subordinate. When they grew closer, I could tell my guess had been correct.

"Jack Hagee," said Lin, "Hung Yee. Hung Yee, Jack Hagee."

"This man is permitted?" asked the woman with a dignified but suspicious tone.

"I believe so," answered the captain.

"Then let us waste no further time. No harm must come to Kon Li Lu—is that understood? None."

And with that, the most dangerous Communist operative in the Far East climbed into one of the two waiting cars with her attendant. As Lin headed for the driver's seat of the other car, he said,

"Get in, Mr. Hagee."

Having no other choice, I did what I was told.

CHAPTER 34

"SO," I ASKED, understandably curious, "what's Sil Hung Yee doing here? I thought this was a closed operation. I thought no one knew what we were up to. How does the large ear of Communism suddenly get a front row seat for the big show?" Lin did not bother to turn toward me, pulling our car away from the curb as he answered,

"There is an old saying here . . . 'Hong Kong faces the west, like a flower to the sun.'"

"Oh, yeah," I answered sarcastically. "Beautiful, that tells me a lot."

"For better or worse, China is the sun Hong Kong follows now. There are over five million people in the Colony, Mr. Hagee. Ninty-nine percent of them are Chinese. Maybe it is as it should be—maybe not. All I know is my orders were to alert Yee Hung over any major happenings in the Lu case. This is major. She was alerted."

"And what's she going to be doing?" This time, the captain turned.

"I do not know, Mr. Hagee," he growled angrily. "Do you understand? I . . . do . . . not . . . know. That is all I can tell you. She is here—she is going with us. Personally, if Kon Li Lu is already in the hands of your Mr. In, I think it better that the 'large ear of Communism' be there to hear the news so that when she judges who is at fault and who is not at least she will have the facts."

The remainder of our ride passed in silence, Peter and I saying nothing to each other—neither of us speaking to Lin. At that time of night the drive from Silvermine Bay up to the Po Lin plateau went quicker than usual. Our car and

Hung Yee's both passed the truck and bus along the way. Both cars arrived at our predetermined rendezvous spot well in advance of the larger vehicles. Everyone exited, gathering next to the cliff edge.

I looked at Hung Yee, impressed with her carefully cultivated looks. It was hard to believe the thirty-seven her CR file gave as her age. She looked twenty-five, twenty-eight, tops. She was thin with practically no hips and a slight chest, but she held herself within a tight sexuality that would have threatened most men big time. It was framed by her thick, long black hair, centering in her amazingly clear eyes. They were black and unblinking and overwhelmingly intelligent, and it was easy to see that they could praise and flatter or cut like a blade at her merest whim. Most men being as stupid as they are, it was easy to see why Auntie Sil was such a successful member of the international confederation of dirty games.

I had only meant to check her out for a moment, trying to figure out what good she could do our cause, but even a moment was too long with a woman that sharp. Having spotted my once-over appraisal, knowing it for what it was despite the darkness of the moonless night, she asked,

"You are the ex-military American . . . the one who does not appreciate the benefits of Communism."

"Yeah, I guess you could say I'm a free market man. But, I'll make you a deal, I won't push my side if you don't push yours."

"I have no interest in deals, Mr. Hagee. You were a member of your government's covert Red Dog Team . . . the Suiciders, I believe . . . yes?" I was amazed—knowing me by name, being able to link me to Red Dog, even knowing the nickname we'd picked up—these were not the kinds of facts one likes the enemy having tucked away in the back of their memory.

Suddenly I was wondering if I was going to be labeled a war criminal. Swallowing my trepidation, though, I answered in the affirmative. She said nothing in return—simply continuing to stand her few feet distant, thinking. A minute later, apparently finished, she called Lin to her side and conversed with him in rapid, whispered Chinese. When they were finished, she returned to her car while the captain came over to me. Taking me aside from the few others there, including even Peter, he asked,

"How would you like to stretch your legs?"

"How'd you like to stop pulling mine?" When Lin just stared, waiting for his answer, I asked,

"All right, what's the deal?"

"Yee Hung has noted that we are going in blind. As a former member of one of your country's special forces teams you possess a level of skill most of us do not. You might be able to make what is coming easier by doing a little scouting work for us."

There was no doubting what Lin was saying. We *did* need some recon and I probably *was* the best man for the job. On the other hand, I wasn't dressed for the part and had nothing in the way of equipment. Before I could point either of those facts out, though, Auntie Sil returned from her car, followed by her aide, his arms filled to overflowing. Walking straight up to me, she said,

"Are you ready to go?"

"I was thinking that I might need a bit more than just the blessing of the big red flag."

"I am aware of this." Snapping her fingers to summon her burdened-down aide forward, she began pulling things from his arms, handing them to me.

"Two-way radio . . . we have another, of course. This rain slicker may fit you—it will be uncomfortable and hot but it is dark and will protect your arms. Besides, considering the cloud cover tonight, it may prove to be useful to you simply as a slicker."

After that she handed me a serviceable combat knife, two palm grenades, a tourist flyer's map of the monastery grounds, a pad with a pencil attached, and a small flashlight. While I found pockets for everything, I thought about the speed with which Yee had pulled together the things she'd brought me. The lady knew her business—I was willing to give her that much. I also thought about the fact that everyone simply assumed I was going to jump the cliff edge and disappear into the jungle even though I hadn't said word one about doing it. That told me a lot about her, too.

Once I had everything in place and was as ready to leave as I ever would be, I checked out the radio, making sure I knew how it worked, and that its mate was working as well. Yee turned down the volume on my radio's beeper to make sure my position wasn't accidentally given away by someone on their end trying to signal me at the wrong moment.

Then, just as I was ready to leave, the sexy ear of Communism stopped me, handing me a hip flask. No one who's ever been in the service has to have that one explained to them. I did give her a short look, however, and then figured what the hell, she wouldn't be offering if she wasn't looking for takers. Accepting the flask, I took a healthy swig and then passed the bottle back to her, giving her an honest "thank you" along with it. She accepted both, taking her own healthy swig, drinking to bless my success. I was impressed.

It wasn't enough to make me reverse all my ideas on Chinese Communism and all the damage it had done in the world, but it did fit in nicely with my theory on life that there are no absolutes. Sil Hung Yee was a tough, sexy woman holding her own on a rough playing field. Figuring one good gesture deserved another, I said,

"There's an old custom that we have in the West . . . when a warrior goes into battle, he carries a token given him by a woman he admires. The idea is that he can't die until he's returned it to her. If it won't upset anyone on the central committee, I'd like to ask the honor of carrying your standard off into the jungle with me."

Yee looked at me for only a second, then with just the barest traces of both hesitation and a smile, she unknotted the scarf around her neck, a long, black silk affair with dark red, unbordered stripes. Handing it to me without any endearing flourishes, she said,

"You are something of a romantic for a hired killer, Mr. Hagee. I didn't know your government approved of such things."

"Well," I told her, accepting the scarf, "why don't we just

admit that my way of doing things doesn't sit any better with my government than it does yours and let it go at that?"

She must have been willing to. As I slipped the scarf around my own neck, her smile widened, breaking into one warm and friendly and almost flirtatious. She said nothing further, though, which, considering the fact that her aide was standing nearby, as well as Lin, was probably all for the best.

I realized at that moment how ridiculous I must have seemed to the captain, not to mention Peter. There was no doubt that at least he would be ribbing me for chewing up the scenery when there was a lot more important work to be done. But, I thought, how the hell many times does a guy get to play James Bond in his life? If I was going to throw myself over the hill ahead of everyone else and risk getting my ass iced for no good reason, the least I should be allowed was one stinking minute of self-delusion.

As I finished tucking Yee's scarf in my collar, the notion raced through my head to kiss her hand. I ignored the idea, however, turning away and heading for the edge of the cliff instead. Maybe she would have gone for it, I thought, maybe not. It would have only been more pretense, though, and people's false illusions of each other had been what had caused all the trouble in this case so far. Not seeing where any more was going to help, I stepped over the edge and started to make my way down into the jungle scrub below.

CHAPTER 35

I MADE MY way past the two men guarding the front gates with an ease that told me what to expect from the rest. The pair had set themselves up to the left of the entrance, one sitting, one standing. Their weapons were hidden from the view of someone heading straight up the front walk but within easy reach. To that someone, they would just seem like any two men conversing near a gate. They had the look of hard men, bought with cash and ready to kill. But, luckily for me, neither of them was the type to think much about their job.

They had been assigned to keep anyone from passing the front gate. Therefore, that was all they felt they needed to be doing. The way they stood their post—one in a yellow shirt, the other in white, spending more of their time watching the sky for rain than their surroundings for intruders—told me they weren't professionals, that they had little to no training, that they were just two more stupid guys who thought guns and muscles were all you needed to get any job done. I always bless their type. They make things so much easier.

Coming into the monastery proper from the right side of the gates, I entered a tiled over portion of the fields. The place was covered with little tables, each one holding a different potted plant. I wondered if it was a nursery for new plants or an area of offerings to the Buddha. I'd seen enough monasteries throughout the Pacific to know either was possible. The difference was that a nursery wouldn't have an attendant but an offerings area would. Sure enough, after inspecting the first few tables I found one with two oranges and an apple on it.

That meant it was a site that should have had a monk in attendance at all times. Since there was no one to be seen, I could only conclude that Smiler had had all the monks rounded up. That was bad. It meant he was playing for keeps and that nothing else mattered to him except the money.

"Oh well," I muttered under my breath, telling myself, "it's not like you expected anything else."

Sitting back on my haunches for a moment, I pulled my radio, getting in touch with Lin and the others. The truck and bus had arrived only a few minutes earlier. I told them about the two gate guards and let them know that everyone else must have been herded off to one of the main buildings. I also cautioned them that Smiler would have been an idiot not to have positioned someone somewhere up on the Buddha's mountain. Lin asked me what I thought they should do. I told him.

"Let me get in further and tell you where everyone is. When you hit the front you're going to have to do it fast and furious. At least if you know where the bulk of the enemy is, you'll have a better chance of pulling this off. Especially since everyone seems to want ol' Li Lu alive."

"Got it," answered Lin. Then he asked, "Is it raining there yet?" When I told him it wasn't, he said,

"It will be. We're in it now. It looked as if it were moving up the mountain which means it's headed in your direction."

I thanked him for the news. Lin told me I was welcome, then said that since they had the rain as further cover, they were going to pull forward to the last turn before the monastery. We agreed that they would move forward on either my radio signal or if they heard anything go wrong. It seemed safe to assume that if they heard shooting or explosions that doing things the safe way was out the window. My only hope, of course, was that those activities wouldn't be drowned out by thunder.

Having no use or time for such worries, however, I slipped the radio back in my pocket, glad to be silent once more. Even though I could neither see nor sense any other guards around me, I wanted all my concentration on finding them before they found me. Sliding as quietly as possible out of the offering area, I moved toward one of the large temple buildings, hugging the shadows, desperate to stay unseen. Most of me was coated with sweat by that time, the rain slicker sticking to my body right through my clothes. The grime of it and the humidity were making me itchy all over, but I ignored the distraction, shutting off that part of my brain, concentrating on finding Smiler and his forces.

The first of the large buildings proved to be nothing. No one was in sight. Their were no incense sticks in the burners, and even the sand inside them was cold to the touch. No one had been around for hours. I slid through the temple, its glaringly bright oranges and yellows muted by the total darkness of the night. Then, as I slid out of the back side of the temple, the rain hit the monastery.

It slammed down out of the sky without warning, without even a cool-breezed break in the humidity to announce it. I stepped back into the temple to watch the outside world, just to see what the sudden waves of stinging cold water might stir up. Nothing moved in front of me, but hearing noise from behind, I stepped back through the open temple, checking out the area from which I'd just come. Unbelievably, I spotted the two gate guards—or at least their bright-colored shirts—racing through the rain for shelter. Knowing there was going to be no better moment, I radioed Lin, telling him what had happened.

"I've swept the right as far as the first temple. I'd say come in now—fast. Boil in to the right toward the bigger buildings. I'll head that way now."

"Got it," he answered, the words almost lost over the sound of his starting engine. "One more thing, you've made it this far—try to keep yourself alive, will you? I don't need any dead Americans to explain."

"Your concern has touched me deeply," I answered, half whispering, half laughing. Neither of us said anything further, though. Knowing the worst was coming I slipped the radio into my pocket and headed again for the back of the temple. Slipping out the other side, I ducked low to use its extended marble railings as cover and made my way back down to the ground level. I slid carefully along the wet stone walkways until I found myself in line-of-sight with the monastery's kitchen/cafeteria. Before I could go further, though, dozens of men burst out of the large front doorway, all of them waving guns and running for the main gates.

Suddenly my blood went cold. I had just radioed to call the rest of our forces in and now instead of coming in on a bunch of unsuspectings they were riding hell-bent into a trap. How? I wondered. Did an outspotter see the bus and truck and radio in to Smiler? Who knew? Who cared? I didn't have time for guessing games. In fact, if I didn't want to see everyone else slaughtered, I didn't have any time at all.

Reaching into my pocket, I pulled out the two grenades Auntie Sil had given me, unpinning and hurling the first into the middle of the thickest group within range. The resulting blast sent three of them flying, driving the rest to ground instantly. At least, I thought, getting the second egg ready, ducking down under the hail of lead the thugs sent off in every direction, the noise would reach Lin and the others and give them some kind of warning. Until they could get inside the monastery, however, it was up to me to provide a distraction—to hopefully convince the men all around me that I was more than one water-soaked private detective with fewer bullets than they had bodies.

I let fly the second grenade, unable to even watch its results. Scrambling on all fours in the dark rain for better cover, I made my way through the stone courtyard like a frightened spider, desperate to find some place bullets weren't landing. Turning the corner around some building I couldn't identify as anything other than shelter, I tried to catch my breath as I pulled out my .45. Not hesitating, I fired twice around the corner behind me without looking. Then I took a quick peek to see if I could spot any targets and fired twice more.

That brought a fusillade of bullets, a lot of it from fully automatic weapons. I was gone by that point, though, racing around the building, trying to double back toward the kitchen/cafeteria. I came within sight of it at the same time

I ran into two of Smiler's men who had pretty much the same idea as me in reverse.

The Buddha gave a little smile and granted me my first break that night. The one with the best shot at me took a step to steady his position and slipped on the slick flagstones, stumbling into his pal. I pumped my last three shots into the two of them, hoping I was hitting something vital. Not waiting to see if I had, though, I kept moving toward the pair, pulling free the knife Yee had given me at the same time.

The second man pushed his buddy into me and onto the knife. Not bothering to try and wrench it free, I let it fall away with the body, directing my attention to its pal. Shooting my left forward, I slammed it into his face with all the strength I could muster, going for a knockout. Not knowing if I had it I hit him again, a roundhouse right off the side of his head as it snapped away from me. His feet stumbled backwards then flew out from under him, leaving me time to deal with the first of the pair, lying off to my left, groaning his life out.

Kneeling quickly, I grabbed Yee's knife and pulled it sideways, cutting him deep and wide. His eyes opened as he screamed, louder and more pitifully than when he'd either been shot or stabbed. Pulling the blade free, I kept it moving in a circle, looking to bring it clearly around to cut his throat. He jerked forward in spasm at the last second, however, causing the knife to slide across his cheek and nose instead.

He screamed again, his arms working suddenly, wrapping around mine. Even as he did, his partner began to stagger to his feet, fumbling around for the 9 mm he had been carrying. Not able to unwrap myself from the dying man's grasp, I shouted,

"Fuck this!"

And then, instead of resisting further, I drove my trapped arm elbow-first into the hole my .45 had made in his side. His response was to throw open his hands, releasing me just as his partner found his feet. Throwing myself forward from my kneeling position, I just managed to wrap my arms around my target's legs, taking him down again. Adrenaline pumping, I grabbed upward, clawing at his body with my fingers, dragging my hands to his throat.

Seizing it, I lifted his head up from the ground and then brought it down again, slamming his brains against the pavement as hard as I could. Then I wrenched his weapon from his grasp and drove the barrel of it into his chest. Pulling the trigger I felt my wrist go numb as an automatic burst emptied the weapon into his body. Lead tore through his flesh and organs only to splatter against the stone beneath us and then ricochet outward from a half-dozen different points in his body.

Two traveling in a one-after-another trajectory rammed into me, knocking me up and away. I fell numbly in the rain, panting and cursing, wondering what kind of damage I had just taken. My side was sore as hell where I'd been hit, but somehow I hadn't been injured seriously. Checking my side, I found the shattered remains of Auntie Sil's radio in her raincoat pocket. Dragging myself to my feet, I dropped the dead thug's spent 9 mm, and fumbled through my pockets for a handful of .45 bullets. Then I reloaded my own clip and started on my way for the cafeteria once more.

As I moved, I listed to the gunfire sounding all around me, mostly from the direction of the main gate. It was a noise I once was a lot more used to, but not in such a setting. Bullets were tearing through lacquered wood and cracking marble walls hundreds of years old—wood and walls not designed to repel an army of thugs, let alone two of them. The din also made me wince with paranoia, each bullet triggering a voice inside asking if that was the one headed toward us. It was a battlefield disorder I hadn't had to overcome in a long time, but it was easy to figure why it was hitting me then.

I didn't want to be where I was—my mind knew I wasn't following anyone's orders—it had been my idea to waltz out into a battlefield this time. Revenge and stupidity and an inability to let go of the way a boy thinks about the world had blinded me, sending me off into a deadly game that if I wasn't careful, was going to be the end of me. Fear had me crawling along the ground, pushing myself down into the dirty running water flooding through the monastery's walkways—fear of being shot in the darkness by one of the hornet wild bullets tearing up the air, of running into another pair of Smiler's men and not being as lucky as I had just been, of letting down Carmine and Peter, of not getting back to Sally after having her tell me she wanted me to.

Then suddenly, I pushed up off the ground, cursing the lightning split sky—cursing everyone and everything around me.

"Fuck you!" I screamed, driving myself to get moving. "Fuck you, bastards—fuck all of you! *Fuck you!* I'm not going down!"

Running flat out, I ignored the lead in the air, blocked out the screams of the wounded and the dying, turned my attention away from everything except the cafeteria ahead of me. Charging it straight on, I threw myself through the open front doorway. Rolling across the floor, I came up in a one-knee crouch, .45 to the ready, surrounded by targets—bodies on every side of me.

I stayed my hand, though, in control enough to recognize that I'd come up in the midst of the monks of Po Lin. Coming up on my feet, I saw someone else—a man in a chair, bloody and bruised and looking lucky to still be breathing. I recognized him, too. Kon Li Lu had looked better in his pictures. Walking over to him, keeping my .45 to the ready, I asked,

"Anyone here speak English?"

I knew Lu did, but he didn't look in any shape to answer questions—not even lifesaving ones. Fortunately several of the monks did. It only took a few moments to describe Jackson In to them and to ascertain that he had indeed been the engineer of Lu's current state. They also explained that Smiler had left with the body of his men that I'd seen pouring out to meet the police earlier.

"But," cautioned the monk with the best English, but also the thickest amount of Brit in his accent, "you will not find him, I think."

"Why not?"

"We were kept away from what he and his men were doing here, but if I heard him correctly . . . on the radio," he indicated a transmitter still sitting on a table behind several of his fellow monks, "then he is leaving by . . . plane? No. What is the word . . . ?"

"Helicopter?" I offered with little hope, considering the lack of sense it takes to pilot one in the kind of storm going on outside. Which only increased my surprise when the monk answered,

"Exactly, yes, good. That is it—helicopter."

The monk beamed with pride over his ability to communicate, forgetting for a moment the unconscious man bleeding in the chair behind him. It was all right, I guess—I forgot him as well, trying to figure out how Smiler thought a chopper was going to make it through the storm we were in, and where he thought it was going to pick him up. The entire area was overgrown—even a drop ladder would be impossible throughout most of the monastery . . . except on the Buddha.

Without a further word—with no concern for Kon Li Lu or the monks, or I suppose, even myself, I wheeled around and headed back out into the storm.

CHAPTER 36

RACING TOWARD THE front gate, I moved as fast as I could through the center of the conflict area, forgetting what was going on there, shoving it from my mind. My moment of fear gone, I had only one thought in mind, to catch up to Jackson In. The gunfire had slacked off considerably. I didn't know if that was due to the rain and the darkness or because perhaps most of the combatants had killed each other—nor did I care. All I wanted was what I had wanted since I had left for Hong Kong in the first place . . . to put my hands on Carmine's killer.

Avoiding the main gate, the only place still giving up fairly steady combat noises, I broke to the inside right, curving around toward the big entrance on the other side of the road which led to the Buddha. Crossing over, I found the gate standing open, its lock blown apart. I started up the staggeringly long staircase to the top, unable to even see how many steps lay ahead of me due to the darkness. I took the stairs two at a time, not worried about the noise of my approach. Considering the noise level of the storm, no one was going to hear me coming. Hell, I figured they were going to have trouble even hearing the helicopter.

Minute after minute I fought my way forward, trying to maintain my balance and speed as I covered the rain-slick marble steps while watching for any sign of Smiler. Two tiers ran around the base of the Buddha at staggered points up the mountain. They offered tourists a place to stop and rest, to walk around the mountaintop and take in the view. The little voice inside reminded me that they might offer Smiler a hiding place as well, but I dismissed the thought.

He would have to know he had someone to hide from to be wanting to hide. All Jackson In wanted to do was to get away from the people shooting at him. If he was leaving by helicopter, the only place he was going to be able to do that from was the Buddha's lap. I quickened my pace when a lightning flash showed me how far away that point was.

Once the uppermost tier was only a handful of steps off I slowed down to catch my breath. Moving at half-speed, I tried to get my breathing back to normal, wishing I could fire up another Camel. Knowing I couldn't, however, I shoved the urge aside and made my way slowly and quietly up onto the last walkway. Having two directions to choose from I chose right, making my way through the storm. I walked cautiously. Some part of me knew Smiler was still on the mountaintop, somewhere nearby. By the time I was halfway around the monsterously gigantic Buddha, I knew where that was.

Looking up at the statue, I wondered at what spot on it I would find him. It would have to be either the Buddha's lap or his one horizontally extended palm. Realizing there was only one way to find out, I holstered my .45 and then reached up and caught hold of the stone platform on which the statue sat. Slowly I pulled myself upward over the sheets of slick, smooth stone, inching my hands carefully from one gap in the blocks to another. Then, once I'd reached the top of the platform, came the moment when I had to move up onto the Buddha himself.

The bronze giant sat in the center of an even larger bronze flower which meant I had to reach upward and outward at the same time. I got my hands up into the crack between two of the large, bus-sized petals and then let my feet fall out into space, the only way I could work my way out to where I could climb up and over. Thunder shook the valley as I did so, the effect of it almost making me lose my grip. I didn't, however, getting my left foot up and over the edge of one of the gigantic petals. I hung there for a second, relieving the tension in my arms, checking my breath, making sure I was ready for the next move necessary. That was when I hit a snag. Sil Hung Yee's rain slicker caught on a barb of bronze, a rough shard I hadn't noticed until it pierced the raincoat. I tried to shake it loose, pulling and twisting every way I could, but to no avail.

Then, suddenly, I realized why. The barb had tangled itself in one of the straps of my shoulder holster. Half up onto the petal, it was clear I could go no further without first losing both the jacket and the holster. Realizing there was no time to debate the situation, I tightened my grip with one hand, letting go with the other. As my weight dragged at me, I braced my feet over the edges of the two petals I was in between, trying to plant them against the wet bronze so I could shed the slicker. After that I fumbled my .45 free of its holster awkwardly with two fingers, silently cursing the fact it was strapped on under my free arm. After getting it, however, then I had to wonder what to do with it. Let it drop somewhere out of sight on the other side of the petal or keep it with me. Opting for control I slid it into my pants and then started working on shedding my coat.

The first sleeve was hard enough to lose due to how much of me was stuck to the slicker by first sweat then rain. I got it loose, however, and then the holster behind it. Shifting arms, I fumbled around until I got a new hold, then struggled my other arm out of both the coat and holster, hearing them drop down to the platform below behind me. Pulling myself up, I was almost over the top when the butt of my .45 caught on the edge. I stopped moving instantly, but it was too late. The bulky automatic slid out of my slacks and bounced away, falling noisily onto the marble below.

Not having a spare moment to curse my luck, I strained and threw myself up and over the bronze petal I was hanging onto, just in time to avoid a crashing attack. Smiler landed next to me, stabbing at my back. I let myself drop and slid down to the base of the Buddha, avoiding the blow by a hair's breath. Not being able to regulate my speed, I slammed into the statue roughly, numbing my left arm instantly. Smiler came down right behind me, looking for another opening. Making it to my feet as best I could, I faced off with him, saying,

"Good to see you, boss. And guess what—you didn't waste your money. I know who the fucking bad guy is."

"I don't need this, Hagee," he answered, wild and mad and burning with anger. "We can pass this shit on, you know."

"You fucking two-bit," I snarled, pulling Auntie Sil's scarf free from my neck with my good arm. "Don't start kidding yourself. You're not going to spend a dime of Li Lu's dough."

And then, Smiler laughed. Standing in the rain at the feet of the Buddha, he threw back his head and howled, obviously up on some joke I was missing. It didn't bother me. Every second we stalled gave my arm a little bit more time to come back to life. A handful of seconds too late, Smiler said,

"And I thought you were some kind of wizard."

"I am. That's why you're going down. Stupid move blowing up my place," I said, stalling out for the precious seconds my arm needed. "Did you honestly think I wouldn't find out about the weapons?"

"You were supposed to, Big Hagee. Motivation. I knew there was no way to find the money. Everyone had tried that. I was counting on you finding them, stirring things up—like Li Lu's guilt. I knew you would send him to the weapons, and that if I watched them I would find him. And I did."

"Yeah," I admitted. "You did. And now you're going to pay for it." His knife hand coming up, Smiler took his last chance, telling me,

"Fuck you, Hagee. You can just die stupid."

And then he came at me, screaming his rage while the thunder pealed through the mountains. I dodged his attack, stepping to the side, hitting him blunt-fisted in the back of the head as he went by, the black silk in my hand trailing like a pennant in the wind. He wheeled around, his slick shoes slipping on the wet bronze. He had hoped to knife me before I could move, but the speed of his reaction merely sent him flying off balance. Even with a knife—even with me only having one arm—Smiler was going to be no problem.

I moved forward, waiting for him to try to make it back to his feet. As he began to rise I kicked him in the side of the head. The blow sent him crashing onto his back, his knife spinning off into the darkness.

"That was for Maurice," I told him, moving in slowly, kicking him again. "That was for Francis."

Lightning flashed as Smiler dragged himself upward, reflecting off the Buddha, illuminating us both for a moment. I could see the blood pouring out of his nose and mouth. Grinning, happy at the sight, I let him get halfway erect and then closed on the shadow form I could make out in the rain and slammed him with a right, then a left, just to see if I'd shaken the numbness. He went down again, staying there this time. Not caring if he was up or down, I walked the two steps it took to put me beside him, then pulled back and kicked him in the ribs, hard enough to break a few, growling,

"And this one . . . this one's for Hubert." Then I kicked him a few more times, adding,

"So are these."

Then, not seeing the point in prolonging things any further, I dropped down onto his back. With a single motion I was able to wrap Auntie Sil's scarf around his neck. Jerking it upward, I pulled it up into the flesh of his throat, cutting off his air before he could fight back or beg. I wasn't interested in either. I just wanted him dead.

As the rain continued to slam against us, hammering the Buddha, making its thick bronze ring, I twisted the scarf tighter with one hand. At the same time I used the other to smash Smiler's head against the flower petal we were on, feeling his face crumple with each blow. The fight went out of him after the second, the breath went out of him after the third. I made the scarf tighter anyway, fueled by hate and just not caring.

When I was sure he was as dead as he was going to get, I stood up again, pulling him with me. Crawling up the flower, I dragged his body behind, somehow getting us both back up to the edge. Then, without even waiting to catch my breath, I scooped his carcass up and hurled it over the side, watching it disappear into the rain, hearing it thud against the stairs far below.

"And that was for Carmine," I spat.

And then I just sat back against the bronze petal I had climbed, letting the rain pelt me—not caring anymore. I could hear gunfire still coming up from below, but I didn't move—I was just too tired to do anything else.

EPILOGUE

AS THE PLANE taking Peter and I back to the States finally began its last taxi run, I heaved a massive sigh of relief. After all that had happened, all I wanted was to find Sally and wrap myself in her arms and hide away from the world for a hundred years. I knew something would probably interfere with that plan—something always does—but like Grampy had once said, a man's gotta have hopes, he's gotta have dreams.

As I pushed my way into the back of my seat, I reviewed my other hopes besides those concerning myself and Sally. Some of it was easy to see happening—some of it was going to keep my fingers crossed for a long time. Out of them all, I centered on the ball Lin, Yee, and I had set into motion—our explanation of Jackson In and Kon Li Lu's deaths. If that one continued along the track we'd set it, then everything looked like it would be all right.

Smiler's helicopter never arrived. The next day, it had only taken an hour's worth of investigation to find that it had crashed into the ocean less than a mile from its departure point on Hong Kong. He was an idiot for thinking a chopper could fly through the storm that hit the islands that night. But then, he was an idiot for thinking a lot of the things he had thought—for thinking Sing would betray what Li Lu had started rolling, or that he could kill my friends and get away with it, or that I could be bought . . . period. Especially that.

We all took our cue from Sil Yee. Her report to her superiors on the Chinese mainland is the one we all backed, hoping for the best. In it she told how patriots like Tai Sing and Chinese-American Jackson In fought to get to the bottom of the Kon Li Lu mystery. It was unfortunate, of course, that In's body was lost when his helicopter crashed. Perhaps, her report suggested, if he and his extra men had been able to reach Po Lin, that those thugs that had Kon Li Lu might have been stopped before they could kill their captive. Li Lu died without revealing where his billions were, all of the thugs died in the ensuing gun battle, and now no one was left alive who had any idea where the money was. It was lost forever—most likely already stolen by officers in whatever banks it had been hidden. At least, that was what the report said.

It was Smiler's body that filled Kon Li Lu's coffin at the memorial service held by Sing and Fel and Iris—Smiler's body that was cremated afterwards—Smiler's ashes that were sprinkled in the waters of the Tathong Channel— escaping into the ocean like old Whut Yuen. As for Kon Li Lu, he did not die, of course. Transformed into a never-before mentioned, long lost son of Li Tsim, he would work as a waiter in the Five Great Grains, saving for his return to the life of a college student. There was also his plan of becoming Felecia's son-in-law, a plan Fel was apparently quite happy with—just like everyone else.

By the time I'd dragged myself and Smiler's body down from the Buddha's mountain, the others had dealt with Smiler's men while the monks had dealt with their handi-work. Kon Li Lu had been roughed up, but he would live. And that was when Lin and Peter and I started to get the whole story. The reason why no one could tell whether the three billion dollars was being saved for the battle against the Communists or squandered on roulette wheels was because both cases were true.

When Lu had discovered that buying weapons got people killed, he had gotten depressed about the whole thing just as Peter had said. For a short while he gave up his dreams and just ran off with Iris, blowing cash in the gambling dens of Macau and the such. But then, after another drunken night, what he could actually do with the money came to him. He had never promised people to overthrow the *Communists* with a bloody revolution. He had promised to use the funds he raised to topple *Communism*. Suddenly he had realized, China did not have to be subdued, it could simply be seduced.

Working with Iris and her mother, he had played the dangerous game of getting in touch with first our C.I.A. and then the Communists themselves. Slaner and Yee had been provided by their governments to oversee his new plan, which was to pump money into free enterprise operations throughout Asia. Canton and the provinces surrounding it were already rife with free trade zones—areas where former peasants could move up to the title of bourgeois.

Over the months, Lu had pumped money into any family business or farm concern he could find on the mainland where a group of hardworking people were just waiting for some start-up capital. Some of the businesses had failed, of course, but the point was he had dispersed the money throughout the country to any work-like-a-dogger he could find that just wanted something better. The big voices in Beijing could not officially approve what was happening. Indeed, they could not even afford to officially know that it was happening. But, in the long run, it had the potential to give everyone what they wanted.

Americans wanted to see the fall of Communism and the rise of democracy. So did the Chinese for that matter. Kon Li Lu had done the best thing he could to help that along. Instead of starting a war that would have merely redug the old trenches and gotten everyone looking through their gunsights for imperialists he became a venture capitalist, getting everyone hopped up for building bank accounts instead of walls.

Not surprisingly, he had given almost all the money away, forgetting that he was Chinese and that he could have kept enough to start his own mainland business. Maybe he felt he'd used his share up at the blackjack tables. Maybe he simply *was* the hero of Tian'anmen Square. Whatever, he had done his duty and whether it worked or fell apart or only just started a small ball rolling that none of us would live to see the effects of was beside the point. Slaner had written his report to match Yee's, both of them backing the official lie that Kon Li Lu was dead and that the money was lost and no one should point their fingers at anyone else.

As for Sing, he was happy to keep quiet, feeling the noble patriot for his part, knowing that come '97 everything he had done would work in his favor. Lin felt much the same way. I didn't see him becoming Sing's dim sum companion anytime soon, but then stranger things have happened. I left Fel with an improved opinion of me and Iris with the promise that I would come back to see her first baby.

As for Lu, once he finally got to talk, he was inordinately grateful to me for having taken care of Iris when he couldn't. He asked me what he could do for me. Thinking about it, I told him what had brought me to Hong Kong in the first place. I told him about Sally and about the rocket which had killed Francis and Carmine. Then I told him about Carmine's wife and kids and that gave him an idea.

Before I left he set up a deal with one of his mainland success stories, a toy factory in the special economic zone in Shenzhen. From then on, the factory would be sending a batch of toys to Carmine's wife. The idea was that she would have her kids and their friends play with them and then send the factory a report on how much they liked them. This would give the toy makers some idea of how the American marketplace would react to their products. For each report she would receive a check that would at least cover the rent and groceries. It wasn't the same as having Carmine, but it was something.

On the morning of our flight, Sing had gathered all the concerned parties at his restaurant for a farewell feast. Everyone showed up but Sil Hung Yee, which I could understand, but found to be a disappointment all the same. Those of us that did show, we ate everything in sight until it was time to leave. Then Peter and I stood up and shook hands all around, I kissed Iris on the cheek, and that was that. Sing told everyone to keep eating and then escorted us to the basement where one of his cars would take us to the airport. That was where we finally saw Sil Yee.

"So, all the stories are true," she said. "Western men just

play with a woman's virtue and then slip out of town on the first plane."

My face broke into a smile. I was being teased and I knew it. I had wanted to see Yee again, wanted to thank her for her faith and cooperation, wanted to let her know how impressed I was with the Communists for not trying to put the nab on Li Lu and his billions, for letting someone help the people for once—something in which most governments, hers, mine, or anyone else's, usually have no interest. Swallowing all the hyperboles, however, I reached into my carry-on bag and pulled out a small rectangular box, passing it over to Yee.

Her eyes grew a tad wider and she almost broke into her own smile. Being a woman and not a girl, however, she couldn't go that far without seeing what was inside first. Slipping off its ribbon, she opened the box, pulling out her scarf. I'd had it cleaned and pressed at the hotel. They'd done a nice job. Holding it up to the light, looking for wrinkles, or maybe blood, she said,

"The standard taken into battle—the weapon that brought down the millionaire gangster dog who would have betrayed his friends, his business partners, and his own people, all just for more money." Wrapping the scarf around her own neck once more, she said,

"For an American, you certainly know the way to a Communist's heart."

Then she graced me with the smile I'd been waiting for, letting me know she understood everything I wanted to say, saving both of us the embarrassment of me actually saying it. It's easy to love a woman who knows when to let you off the hook.

After that she gave us all a little bow and then left, driving away in a small red sporty number. Peter and I shook Sing's hand and left right behind her. Number one cab driver Jimmy Wing got us to the airport in plenty of time, and soon after we were on our way for home. As our jet finally got itself into the air, Peter asked me,

"So, how'd we do?"

"Well," I told him, "we'll get our daily fee plus half

again, and expenses from the C.C.B.A. We did Rice his favor which is points earned. We took care of Carmine's family which is points of a different kind and we proved that we work together okay, which isn't bad, either."

"It's no four hundred and fifty million dollars," he answered, to which I said,

"No, but it's better than being dead."

He agreed and then we settled down to simply discussing what had gone right and what had gone wrong and what we would do once we got home. In the middle of making our plans for my new, expanded agency, he said,

"You know, it's funny."

"What?"

"I always thought you'd be sitting in your one-man office until the end of time—the last single op agency in town. I guess nothing lasts forever."

I sat in my seat next to Peter's, nodding my head, thinking about the case we'd just finished. A lot of things had changed. A sweet little girl had turned into a woman. I'd lost some of my notions about Communists and about my career, my life my future and God knew what else.

After acknowledging all of that, we talked for a little while longer and then I put my head back, trying to get some rest. Instead I thought of sitting in Leslie Stadler's living room, lecturing her on good guys and bad guys and killing and wondering what she'd think of me now. I wondered if she had a crush on me, like Iris, or if she'd already forgotten me, or if that wouldn't happen until she met her own Kon Li Lu. If she was that lucky.

I thought about all the things that were different now, and wondered why that was always the way. Before I could go on for too long, however, I fell asleep, staying that way for almost the entire flight home—something else I'd never been able to do in the past.

Yeah, I thought when I woke up, nothing lasts forever, all right.

EXTRAORDINARY
——— HARDCOVER
——— MYSTERIES
——————— FROM

BERKLEY
PRIME
CRIME